# MAGIC REDEEMED

### Hall of Blood and Mercy Book 2

## K. M. SHEA

MAGIC REDEEMED
Copyright © 2020 by K. M. Shea

Cover Art by Natasha Snow Designs
Edited by Deborah Grace White

ISBN: 978-1-950635-08-5

www.kmshea.com

*For my Champions.*
*I hope you enjoy Killian's active eyebrows.*

# CHAPTER ONE

*Hazel*

"Therefore, it's been decided that it's time you face an opponent in a real fight. As such, Gavino will not be holding back."

I had been fussing over my chisa katana—which is basically a smaller version of the Japanese katana—so I clearly had misheard Celestina's plans for the day's training session. "I'm sorry—say what now?"

Celestina tapped a finger on her clipboard. "You're skilled enough with your new level of magic that you can now fight toe-to-toe with one of us."

I slowly blinked. "By us you mean a *Drake Family* vampire?"

"Yes."

"A vampire from the *Drake Family*," I said again. "The deadliest vampire Family in the Midwest. And you think I—who only unlocked my full magic potential *two months ago*—can survive fighting one of you?"

The white of Celestina's smile magnified the tawny bronze color of her skin. "Precisely."

"Are you crazy?" I demanded. "There's no way I can keep up!"

"Gavino is the lowest ranked member in the Family who is currently in Drake Hall," Celestina said. "If you use your magic correctly you should win."

"*Win?*" My voice went up several octaves.

Gavino—who had the shoulder span of a defensive lineman and the height of a troll, making him heavily muscled for a vampire, which are usually more on the lean side—bowed slightly to me. "May we fight nobly."

"Aren't you *offended* by this?" I asked.

I had sought sanctuary among the Drake Family long enough to know most of the vampires by name, if not personally. I knew Gavino pretty well because he usually stepped in as my trainer for the day if Celestina—the Drake Family's First Knight—or Josh—the Second Knight—were too busy.

Gavino tilted his head as he considered my question. "Why would I be offended? There is nothing but valor in a proper fight."

"I'm a wizard," I said. "The idea that I could beat you is a joke."

Wizards are considered the bottom feeders of supernaturals. Sure, we can do magic, but we can't match the speed of a vampire, or the brute strength of a werewolf. The only kind of being we could reasonably defeat was the fae—and that's because as wizards our ability to use magic cancels out a lot of the spells and enchantments fae use on their opponents.

However, through the rather...*unusual* teaching methods of the Drake Family, I'd come to see that wizards could be more powerful. The trick was training. For the most part, we wizards were content to summon balls of fire and flick them at our opponents. But the Drake Family had me wrapping electricity around my katana—which packed a heck of a punch and was a lot harder to evade than a single firebolt.

I could see how we wizards could fight far better than we were taught—with enough training we could probably beat off a werewolf and maybe defend ourselves from a lesser vamp. (I had actually killed a crazy vampire named Solene who was on a murdering spree when I unlocked my magic two months ago.) But.

*But*!

Fighting a Drake vampire—the most powerful vampire Family in the Midwest, who trained harder than werewolves and were versed in everything from martial arts to sidearms? I didn't stand a deer's chance in a werewolf den.

"You won't win with that kind of attitude," Celestina announced.

Gavino sagely nodded. "The mental battle is equally as important as the physical fight."

"How about we wait another week or ten?" I suggested.

Celestina pursed her lips—not a good sign.

"Um—Killian! Does Killian know about your plan?"

"His Eminence suggested the plan," Celestina said.

"*Why* would he do that? I don't recall pissing him off recently." I gripped the hilt of my katana with worry.

"He is not angry with you; rather, he *believes* in you," Gavino said with great conviction.

"He *believes* it would be funny to watch you crush me, is more like it," I muttered.

"Hazel," Celestina said. "You are fretting over nothing. You've had practice matches with us before."

"Yeah—but as you said they were practice. If Gavino is serious I'm going to *die*."

"Don't be silly." Celestina tossed the tail of her hair—wound in a French braid—over her shoulder. "You'll have to stop him before it comes to that."

I could tell my complaints weren't going to get me anywhere, which meant one of two things.

1) Despite Celestina's assertions, Gavino *was* going to take it easy on me, or

2) I'd have to do my best and get pounded in the process,

which would hopefully make Celestina—or more importantly *Killian*—realize I wasn't as good as they thought and adjust my training accordingly.

Either way, I was in for a rough time. But I wasn't going to take it sitting down—oh no, I'd scratch and claw my way through this if I had to.

Because no matter how questionable the Drake Family training methods were, they got results. And I *needed* to keep getting better, because eventually I'd return to House Medeis and be in for the fight of my life.

I followed Celestina over to the mat-covered area the vampires used for their matches, unsheathing my chisa katana and setting the scabbard on a bench before I joined Gavino at the center.

I took a deep breath and adjusted into a proper stance, then tapped my powers. Wizards used magic by pulling it from the air and filtering it through their blood. It made my mouth taste tangy —like that zing-y feeling pineapple leaves on your tongue.

My body temperature rose as my magic flowed around me, and I felt the tell-tale warmth of my wizard mark surfacing on my skin.

A wizard mark was kind of like a magic-sensitive tattoo that only showed up when we tapped into magic. It was usually a pattern of swirls, shapes, or spikes, but more important than the design was the size. When my magic was sealed, I had one swirl under my left eye.

Now, with my magic unbound, my mark extended up into my hairline and brushed past my jawline and down my neck.

Gavino cracked his knuckles while he waited, watching me with something that looked like approval.

Celestina settled her hands on the fitted waistline of her black suit. "Ready? Then begin!"

I dove sidewise as I flung a fistful of blue fire at Gavino.

He, of course, already wasn't there.

Vampires are *fast*. They don't have great defenses, but they move so quickly it doesn't matter because they're on you before you can get a good hit in.

Rather than stop, I darted in an unpredictable pattern as I wrapped my sword in magic. I whirled around, and Gavino leaned back slightly to avoid the magic-charged blade, then leaned in to grab me.

I couldn't recover and bring my sword up fast enough. But as his fingers bunched around my shoulder I kicked at his side with my right foot, which was encased with blue fire.

Gavino grunted, and the smell of burnt fabric tickled my nose.

Unfortunately, he didn't let me go. But my kick had bought me the precious seconds I needed to reverse my katana so the edge of the blade faced him. I flicked it up in a diagonal slash.

Gavino leaped backwards to avoid the blade that hissed and spat blue colored electricity.

"Neatly done," he praised.

I didn't reply—I was too busy trying to *survive*—but I tried to press my advantage and used my sword to swing a bolt of lightning at him.

Gavino ducked it, then closed in on me within the blink of an eye. He had one hand wrapped around the hilt of my katana—completely covering my much smaller hands—and grasped my shoulder with the other.

I tried to heat my hands with some magic shaped into blue flames, but before I could get a good roaring fire, Gavino plucked my katana from my hands and flung it away.

In one smooth movement he scooped me up, holding me upside down with my arms pinned to my waist by his arms as he held me securely against his super ripped chest.

See? What'd I tell you—totally going easy on me!

But there was no way Celestina was going to call the match here, which meant I was about to experience some pain.

My mind raced as I thrashed, trying to wriggle my way out of Gavino's grasp.

Filtering magic into fire didn't seem to bother him too much —it obviously hurt when I'd kicked it into him, but he was way more wary of my katana. But was that because of the cutting edge on it, or the magic electricity I swaddled my blade in?

Only one way to find out!

I breathed out, pushing magic out of every pore in my body and transforming it into electricity that crackled and popped. I didn't know how much power I needed to get Gavino to let me go, so I used quite a bit. Enough that I couldn't hear anything besides the crackling fizz of the stuff.

Gavino let me go—great! Unfortunately, I couldn't disentangle my arms, so I mostly fell on my head—that was bad.

I groaned, pain blossoming in my head as I rolled slightly, looking up just in time to see Gavino—still crackling with electricity—go limp and fall *directly* on top of me.

Getting dropped on my head was no joke, but having the bulkiest Drake vampire land on me?

Yeah, that hurt *way* more.

I lost all the air in my lungs, but trapped under his massive hulk I couldn't wheeze for more, either. I tried to move—to claw my way out from underneath him, but Gavino weighed too much, and my body wouldn't listen to any commands.

My ears rang, and my vision grew fuzzy and dark.

————

WHEN I CAME TO, Killian Drake was crouched at my side. His red eyes—which were closer to black with flecks of red most of the time—were narrowed, but once he confirmed I was conscious again he straightened his shoulders.

"I believe you are the first person to have knocked yourself out by dropping a vampire on your head. Well done," he said in his irritatingly rich voice.

I groaned, and my fingers twitched as I tried to move my arms. "I didn't think *one* zap would hurt him that much."

"Given that Gavino is *still* unconscious, it appears your 'zap' was the equivalent of a lightning bolt." Killian's British accent was so faint it was nearly indiscernible from American English, but I could hear bits of it in his dry tone. "Can you stand?"

My fingers were finally listening to me enough that I could boost myself up on my palms. I sat there for a moment or two, wincing when I saw Gavino spread-eagled a few feet away. "How badly did I hurt him?"

"He will recover," Killian impassively shrugged. "Whatever inner damage you did, he is likely healing right now."

I shuffled so I was on my knees, then pushed myself into standing. I wobbled a bit and almost fell, but Killian grabbed me by the elbow and twitched me so I smacked into his chest instead of collapsing on the ground again.

And then Killian Drake—Elder of the Drake Family and Eminence of the Midwest, indisputably one of the most powerful vampires in America—sniffed my hair.

He'd been doing that a lot more since I had unsealed my powers and killed Solene after realizing she'd been behind the murders of blood donors, servants to Families, and some vampires. I wasn't sure if all the new magic in my blood made me smell worse, or what.

Wizards, you see, have *one* natural defense against vampires. There is something about the magic in our blood that smells awful. We're talking roadkill rotting on a sizzling hot day awful. The smell protects us wizards, because no vampire can fight their gag reflex and drink from us, or they probably would have drunk us to extinction centuries ago.

There's a way to get around it—but it requires the vampire and the wizard to unconditionally and absolutely trust each other. Apparently this pleases the magic in the wizard's blood? I don't know. It kinda sounds like the longings of a *Twilight* fan, but I know it's real—just rare—because there have been historic cases of it.

All of this is just to point out how weird it was that Killian had been sniffing me. (Because why on earth would he want to go around taking whiffs of roadkill?)

I tried to tug my elbow from Killian's grasp, but he didn't let go. "Thank you, but could you release me now?"

"Why? Does my closeness make you uncomfortable?" Killian purred as he further invaded my space, going so far as to rest his forearm on top of my shoulder.

Killian was handsome—like, outrageously so. In general, most vampires are good looking—it's another tool for them to use in luring their prey in. But Killian was exceptional among his kind *and* took care to have a modernized look with his artfully mussed dark hair and all of his stupidly expensive designer suits.

But I could admire the beauty of a wolf and still be keenly aware of its teeth. It was the same for Killian.

So even though he smiled down at me and crowded my space with enough pheromones to twitterpate a rock, I stared at his crisp white dress shirt—which was rolled up to his elbows—and frowned.

"You aren't wearing a suitcoat?"

Killian's chuckle started in his chest. "Want me to pull off a few buttons to give you a show?"

"No thanks." I patted his chest the way I might pat a horse. "But I would like to request a uniform change—for me."

Killian nudged me slightly backwards so he could inspect my clothes. "You need a new set of workout clothes?"

"I'd like something that will keep me from bruising and scraping so easily," I said. "Regular cloth isn't going to cut it."

"You do flail about," Killian acknowledged. "Fine. I'll have someone look into it. Though I don't know what sort of durable clothes they'll find in the *children's* section."

He smirked when I squawked my anger.

If I wore the right shoes, I was about five feet. My mom—when she was alive—had called me petite; in reality I was irritatingly *short*. I found it annoying because it was way harder to head-butt someone when they were over a foot taller than you, and before I unsealed my magic that was one of my best defenses.

There was a choking noise behind me.

I twisted just enough to see Gavino coming out of it, his limbs twitching.

"Gavino?" I tried to take a step closer to him, but Killian still hadn't released me. "Are you okay?"

The big vampire groaned as he sat up. "That was...ugh." He groaned again and leaned back on his elbows, scrunching his eyes shut. "That was *magic*?"

"She thumped you good." Celestina patted the bigger vampire's shoulder. "Don't get up too quickly."

Gavino nodded, breathed a few times, then slowly stood. When he caught sight of Killian he bowed, more of the liquid grace of vampires returning to his movements. "Your Eminence."

I nervously bit the inside of my cheek as Gavino stood straight again. "I'm sorry," I said.

Gavino blinked. "What do you have to be sorry for?"

"I didn't know how much magic to use—I guess that's something I should practice."

He shook his head. "It was my loss. Thank you for the fight, Miss." He bowed to me—just his head, not with his whole body as he had to Killian—but it still shocked me. "It is an honor to be under you."

"But—what? What?" I glanced up at Killian for direction.

"You've beaten Gavino—admittedly while almost killing yourself in the process, but a win is a win," Killian said.

"So?"

"So you are now ranked above him."

I sucked my neck into my shoulders. "You're joking."

Killian lifted an eyebrow. "Rank is never a joke in Drake Hall."

I uneasily peered back at Gavino, who gave me a slight smile. "It's true, Miss."

I narrowed my eyes. "You've always called me Hazel—or the wizard."

"When you were ranked below me. Now I must give you the honor due to your station." Gavino said.

"But I'm a *wizard*! And you were going easy on me!" I complained.

"Not at all," Gavino insisted. "You won outright."

I pressed my lips together and started to plan my rebuttal, but Killian stopped me before I could go any farther.

"I think you have done enough training for the day." Killian cast an indolent glance over my head.

Celestina bowed deeply, but a wide smile stretched across her lips. "Very good, Your Eminence."

"For real?" I said. "But it's a Tuesday. Gavino makes my arms into noodles with weightlifting on Tuesdays."

"It's fine." Killian slid his arm off my shoulder and pressed his hand between my shoulder blades, effectively scooping me away.

Celestina wiggled her fingers in farewell at me.

I dodged Killian's touch so I could reclaim my katana and scabbard, but I rejoined him in the dim hallway outside the gym.

"What did this battle teach you?" Killian prompted as he sauntered down the hallway.

"Not to clobber a vampire when he can fall on top of me."

The corner of Killian's lips quirked in amusement, but I only vaguely noticed as I mulled over the fight.

My observation was obviously right, but it was more than that. I needed a way to keep vampires from moving into close combat range. They were their most deadly up close.

But magic shifted into flames—a wizarding classic and perhaps the most used skill among my kind—hadn't done much.

Electricity was obviously a bigger contender, but if only I could use a shield of some sort...

I tucked the thought away for some later musings—it wouldn't be good for my health to get distracted around Killian. "Where are we going?" I followed Killian up a large staircase that took us out of the basement—where most of the training rooms were located.

"My office."

We reached the top step, and I had to trot to keep up with Killian as he moved through Drake Hall. "I want a cookie."

Killian looked down at me and raised both his eyebrows.

"The kitchen staff made peanut butter cookies this week. They're *amazing*."

Killian rolled his eyes. "Do you want some chocolate milk to go with your cookies?"

"Just because *you* don't imbibe in regular food doesn't mean it's not worth launching a campaign for it," I said. "I'll get you a blood pack and meet you at your office?"

"If you think I'm going to let you run loose in the hall like a rabid, starving racoon, you are gravely mistaken," Killian dryly said.

"What?" I huffed, but Killian walked too fast for me to stop and call him out. "You've let me 'run loose', to quote you, for weeks, and this is the first time I'm hearing you complain about it."

"This is also the first time you dropped a vampire on your head," Killian said.

Now I did stop—I was too shocked to keep up with him. "Are...are you *concerned* for me?"

Killian stopped as well and slipped his hands into the pockets of his black pants so he looked like a posing model. "The health of my wizard and attack dog in training has always *deeply* concerned me. I have worn myself out in my worry for you." He wasn't at all convincing. Even though he had sorrowfully tilted his eyebrows, his voice held the obvious musical tone of mockery.

"Yeah, yeah. I'm sorry I ever thought you were capable of sympathy," I grumbled.

"Perhaps it occurred to me I ought to keep better tabs on you after you almost killed yourself by toppling a vampire on top of you," Killian said.

"You aren't going to let me forget that, huh?"

"As long as it amuses me, no."

I twisted slightly to the side so I could hide my expression from Killian and sneered at him.

My good spirits returned, however, after Killian made a turn where the sections of the hallway met, and he moved in the direction of the kitchens.

"Which reminds me. I know Gavino meant it as a joke, but it's totally not funny that he bowed to me and called me Miss."

"That wasn't a joke. You now rank higher than him." Killian pulled his cellphone from his pocket and frowned at the number. He ignored my snort of disbelief and answered his phone. "What?"

Silence for several moments, then Killian stopped. "Bring it here. She's with me."

Being the only she around, I roused myself in self-interest and peered up at him. "Something happen?"

"Of a sort." Killian stuck his hands back in his pockets and turned to face the direction we'd come from—though he didn't attempt to backtrack.

I used the moment to secure my katana scabbard to my weighted sword belt, then edged around Killian in a wide circle, trying to choose where I'd stand. Given this was Killian I was dealing with, there was a distinct possibility this was all an elaborate setup and he was about to throw a three-headed dog or something at me for "training purposes." (He had once flung me off the third floor of a building in the vague hope that it might unlock my magic. Spoiler: it didn't. But it DID make me paranoid about standing anywhere close to a ledge with vampires.)

Before I could find the safest/most suitable spot, Killian snagged me by the wrist and tugged me to a stop at his left side.

Shortly after, two Drake vampires appeared, frog-marching a young man between them.

The unexpected guest was most definitely human based on the way he gawked up at his guards and gaped at the mansion's interior design.

He looked a few years older than me, but where my parents' deaths, my cousin leading a coup against me, and coming to live in Drake Hall had matured me by centuries, this guy still had that sparkling naïve light in his eyes—the foolishness of youth, a jaded part of me wanted to say. He wore a nice charcoal suit, but living in a house of designer labels had made me immune to the charm of fancy clothes, so there was no telling what his job was.

His vampire escorts each had a hand rested on his shoulder. They pulled him to a stop short of Killian and me.

"We intercepted him on the driveway, Your Eminence," the vampire on the right said.

"He drove a Volkswagen bug onto Drake lands," the vampire on the left—a female vampire named Julianne—reported.

Both of Killian's eyebrows quirked—but this was not the quirk of amusement, but a thoughtful one which was far more dangerous. "I see," he said. "And who are you?"

The human obviously had no idea how much danger he was in, because he smiled brightly as he thrust his hand out. "Riley Nelson at your service, Mr. Drake!"

Killian stared at Riley's hand with the same enthusiasm he probably afforded a dead fish.

Rather than give the vampire time to say something nasty, I hurriedly shook Riley's hand in his place. "I'm Hazel Medeis—Adept of House Medeis. What brings you to Drake Hall?"

"You, actually! I'm the intern for Schuman and Shafer's Law LLC." Riley cracked open his briefcase.

His vampire escorts eyed Riley, but a head tilt from Killian had them backing away.

I, meanwhile, tried to figure out what a law office would want with me. (What, was Mason trying to sue me to get control of House Medeis?)

Riley slid a letter from his briefcase and offered it to me. "They told me to deliver this letter directly to you—they said they couldn't chance it getting waylaid."

I studied the letterhead, and the name finally clicked.

Schuman and Shafer's were the lawyers my parents had used for their will and legal documentation.

I had worked with them when they submitted the will to probate court and took inventory of my parents' estate. They also served as the executor of my parents' will and had approved the final bill payments.

I hadn't given any thought to them in weeks—months, even— since they had submitted the last funeral bill.

"My employers wish to warn you that they can no longer delay petitioning the court for authority to officially execute your parents' will." Riley said.

"What does that mean?" I asked.

"They'll transfer remaining assets to the will beneficiaries— chiefly, you," Riley said.

"Why is that a problem?" Killian placed a hand on top of my head and watched Riley with narrowed eyes.

Riley grimaced and slightly shook his head.

"It's Mason," I said. "He's going to be a pain, isn't he?"

"Rather, it's likely he might organize an attack on you once the assets are distributed," Riley said.

Killian lightly squeezed the top of my head. "Assets?"

"My employers will draw up a new deed for House Medeis and bestow it on Hazel, as well as liquidate all assets and transfer them to the proper recipients. We also have in our care a package that was to be passed to you, Miss Medeis, upon your parents' death."

I sighed. "It must have the signet ring—which is why Mason will attack me. Momoko and Felix—my best friends from House Medeis—said he's been bothering the office about it."

"Mrs. Schuman and Mr. Shafer said they were able to hold Mr. Mason off due to his ignorance in human law, but legally speaking can't afford to delay the legal process any longer," Riley explained. "The court still needs to approve the request. But it is likely to be a speedy process. My employers would like to schedule a private meeting with you next week to give you the new deed to House Medeis as well as the rest of your parents' assets."

"They'll be ready next week?"

Riley nodded. "Indeed! Here is a business card—please call to set up an appointment."

I took the card. "Thank you for delivering their message, Riley."

"It was my pleasure!" Riley beamed. "I've only seen vampires on TV, so I wasn't about to pass up this opportunity!" His forehead puckered slightly. "Although Mrs. Schuman and Mr. Shafer seemed relieved when I volunteered to take it."

Probably because they had some experience with supernaturals and knew just how dangerous the Drake Family was.

I glanced first at Killian and then Julianne and the other vampire guard to see if they were offended by Riley's puppy-like exuberance.

All three of them were staring at the intern with a mix of disbelief and confusion.

I needed to get him out of here before he accidentally insulted them. "Great, I'll see you back to your car!"

"No need!" Riley cheerfully said. "I'm certain I can find my way! Have a most excellent day!" He smiled first to me then Killian before he marched back up the hallway, Julianne and the other vampire guard trailing after him. "Oh, are you coming with? How excellent!" I heard him say before he fell out of my hearing range.

Julianne was one of the more cheerful vampires...so I didn't *think* she'd harm the bubbly intern. I pressed my lips together as I considered following the human intern anyway.

"How can any of this affect Mason?" Killian asked, rousing me from my thoughts. "You were the Heir. He cannot hope to claim your birthright."

I was a little surprised he didn't immediately get the implications of my parents' will, but then again, he was part of an *immortal* race. Vampires didn't die too often, and there was no chance they followed human custom about wills and stuff.

"We wizards have a ton of legalese to protect the House and to handle worldly possessions, which includes the deed to House Medeis, instructions for Ascension—the process where the Heir officially becomes the Adept to the House—and the signet ring, which is required for the Ascension ceremony."

"If he can get the House deed, he can usurp you," Killian stated.

"Yeah, sort of? We're in a bit of a standoff because I have the purest Medeis blood, which will keep the House from going crazy like it would if someone new tried to become the Adept. But Mason must be controlling the House somehow because otherwise it would have snapped by now. If he can get the signet ring there won't be anything stopping him from Ascending—even if I have the House deed and the purest blood."

"Given your blood, can't you command the House to rebel against him?" Killian asked.

"No—I messed up, and I didn't perform the Ascension ceremony right away, so my connection to the House is non-existent." I groaned and rubbed my eyes. "And that makes me an army of one. Even with my new magic abilities I can't just stroll in and forcibly take everything back. He's got a House full of hostages in my family. My only real option is to go the legal route in the supernatural community. I didn't get any backing, but with my new magic, and once I get the signet ring, that might change."

Killian didn't say anything in response. I wasn't sure if it was because he didn't care, or he didn't think it was likely. Neither response particularly encouraged me.

I rubbed the back of my neck, my thoughts returning to my previous musings about vampires. Curious, I glanced up at him. "What would happen if you kicked the bucket?"

"Assumedly it would mean that the world as we know it is ending and there is a great calamity," Killian said.

"That's not what I meant."

Killian smirked down at me. "Everything would pass to Celestina."

"Everything?"

"She is my First Knight, which automatically makes her my Heir. Vampires operate off strength and purity of blood. I don't believe there is a single vampire Family that has bothered with any of these court papers your parents had drawn up."

"I suppose that makes sense," I said. "I just thought as a race you'd be more organized."

"We vampires are—above all—a prideful race. I'm certain it doesn't occur to even a fraction of my cohorts that they may die and leave a vacuum of power in their Family."

"I'm impressed you can even acknowledge vampires are prideful."

Killian shrugged. "It is to be expected when one is as superior as we are."

I rolled my eyes. "Right. Of course. How stupid of me not to have guessed that."

Killian made a noise of amusement in the back of his throat as he sauntered off.

"Where are you going?"

"You said you wanted a cookie."

I hurried to catch up with him. "We're done? Just like that?"

"Given that I do not care what you do with your little House of traitors, yes."

"Yeah, yeah. Can I use your office phone?" I asked—Killian's office had one of two landline phones in the house. (I was fairly certain he had it only so he could direct all Eminence-related calls there where he simply *didn't answer* them.)

"Why?"

"Because I need to call the lawyers to set up an appointment."

Killian stared down at me, his forehead wrinkled slightly.

"Because I don't have a phone," I reminded him.

"You *still* don't have one?"

"How would I have gotten one?" I complained. "It's not like they're growing on bushes outside. I don't have a way to order one online since I don't have my wallet or access to any money, and Celestina said I can't leave Drake Hall unless it's for an outing with *you*!"

Killian sighed in irritation. "Use the phone after we get your cookie, I don't care, just stop complaining."

"Thank you!"

# CHAPTER TWO

*Hazel*

The following week I dropped by Mrs. Schuman and Mr. Shafer's law offices for the "asset transfer". This basically meant I had to sign a ton of forms, and we went through paperwork for *hours*.

By the time it was over, the handbag Celestina had lent me was stuffed with papers.

"I believe that is just about everything, Miss Medeis." Mrs. Schuman set her hands on her hips as she surveyed the completed paperwork.

Mrs. Schuman was a short, stout woman built like a bulldog. After meeting her, I wasn't at all surprised she managed to hold Mason off. Her voice was short and gruff, and when she frowned, she frowned with her *whole body* and made you feel like a bug. But she had a heart of gold, and when she smiled—as she was now— she brightened the room. "We gave you the deed—which is, of course, the most important thing."

Her business partner—Mr. Shafer, a tall, willowy man who

didn't speak much—loomed behind her, meticulously going down his checklist.

I scrubbed my face as I stared at the sea of paperwork I'd shoved in Celestina's handbag. "Don't you have the signet ring?"

Mrs. Schuman shook her head. "No—we gave you the information for their vault in Tutu's Crypta & Custodia, didn't we?"

Mr. Shafer nodded and tapped a spot on his checklist.

"Yes, I just thought my parents would have left the House signet ring with you since you have *everything* else."

"The will dictates that you are to receive the ring, but your parents never officially told us where they kept it," Mrs. Schuman said. "It was safer that way. We had access to the House deed. To have it *with* the signet ring could have been dangerous given the importance of House succession. In this unfortunate case, it seems your parents prepared well."

"I will check Tutu's Crypta & Custodia, then." I slowly stood and adjusted my black suitcoat. (It was the only thing besides workout clothes that I had to wear.)

Tutu's might sound a little ridiculous, but it was one of the top magical vault providers in America.

Supernaturals *needed* vaults—we had too many powerful magical items, family heirlooms, and artifacts that could be stolen and cause a lot of damage. Some stuff was on a city-destroying level, and others were more like the signet ring—a life-or-death matter for those it affected.

I couldn't Ascend without the ring, and if Mason got it first, he'd be able to stake a claim since he had the rest of House Medeis under lock and key and help from a lot of wizarding Houses that supposedly had been our allies.

"I regret to say such a thing, but is it possible the ring is *in* House Medeis?" Mrs. Schuman rested her hand on the sole patch of her desk that wasn't covered in papers and manila files.

I straightened my tie, then picked up my borrowed handbag.

"It's not very likely. If it was under the House's guardianship it would have shoved it in my face every chance it had. My parents had a safe, but it was for paperwork only—like birth certificates and social security cards—and again the House would have pushed me to it. The only way it could be in the House was if my parents gave it to a member of the House to hold for safekeeping, but that's impossible because if it was one of my family members they would have given it to me, and if it was someone under Mason's thumb he'd already have it."

"A wise statement." Mrs. Schuman offered out her hand. "We wish you luck, Miss Medeis. We'll keep Mason hoodwinked as long as possible, but we have to post a notice with the Curia Cloisters for their record keeping. I imagine he'll figure it out after that."

I shook her hand, then Mr. Shafer's. "Thank you for everything you have done—both of you."

Mr. Shafer smiled and waved before he began organizing papers.

Mrs. Schuman saw me to the lobby of the office building they rented rooms in, where Josh was waiting for me.

Josh was Killian's Second Knight and the most unlikely vampire ever.

He was about average height—which made him a little short for a vampire—and though he had the classic vampire good looks with black hair, pale skin, and the tell-tale red eyes, his mannerisms and way of talking totally threw the stereotypes out the window.

For starters, he's pretty obsessed with death for someone who is *immortal*, and he has enough weapons to arm a small army.

Josh also happened to be my third trainer. He usually coached me on sword fighting, but he sometimes took over for my martial arts training if Celestina was busy.

Yeah, I don't understand why Killian uses his top two

vampires as my nannies either. I think it's because he wants a quality product out of this, but he's so mercurial it's hard to tell for sure.

Josh had been staring at the unlit fireplace in the lobby, but he stirred when I approached him. "You have finished your business dealings?"

I slung my borrowed handbag over my shoulder. "Yeah. I need to stop by Tutu's Crypta & Custodia, but it's already pretty late."

"How could you say it is late, when the blush of night hasn't yet murdered the light of day?" Josh unfolded a black umbrella before he joined me outside, standing in the orange glow of the evening sunlight.

Contrary to popular belief, vampires didn't instantly die or turn to ash if they were touched by the sunlight.

It was super uncomfortable and it did a number on their speed and natural power, so most vampires avoided it. Of course, Josh was a member of the Drake Family, and Killian never did anything by halves, so naturally he had his vampires train *outside* in the afternoon sunlight some days.

I hefted the handbag strap farther up my shoulder. "Are we going to wait for someone to drive out from Drake Hall and pick us up?"

"No." Josh slipped on a pair of sunglasses. "His Eminence was in town this afternoon for a meeting. I believe he is en route."

"*Killian* is picking us up?"

"Indeed."

"That's...something," I lamely said. I looked up and down the city street—which was still bustling with traffic—but paused when I saw a woman leaning against the brick edge of the office building.

She was on her cellphone and watching me, but when I met her gaze, she spun around...but not before I saw the House Tellier coat of arms that was printed on her T-shirt.

House Tellier was one of the wizarding Houses that helped

Mason pull off his coup. Which meant it was probably Mason she was talking to on her phone—or if not him, one of the Tellier rats who was going to scurry off and report back to him.

So much for misleading Mason as long as possible.

But if he was going to be a total idiot and try attacking me in public, I'd rather *not* make it near Mrs. Schuman and Mr. Shafer's office after all the help they'd given me.

"Hey, Josh, could we cross the street?" I asked.

"If you wish." Josh led the way to the crosswalk, dutifully pushed the button, and waited for the light to change.

The House Tellier wizard watched us, but she didn't try to follow, even when we walked a few blocks to a city park.

I kept a death-grip on my handbag as I considered tapping magic—even though wizards were supposed to avoid using it publicly. Though I didn't see Mason or his goons, it didn't mean they weren't on the way.

I tilted my head, feeling for the tell-tale sizzle of wizard magic.

Josh watched me from under the rim of his umbrella. "Is something wrong?"

"No—" I froze when magic brushed my senses. It wasn't the zesty feeling of wizard magic, but the floral flavor of fae magic—which tasted like rose-scented bathwater.

I turned in a slow circle, my eyes carefully tracing our surroundings. "There's a fae somewhere nearby," I whispered, knowing Josh would be able to hear me.

Josh didn't move, but the air around him sharpened.

I casually drifted closer, freezing momentarily when I saw the man standing just to the side of a small copse of trees. He was eye catching with his silvery hair and copper toned skin, but I'd seen him before. He was a fae from the Night Court—the fae Court that loathed Killian and his vampire Family. "I see Ira—my three o'clock," I muttered, standing still for a few long moments before moving to face the curb where Killian would hopefully soon arrive.

Josh briefly twisted, as if addressing me. "I see him."

"What do we do?"

"Nothing."

"Seriously?"

Josh nodded at the street. "Because backup has arrived."

The Drake motorcade pulled up to the curb. Today it consisted of three black luxury SUVs—though it was anyone's guess which car Killian was actually in.

The back door to the first SUV popped open, and Celestina slid out. "I'll take your handbag, Hazel. Killian wants you in his car."

I shook my head. "Given all the papers, I'd rather keep the handbag with me."

Celestina chuckled. "Very well. Would you like—"

"Killian's pet is still alive, what a surprise."

I slowly turned around, narrowing my eyes as I watched Ira amble closer to us, bringing the cloying floral taste with him.

Josh narrowed his eyes. "Is that a *threat*, Consort Ira?"

"Not at all. I was merely observing my surprise at one helpless wizard surviving in Drake Hall for so long." Ira smiled, handsome in a cloying sort of way.

"Drop whatever spell you're weaving," I warned him.

Ira paused when he reached the sidewalk and sneered at me. "You really think *you* could stop me?"

"No," I said. "But I don't particularly feel like hanging around to answer police questions when these two disembowel you." I nodded first to Josh—who rested a hand on his broadsword—and then to Celestina—whose hand had drifted to the pocket that held her gun.

Ira scoffed. "Even Killian Drake could not survive the public uproar of murder in a public place."

"I doubt that. All it would take is a few photos of him in dark suits staring at the moon and he'll have the public swindled that it's part of his dark, brooding charm. He'd probably get his own Netflix series or something." I squinted at the fae. "You don't have the right look to pull off dark and brooding though—sorry. You're more of a pouter."

Ira's natural fae beauty twisted into something ugly. "Careful, *pet*, lest you say something you come to regret."

"Touch my wizard, you'll start a war." Killian snaked an arm around my waist and scooped me against his side, his appearance as stealthy as it was sudden.

Ira raised both of his eyebrows. "You have such strong feelings for her, do you? How shocking. Killian Drake has grown *fond* of a rat-blood."

I stirred, intending to complain that it wasn't really fair of him to call me a rat-blood—it's not like my blood smelled like roadkill to *him*. But Killian must have guessed my idea because he raised his hand to brush the back of my neck and smashed my face into his suitcoat, muffling my complaint.

"Haven't you heard? She's unsealed her powers—which rival her parents'. That makes her a great deal more useful than most fae." Killian let me go long enough that I could glare up at him and witness his smug smirk.

Ira started to snarl, then he forced a brittle, seething smile as he reined in his outburst. "If that's so, then you really ought to be careful with her and mind your precious pet, hadn't you?" Ira's eyes flickered with something wild. "Accidents happen. It would be such a shame if something happened to her."

I had switched to gripping Killian's suitcoat with a death-grip as I stared at the Night Court Consort. Had he just threatened me? In the middle—okay, no—late hours of the day? In a *park*?

Sheesh. No wonder my parents hated politics.

But that revelation delivered a prickled reminder that I was avoiding thinking of my parents. Thankfully, all of my thoughts screeched to a halt when Killian laughed.

Like, he actually tipped his head back and *laughed*.

Ira, myself, Celestina, and even Josh eyed Killian with varying degrees of puzzlement and concern.

When his amusement finally subsided, Killian turned back to the car. "Wizard, come."

"If you snap your fingers I *will* bite you," I muttered, though I did turn to follow him.

When he slid into the back seat of the middle SUV, I made a beeline for the front passenger seat.

"In the back, Wizard," Killian called.

I sighed and let my shoulders droop, but reluctantly closed the front door and clambered into the back seat.

When I first arrived at Drake Hall I didn't like sitting in back because I knew if I breathed wrong, he'd kill me. Now I didn't like sitting in back because being seated next to Killian and his dazzling looks in an enclosed space was a mixture of danger and nausea. (I mean, he *knew* he was handsome, and he wasn't above using it.)

The door closed behind me—our driver's work most likely, given that the door locked behind me, too. Which was petty! I hadn't clawed my way out of sitting in the back with Killian. Yet.

"What was that about?" I peered through the window. Ira was still in the park, though he'd slunk back toward the playground equipment and watched us pull away over his shoulder.

"With such a vague question I have no possible way of knowing what you are talking about," Killian carelessly said.

"Why did you laugh at Ira?" I asked.

"Because it's *hilarious*." The sparkle of humor had returned to his voice.

"In what way?"

"The fae are obviously intimidated by you at the very least— I'd say they must be even afraid, or he never would have uttered that ridiculous threat."

"It didn't feel ridiculous to me."

"No, but you take self-preservation quite seriously—except when you decide not to." The last line he uttered with more of a sneer.

"Huh?" I very intelligently replied.

"Occasionally your tendency to be a virtuous idiot will make you fling yourself into dangerous situations you should actively *leave*."

"Are we finally talking about Solene?"

Killian said nothing and stared outside.

We had talked about the crazy vamp when I had woken up after the fight. Killian had read me into the situation, then gave me the dire warning that we'd talk about my stupidity in attacking Solene at a future date.

Except we never did. And while Killian never hesitated to allude to the incident and how stupid he thought I was to do it, he would never go farther than aggravated hints.

I looked into the rearview mirror, my eyes meeting the gaze of the vampire driving the car, shook my head, and shrugged.

The vampire only blinked back, but before I could try any other expressions out, Killian tossed something black at my face.

I caught it before it beaned me in the nose—thank you, Celestina, for all the training—and frowned. "What is it?"

"I thought it would have been obvious," Killian said.

I turned the object over in my hands. "This is a smartphone."

"Congratulations, you're a genius."

I swiped the screen, unlocking the phone. It had a bunch of numbers in the phone book, some basic apps, and someone had changed the background picture to a blue-hued lightning bolt—Celestina, maybe?

"You got me a cellphone?"

"It seemed better than having you run around stealing Drake cars."

"I *borrowed* Rupert's car—he got it back!" I studied the phone with a slight frown. "Is this really okay, though? Do I need to pay for the plan?"

Killian's brows arched up. "Why?"

"Well...this isn't going to be one of those favors that I really regret later because the price is too high, is it?" I asked.

Killian shrugged slightly and draped his arms over the back of the seat. "That's more a fae's style. And as stupid as you were in the execution of it, you've earned *some* of your keep."

I stared down at the phone, surprised. Killian had never been hesitant to drop cash on me, but it had always been for things that were necessary—like clothes. He hadn't bought anything personal like this. "Thank you."

"We'll see if you're still thankful tomorrow."

I eyed Killian, my suspicions renewed. "Why?"

Killian's smile was so predatory, it made the hair on the back of my neck stick up. "We're going to visit an old *friend*."

———

AFTER SUNSET THE FOLLOWING DAY, Killian dragged me to a small grocery store on the edge of town.

"We don't need a cart?" I asked.

We passed through the doors that dumped us in the fruit section, and Killian gave me a withering look. "I already told you, we're here to find an old acquaintance. Why would we need a cart?"

"I don't know, the kitchens might be out of milk and eggs or something," I said. "I was being *thoughtful*."

"Mmm. Come on." I lingered for a moment, looking back, but none of the Drake vampires had followed me in. Whomever we were meeting, they must be relatively harmless.

I hurried after Killian, gazing longingly at the glazed donuts in the bakery display, then shivering as we tromped through the chilly meat section, followed by dairy. We walked the length of the building before darting into the freezer aisles—specifically the ice cream section.

An old man stood in the abandoned aisle, pressing his face against the freezer doors so he could view the ice cream flavors. "Rocky road—shall you seduce me again, you flirt? Or perhaps tonight is the night of mint chocolate chip?"

The old man was pretty eccentric—not just because he talked to ice cream flavors. Dressed in long draping robes that were a beautiful silver color and accented with dark blue embroidery of stars and crescent moons, the old man could have been mistaken for a video game character.

"Oh, it's the Paragon," I said.

The old man twisted around. "Oh—it's *you* again," he said when he saw Killian, though he paused when he noticed me. "And you brought your wizard?" He twisted the ends of his long silvery mustache—he must have used scoopfuls of beard wax or something to get the ends to curl. He looked like a ridiculous cartoon villain.

"Paragon." Killian inclined his head to *the* most powerful fae in America—although the Paragon himself told me he was not a fae ruler but representative, which basically meant a professional fae wrangler.

The Paragon squinted at him with suspicion. "What do you want now? I heard the rumors that your wizard successfully broke her seal—well done, by the way, Hazel."

I grinned. "Thanks!"

"She needs your advice."

"I do?" That was certainly news to me.

Killian ignored my question. "Take us to your workshop."

"*No*," the Paragon groaned like an irritated teenager. "I'm picking my *ice cream*. You can wait!"

"Paragon," Killian said in a warning tone.

"Fine—but you owe me an ice cream cake for this." The Paragon dug a pink unicorn coin purse out of a pocket in his robe and flicked it open. A gust of wind slapped at my face, making me close my eyes, so I didn't get to see the Paragon's personal pocket realm settle around us.

When I opened my eyes, however, the grocery store was gone, and we stood in a strange hybrid of modern tech toys—like a sleek gaming system—and ancient magic shown by the Paragon's personal desk which was formed by *living* trunks twisted together.

He'd made a few changes to the room—it was still stuffed with bookshelves, but it had a wood floor now, and he'd swapped out paintings and artifacts around the room.

The most noticeable thing that hadn't changed, however, was the massive velvet pet bed that claimed the middle shelf of the biggest bookshelf in the whole workshop. Lounging on that bed was a gloriously hairless sphinx cat. She was flat on her back, displaying her flabby belly and pink skin to the world, though she looked up after we arrived, making the tiny gold bell on her purple collar jingle.

"Hello, Aphrodite," I said to the cat.

She flicked her tail a few times, then let gravity drag her head back so her bald chin jutted up into the air, somewhat resembling a lazy hobgoblin.

"What a rare occasion!" the Paragon gushed. "She's invited you to give her scratches under the chin!" He gave me a smile of rapture as he pointed to his cat. He was, I'd learned on my previous trip to his workshop, one of those *really* intense pet parents. Which meant I had better pet the cat, or we'd never get what we actually came here for—whatever that was.

I reluctantly approached Aphrodite's bed and carefully stroked her cheeks. It was kind of a weird sensation. I mean, my brain told me Aphrodite was a cat, and therefore I needed to expect fur, but given that she was hairless I was just rubbing her skin.

Aphrodite didn't seem to care, thankfully. She let out a very loud "*Mmmert*" and then curled into a massive ball that consisted of mostly her hindquarters and belly.

Killian leaned over my shoulder and peered down at the feline. "You need to stop feeding this thing so much."

"She needs no such thing! Aphrodite is a *beautiful* and *stunning* example of her breed!" the Paragon said.

"You're right about the stunning part," Killian deadpanned.

"Killian, why don't you explain what we need to talk to the Paragon about?" I asked, hoping to divert the conversation before things got...weird.

"I already said what—you need his help."

"I find it intriguing you have again ventured here for Hazel's sake." The Paragon removed his spectacles and wiped them on his robes. "You must care for her an awful lot."

"Or perhaps it is merely that if I'm going to train a wizard I want to get the maximum benefit out of it," Killian said.

"Yeah, of course," I said, having expected that reply. "But I don't know what you think I need his help with."

Killian shrugged, probably loosening more of those irritating vampire powers or pheromones or whatever given how smooth the motion was. "Magic," he said.

Now it was the Paragon's turn to frown. "But she unsealed her magic."

"Yes, and though she has great potential, she uses it the same way all wizards use it—fireballs, a few bolts of electricity, the usual. She's gotten rather good at wrapping her sword with electricity, but there must be more extensive methods and skills she can learn," Killian said.

"Is that really possible?" I looked from Killian to the Paragon. "Wizards are pretty limited in the kinds of magic we can do. We can create magic versions of fire, water, wind, electricity and all those sorts of elements, but it's not like we can enchant things like the fae."

The Paragon twirled the tips of his white mustache, flinching when he yanked too hard. "There is truth in both of your words. Killian is right in that there is more to a wizard's magic potential than simply scaling up your attacks, but you are right as well, Hazel, in knowing that you cannot cast spells. You use magic in its rawest form."

"So what else is there?" I asked.

The Paragon shuffled over to his bookshelves. "Your magic can be used in more...hmm...harmful—shall we say?—ways. Techniques and styles that fell out of vogue as the infighting among supernaturals dropped off."

He turned around to peer at me over the rims of his spectacles. "Really, you wizards just lack imagination. Everyone is so anxious to copy everyone else—not a speck of creative thinking in the lot of you." He plucked a book bound in cracked leather from the shelf, grimaced at the dust coating the spine, then buffed it off with his silk sleeve.

"Here." He waddled over to me and held out the book. "This might spark a few ideas. It's not readable, but the pictures are useful. Sit down, and take a look at it."

He marched off before I could ask *where* he expected me to sit —just about every surface in the room was claimed. The nearest chair wasn't *too* full, though. It only had a stack of books on it, and its matching footstool just had a model globe—of a green and blue planet that was *not* earth.

Aphrodite peered over the edge of her pet bed and watched me transfer the books to her bookshelf before I plopped down and opened the book.

The Paragon hadn't lied. The inked words of the book had faded to illegible smudges. Only a few random letters remained, but they weren't even from the English alphabet. It occurred to me about then that this book was quite possibly a millennium old —or older.

I froze with my fingers sifting through the pages, but relaxed when I tasted the flower bathwater scent of fae magic

—probably a preservation spell—and resumed turning the pages.

The illustrations still remained. They were slightly faded, but the use of color made it easier to decipher what I was seeing: rudimentary figures that were supposed to represent wizards, casting a variety of spells.

So far, I only saw what Killian had dubbed "the usual"- a fireball spell- though it had a few more difficult variations- like fire walls. I had watched my parents successfully pull off fire walls, but they had only done it once or twice for demonstrations.

I frowned at the red and orange wall of flames the book depicted and considered it. It would work against werewolves, but not—based on my fight with Gavino—vampires. They'd blow through it so fast I doubted they'd even singe their hair.

There had to be other alternatives.

I turned the page, vaguely aware of Killian's and the Paragon's presence.

"Might I enquire what prompted this field trip?" the Paragon asked.

"I already told you, Hazel needed your help."

"*Obviously*. But something must have goaded you into deciding that she needed to level up."

"I cannot be goaded—though the Night Court did try. Which begs the question *why* do you hang around if you aren't going to actually do anything to rein in the Midwest Courts?" Killian said.

"I'm a representative, not a ruler."

"Then leave. Your presence is giving the Courts an overinflated vision of their importance."

"Can't," the Paragon said. "I'm looking for...something," he added evasively.

"Then *find* it and go away."

"What a rude thing to say when I'm helping your wizard!"

"You gave her a book. That hardly counts. And I'd be a great deal more grateful if you brought the Night Court to heel."

"You set off that bomb long before I arrived in the Midwest." The Paragon snorted. "It's only right that you have to deal with the consequences of your mess. Besides, even if I interfered it's never going to end unless the Night Queen and her consort fall out of power. You really bearded the dragon with that one."

"It's hardly my fault," Killian said. "She should have been better at murdering if she wanted to get away with it."

# CHAPTER THREE

*Hazel*

That yanked me out of my picture-viewing. "*What?*"

"You haven't heard?" the Paragon asked me. "Why the Night Court hates *His Eminence*, that is."

"I assumed it was politically motivated," I said.

"Oh, pooh. Everyone hates Killian because of his power and pushiness when it comes to politics." The Paragon rolled his eyes. "But no, it's much more personal. The Night Court reflects the feelings of their ruler—Queen Nyte and her consort, Ira. And *they* hate Killian because he uncovered that the queen had murdered her previous husband, the King of the Night Court. When he dropped that little bomb on the local fae Courts they stripped the Night Court of some of its power and fae land—which naturally ticked off the queen."

I squinted at Killian. "I thought you don't care what happens between the other races?"

"I don't," Killian said frankly. "Unless I can use it to my advantage, as I did in this case. I informed the fae Courts of the Night Queen's violent pastimes before we were set to vote on a particular law I wanted passed that wasn't going to make it. We had to adjourn briefly so the fae could sort themselves out, and not all of them returned to the meeting, which made it possible to get a majority vote."

"And that's what your real aim was," I said.

"Obviously."

"You know." The Paragon removed his glasses and set them on his living desk. "I don't think Queen Nyte would have been quite so offended about your reveal if you hadn't made her into a foot-note for one of your political pushes. It makes her feel unim-portant."

"She *is* unimportant."

"Weren't you asking me just minutes ago to handle her? She can't be *that* unimportant."

Killian ignored the Paragon and settled his obsidian-red eyes on me. "Read the book, Hazel."

I didn't particularly want to do what he told me, but the book *was* interesting, and I had just found a section that detailed the use of raw magic.

As a wizard, I filtered raw magic through my blood to make it useable. Wizards transformed it into whatever they wanted—lightning, fire, etc—but we could also handle the filtered magic at its purest form.

No one did much with it because it didn't really have any properties to it. It didn't burn like fire or zap like electricity. It just...was. But based on the illustrations it looked like in the past wizards managed to forge it into something useful.

I flipped through the pages, hoping for an illustration that might reveal more and occasionally pausing to listen to the exchanged banter between the Paragon and Killian.

Over the next hour I found several interesting illustrations that seemed like I might be able to use, though it was going to take a lot of experimentation.

"We need to leave." Killian frowned down at his gold watch.

"Thank you for letting me look at this book, Paragon." I scooted off the chair and approached the pair, holding the book out.

The Paragon scratched his cheek, muttering in irritation when he poked himself with his sculpted mustache. "Take it with you and borrow it for now, Hazel Medeis," he said. "I can only assume His Eminence will come barging back in a month or two to upset my peaceful abode again. You can bring it with you then."

I studied the tattered book. "That would be a big help—since it's only pictures, my guesses are pretty cryptic about getting any of this to actually work."

"Splendid. Books love to be read, so everyone will win. Oh—though you must seek Aphrodite's permission, first," the Paragon said.

Killian stared at the fae. "You want her to ask your *cat* if she can borrow a book?"

"Of course! She is the guardian of my domicile."

"What does she do? Make any potential invader stupid at the sight of her bulging belly?"

"You toad! Take that back right now!"

I left the pair and picked my way around a foosball table so I could approach the hairless cat. I saw the way she peered at me over the edge of her pet bed with glittering eyes, so *I* wasn't about to question the necessity of asking her permission or not.

"Aphrodite, can I borrow this book?"

The cat blinked twice, then flipped on her back with an agreeable "*Mmret.*"

"She has agreed!" The Paragon excitedly clapped his hands.

"This is so stupid," Killian grumbled.

"If *that* is how you feel, then begone—go on, now. Shoo!" The Paragon made a shooing motion with his hand.

Killian rolled his eyes as I joined him.

"Thank you for lending me the book," I said.

The Paragon fumbled with his unicorn coin purse. "Of course, of course. Be sure to bring it back when you come again—and bring me an ice cream cake!"

We were battered by wind, and when I opened my eyes we were back in the ice cream aisle of the grocery store.

"Did you find anything of worth?" Killian led the way down the aisle and up to the front doors.

"I think so. I'm going to have to experiment, but it had some interesting illustrations—if I'm interpreting them correctly."

"Excellent." He checked his watch again when we left the store and stood outside under the moonlight. "Celestina will take you home. I have a meeting I need to attend."

"Okay. I'll see you back at Drake Hall?"

"Yes." He glanced down at me.

I wasn't entirely sure what to do, so I smiled.

Killian stared at me for several long seconds. He then abruptly grabbed my hand and stretched it up so he could delicately sniff my wrist. He dropped my wrist and slightly shook his head, his eyebrows furrowed.

"Why do you keep doing that?"

"Doing what?"

"Smelling me."

Killian shrugged. "Read your book when you get home."

This, of course, meant Killian wasn't going to tell me why, which made me a little wary. Did he have a dastardly plan? Or was he trying to figure out if I trusted him? But my trust in him only affected the taste of my blood, it was a vampire's trust in me that affected how my blood smelled to them.

The motorcade pulled up, and Killian slid into the front car before I could so much as blink.

"Hazel," Celestina called from the back car.

I shook my head then trotted to Celestina. Forget Killian's weirdness—I needed to work on my magic *and* track down the House Medeis signet ring. He could have his mysteries for all I cared—just as long as they didn't threaten my life.

———

I THREW myself into practicing my magic with a frenzy driven by the need to get House Medeis back. And it didn't hurt that if I focused on my magic I didn't have to dwell on my parents' actions.

It had been my parents who sealed my magic...and they never told me about it.

I had gone through life picked on, looked down on, and bullied because I had barely any magic at all, even though I was the Heir to House Medeis.

I had *lost* House Medeis because of that lack of magic when Mason—my distant cousin who was also a member of House Medeis—had threatened to kill off friends and family who belonged to House Medeis if I didn't marry him and make him the leader of the House.

Without magic, I couldn't fight back. Everyone in House Medeis—everyone I *loved*—sacrificed themselves for me to see that I made it out alive. They were still under his control, and given his many allies, they couldn't fight back either.

All of this because my parents had sealed me.

To make matters even worse, the condition they put on breaking the seal? It was the desire to *kill*.

House Medeis is a House of peace-lovers. They don't believe in killing—even in self-defense—and they don't look highly at fighting either.

My parents made the condition of the seal something that went against the foundation of House Medeis.

I didn't regret my decision to take out Solene-the-crazy-vampire—which was what cracked the seal on my magic. I'd *never* regret killing a murderer or stepping in to protect those important to me—Celestina, Josh, and yes, even Killian.

But it made me wonder why my parents had done it, when it was something they personally would have abhorred. Had they *wanted* me to live a life without magic and to experience pain that wasn't necessary?

It was easier to push it to the back of my mind and forget about it.

So I experimented with magic and embraced my packed training schedule—and the new clothes Killian had ordered for me. I now had pants and a shirt made of soft but durable fabric that didn't give me rugburn when I skidded in it, as well as a black jacket that had the texture of leather but conformed to my movements like a plant-based material. (They smelled like fae magic, so I was guessing Killian had them made for me.)

"This isn't an official match." I eyed Tasha—the female vampire Celestina had paired me against for the day.

"If you say so, Wizard." Tasha smiled all too beautifully.

"Look, I want to practice a move, but if you're going to be serious about this like Gavino, Chancer, and Dimitri all *claimed* they were, then I can't try out this new type of magic."

Tasha looked as innocent as a summer's day. "Wizard," she said. "They did not *claim* to be serious in their fights against you, they were. It's why you have climbed ranks within the Family."

"Yeah, right." I set my hands on my hips and stared up at the night sky and the moths fluttering around the bright lampposts—Celestina had sent us to practice outside for 'educational purposes'. "Look, can I practice this, or not?"

Tasha gave me a showy bow, which I took as an agreement.

I took a deep breath and extended my katana, pointing at Tasha.

Lightning jumped from my sword and danced in front of me, slowly creating a wall between the two of us.

The lightning hissed and spat when Tasha batted at it. "My," she said. "That is quite dangerous indeed."

I tried to extend the lightning around me to create a barrier, but I couldn't manage it. The lightning was too unstable, and I nearly lost it.

It was certainly better than the fire barriers I had tried—Chancer hadn't even paused at that. It was better than the ice wall I had tried to make—Dimitri had punched through it as if it were tissue paper.

But sweat dripped down my spine, and my temple pounded with the effort it took to contain and control the lightning—which is by nature far more volatile.

Tasha batted at it again, almost shattering my tenuous control.

Nope, a defensive wall of lightning wasn't going to work. I needed a different medium.

I cut off my magic, letting the wall fizzle out. "Thanks, Tasha, that helped *a lot!*" I broke into a yelp when Tasha lunged for me, her red eyes bright.

I ducked just in time, and she barely cleared my head, her nails stirring strands of my blond hair as she passed.

"You said this wouldn't be an official match!" I adjusted my grasp on my katana as I swung around to face her, using my momentum to swing my sword in a diagonal cut.

Tasha was nowhere near me, but it hadn't been my aim to stab her.

Lightning jumped off my katana. Tasha dodged it, but I was already following through with a slice that unleashed another wave of lightning on her.

I *needed* to keep her away from me.

Every time I fought a vampire in close range, things got dicey.

Tasha dodged the lightning again and managed to edge the tiniest bit closer.

Sweat dripped down my back, and I tried backing up. But it's hard to keep the momentum required to push your sword forward *while* backing up, so Tasha was closing in on me even while I directed lightning strikes at her.

She waited for an opening, and got her chance when I finished a diagonal slice and had to adjust my katana.

She struck like a snake, jabbing at my neck with one hand and following it up with a stab at my gut. I ducked to the side and tucked myself into a roll. About a month ago, Josh spent a week teaching me the proper way to roll, so my shoulder struck the ground first and I popped upright with my sword ready and a lightning bolt charged.

Tasha had to retreat as I used my magic and created a lightning bolt that struck from the sky and shook the ground with a peal of thunder. It was the same neon blue as all my magic and was blinding, even though I had raised an arm to block the worst of it.

As soon as the last sparks of the bolt fizzled out, I dropped my arm and stabbed my sword forward. It crackled with electricity, but I realized I was too late.

Tasha had charged in and was about even with my katana. She ducked to the side to avoid it—and its electric tendrils—entirely, and reached for my throat.

Panic buzzed in my blood. Recalling one of the illustrations from my musty book, I yanked on the magic in the air. "No!" I shouted. Rather than trying to channel the magic into anything, I pulled it raw through my body and flung it out in front of me in a sheet of blue.

I thought it might make Tasha pause, or maybe burn her a bit at the worst.

Instead Tasha slammed into it with a painful crunch. Her legs gave out underneath her, and she sagged to the ground with a pained groan as blood that was far too dark to be human trickled from her nose.

Without me funneling into it, the blue magic evaporated. "Oh my gosh—Tasha, are you okay?" I crouched at her side, trying to get a good look at her nose in the flickering light of the lampposts.

Tasha gave me a thumbs up with her free hand—she clutched her nose with the other. "This is your win, Miss."

"*Don't* even *start*," I growled. "We have to get you inside—and there's no way this counts—"

"Every match counts, Hazel." Celestina made me jump when she appeared at my elbow, peering down at her underling. "Is it broken, Tasha?"

"Yeah."

"Badly?"

"It's probably going to take an hour to heal." Tasha's prim and proper voice was oddly muffled by her hand.

Celestina nodded in satisfaction. "Take the rest of the night off, then."

"Yes, First Knight." Tasha slowly stood, then forced herself to bow first to Celestina and then to me. "Thank you for the fight, Miss."

I made a noise in my throat, but before I could say anything Celestina slapped me on the back, almost knocking all the air out of my lungs. "That's our wizard," she said cheerfully.

Tasha nodded—which looked awkward since she was still clutching her bleeding nose—then limped her way back to the house.

I wiped sweat off my forehead with my free hand—as a wizard I always had a naturally high body temperature, but using magic put it into overdrive. "Celestina, this is ridiculous. There's no way I could have beaten Tasha," I said. "Everyone's been going easy on me—is this rank just a farce because you guys feel bad I got beaten down by Solene before I unsealed my magic?"

"No—we haven't been able to openly discuss that matter," Celestina said. "It gives His Eminence anxiety."

"HAH! As if!"

Celestina grinned, acknowledging the absurdity of her statement, then twitched her expression back to something more serious. "However, Hazel, your rank is very real."

"That's impossible. I'm a human, you guys are a race of immortal beings that Killian has trained for decades. There's no way I caught up to you guys in a matter of weeks."

"We've been training you for several months now," Celestina corrected. "And you don't give yourself enough credit. You were scrappy when we picked you up, which gave us a good foundation to work off. Combined with your magic, it was guaranteed you were going to be lethal once you were unsealed. Killian wouldn't have brought you into the fold if you weren't."

That was a pretty good point, actually.

Killian would never waste his time if he didn't think the payout was going to be several times the investment. He wouldn't have been content at making me competent, he wanted a *deadly* wizard at his beck and call.

"It *feels* like we're taking it easy on you because you've grown skilled at such a fast rate," Celestina continued. "And I am not only referring to your magic abilities. Before you unsealed your magic, you almost managed to stop the murderous Unclaimed—a foe other vampires had fought against and lost to—by yourself."

"Yeah, but Solene wasn't the same caliber as a Drake Family vampire."

"But you still did it. And it still counts," Celestina said. "Hazel, you demand a perfectionism from yourself that *none* of us expect. Don't you realize? You stopped Tasha with *one* attack."

I frowned a little. "Yeah, that was...unexpected."

"What *was* it?" Celestina asked. "I saw blue magic, but I don't recall you doing anything like that before."

"It was pure magic. I filtered it through my blood and didn't try to form it into an attack, just flung it out in front of me," I said. "In the book the Paragon has lent me, there's a picture where a wizard is holding swords made of magic. Since there aren't any words, I can't tell for certain if there is anything special about the magic, but based on the other pictures I *thought* it seemed like the blades were made of raw magic. I thought if raw magic was strong enough to form swords, a blast of it might be powerful enough to knock Tasha off balance."

I scratched my chin as I considered the matter. "But it did so much more than that, which opens up the possibilities. I wonder if I could use raw magic to create a shield...it technically should be more stable than electricity."

"Ahhh, yes. I saw your lightning strike." Celestina turned to the cleared area where Tasha and I had fought, zeroing in on the burnt husk of a bush that had taken some of the lightning bolt damage. "I appreciate your enthusiasm, but I would prefer that you refrain from blowing Drake Hall to smithereens in your efforts to win your match."

"One bush hardly counts as Drake Hall."

"Only because you fought Tasha outside instead of inside," Celestina countered.

"Fair enough. I'll apologize to the gardeners tomorrow." I stretched my arms above my head. "But instead of another match, could I try to re-create that magic shield?"

Celestina tilted her head. "I suppose so."

"Great, thanks! Oh—and Celestina?"

"Yes?"

I scuffed my foot on the burnt lawn. "When do you think I could have a night off so I can go check out my parents' lockbox at Tutu's?"

"You'll need a vampire escort," Celestina said.

"The fae won't jump me at Tutu's," I snorted. "The staff would kill them first."

"No, but once you exit Tutu's it is quite possible the traitor who controls your House may be waiting to jump you."

I grimaced. "Oh. Yeah, that's true."

"Indeed," Celestina said. "And you may have a night off as soon as you clear it with Killian."

"But Killian knows I need to go to Tutu's—he seemed fine with it."

"Yes, but he may wish to go in with you."

I squinted at her, confused. "*Why*?"

"I don't quite know," Celestina admitted. "But I don't intend to question it as I might be able to get a pedicure or something while he's off playing with you."

I laughed. "You're the best, Celestina."

"I train for it."

———

THE CAR ROLLED to a stop in front of Tutu's Crypta & Custodia. To humans, it would appear rather benign: a brick building with glossy red trim and spotless picture windows.

But those of us who were supernaturals could see the truth.

The building really was made of brick, but every square inch of the place was covered with glowing seals and wards.

Tutu's was founded by a dragon shifter.

Dragon shifters are super rare—I don't know if even a hundred of them are alive today—but they are also supremely powerful because they're the only kind of shifters capable of casting magic.

As a result, they were pretty enterprising, and filthy rich. Tutu's was actually a chain...*store* I guess you could say. But it was also the highest rated option for magical lock up because of all the wards its dragon founder put on her buildings. Wizards and fae couldn't pass through dragon seals, and she shored up her other openings with wards from fae, and hired enough shifter, fae, wizard, and vampire guards to staff Fort Knox.

I climbed out of the car and turned around, surprised to see that Killian was also climbing out of the vehicle. "I thought you said you weren't coming in?"

"I'm not." Killian looked at Tutu's with great disdain. "The inside is so gaudy it's offensive. Besides, I have a meeting I have to phone in to."

"Then why aren't you staying in the car?" I asked.

Killian raised an eyebrow at me. "Is there a reason you *want* me to stay in the car?"

"No, it just makes the most sense."

"Then stop worrying about my business and go see to yours." Killian put his back to the building—which *hummed* with magic— and answered a call on his smartphone.

Was it really wise to leave Killian out here alone? What if a human accidentally offended him, and he decided to maim them?

I peered up and down the street, hoping a Drake vampire would emerge to watch their leader, but I didn't see any in the swirl of people walking up and down the sidewalks.

It was really easy to tell who was supernatural and who was not. Anyone familiar with supernaturals glanced at Killian, paled, and moved to walk on the other side of the street. Only oblivious humans walked past him. Two young women even tossed their hair and giggled at him as they strutted past.

Conversely, they didn't seem to hear Killian's phone call, or it might have put a dampener on their interest.

"I don't care. Fail me again, and I'll have you staked under the noon sun," Killian said in his too-pleasant voice that always meant pain was coming.

I shivered, but relaxed when I recognized Manjeet and Sigmund—two Drake vampires—crossing the street.

"We had to park," Sigmund said when they reached me.

"No worries. Wish me luck!" I winked and slipped through the revolving bank door, holding my breath when I stepped into the fluorescent script of the dragon seal. It was a burst of heat on my skin, but faded as soon as I passed through it.

The interior of Tutu's vaguely resembled an old-fashioned bank. Tellers stood behind gorgeous wooden stands that were fenced in with iron bars, and velvet ropes indicated where lines began.

Everything looked beautiful—the stands had elaborate carvings of dragons and piles of money, and the iron bars had fancy decorative swirls at the top and bottom—but there was no hiding that every bar, every piece of furniture was covered with seals and wards. Even the frames of the artwork hung on the brick walls had dragon seals plastered to them.

This is what made Tutu's safe. No one—and I mean *no one*—could break in and survive.

I waited in line for a teller—a lean young man who was probably a werecat based on the unnatural luminescent green of his eyes and his silent movements. He smiled and set his hands on the glossy wood stand. "Welcome to Tutu's, how can I help you?"

"Hello." I smiled politely as I set my folder—which contained the House deed and other official papers—on the stand. "I'm Hazel Medeis. I inherited my parents' vault, and I wanted to open it up today."

"Of course. I assume you have the necessary legal documents and a photo ID?" the teller prompted.

"I have the documentation." I opened the folder and slid it in the rectangular gap left between the wooden stand and the iron bars for that purpose. "Unfortunately, I don't have any ID, and I can't really get any right now."

I'd left my wallet behind in House Medeis. Mason went through my room and took my wallet, phone, and personal stuff when I fled, so there was no way I was getting it back until I kicked him out.

The werecat frowned. "That is going to be a problem." He opened the folder and flipped through the documents. He found the document that proved I had inherited the vault, then turned to his sleek black computer and pounded on the keyboard for what felt like forever.

"I can verify that Rand and Rose Medeis have Hazel Medeis listed as a beneficiary, and your paperwork confirms that Hazel Medeis has inherited everything as is proper. However, without any legal ID confirming your identity, we cannot give you access to the vault."

# CHAPTER FOUR

*Hazel*

"Could I bring my parents' lawyers and have them confirm my identity?" I asked. "Or do you have a wizard on staff who can confirm my wizard mark?"

"We need legal documentation, unfortunately," the teller explained. "Fae glamor can be used to trick others into *believing* you are someone else, and your wizard mark proves you are a wizard, but not your personal identity unless you get a confirmation from Wizard Registration that proves the match. If you don't have a voucher from Registration, we need a photo ID and then use a magic process to test your blood."

"I can get my ID, but I need to get into the vault first to get my signet ring so I can reclaim House Medeis," I said.

"I'm afraid we can't allow that," the teller said. "Company policy."

"Can I make an appeal for a special case?"

"Yes, the appeal process usually takes several months." The werecat ducked behind his stand, then reappeared with a packet of papers.

I took them, holding in a sigh at the size of the stack, and took my folder back, too. "Thanks for the help."

"It was my pleasure—though I am sorry we cannot do more."

I nodded and was about to step back, but then paused. "No one besides me can be granted access to the vault, right?"

The werecat glanced at his computer. "Hazel Medeis is the inheritor, but the Adept of House Medeis automatically has access as well."

"I'm the Adept, but I'm guessing I need legal proof?" I asked.

"You need a photo ID and to be the registered Adept, yes," the teller said.

I finally let a sigh escape me. "Go figure. Thanks anyway."

"Of course. Have an enjoyable day."

I clutched my papers as I left the building through the revolving door—the dragon seal dropping a kiss of warmth when I passed through.

Killian was still on his phone. I don't know if he could smell my nasty-scented blood, but he turned around when I stepped onto the sidewalk.

I smiled at Manjeet and Sigmund—who backed up a few steps.

Just before I reached Killian, he wordlessly hung up his phone call. "That was faster than expected."

"Yeah, well, I didn't get to see the vault. They need a photo ID, and I left all of mine in House Medeis when I was fleeing for my life."

"What will you do next?" Killian asked.

"I don't know. I've got time, though. The ring has to be in that vault, and Mason can't open it since he's not the Adept, so he can't claim it either. Can we go home?"

Sigmund jogged off—probably to get one of the cars.

Killian studied me. "You are upset."

"Frustrated." I puffed my cheeks out with my sigh. "It just seems like I can't get anything to go right with House Medeis."

Killian stared at me. In fact, he stared at me so long, I was starting to feel awkward, so I peered out at the street, which was gold with the setting sun. "Did you finish your phone call?"

"No."

I whipped back around to gape at Killian. "Then you just *hung up* on them?"

"Yes." He tilted his head as he stared at me. "Have you started wearing perfume?"

"No," I sourly said. "Rupert already complains enough about the smell of my blood. He'd be unbearable if I tried to cover it up with a human scent. Why?"

"Hazel?"

Recognizing the voice, I whipped around and almost dropped my papers. "Momoko?"

Momoko booked it down the street. She craned her neck, wildly looking around, as she skipped the last few steps to me. "Hazel, thank goodness."

She reached out to grab me, but Killian—with his hands on my shoulders—tugged me out of reach and managed to half scoop me behind him.

"You know this human?" he asked me.

"Momoko—it's fine, she's one of my best friends," I said.

Killian stared at her. "Your best friend from the House that betrayed you?"

"Everyone from Medeis saved me—Mason was the traitor. Come on, you know she's safe. You let her visit me in Drake Hall."

"Do you really think I bothered to remember the faces of random wizards?" Killian asked.

"Yes," I bluntly said.

Momoko had shrunk during our conversation, but at my response she bulged her eyes at me in shock.

Killian also turned slightly so he could look back at her. "Don't take too long." He released his hold on my shoulder and let his hand slide down my arm before stepping away to speak to Manjeet in a lowered tone.

Momoko threw herself at me, wrapping me in a fierce hug.

Tears stung my eyes, and I sniffed as I hugged her back.

When Momoko finally released me, she left her hands on my elbows. "Are you okay?"

"I'm fine." I wiped at a tear—seeing Momoko was like crashing into a wall of homesickness. Exhaustion and determination had kept it at bay, but seeing her made me realize how much I missed everyone, and how much I missed House Medeis.

Momoko didn't look convinced. She scratched her arm—the blasted magic-blocking cuffs Mason made the whole family wear so they couldn't use their magic and fight him glittered in the fading light. "I'm so glad I saw you—I was about to leave."

"What do you mean?"

"When we overheard Mason say you'd gone to the lawyers we knew it wouldn't be long before you'd come to Tutu's. We've been taking shifts hanging around."

I frowned. "Why don't you just come to Drake Hall?"

Momoko winced. "Mason found out about that, so it's not really an option anymore."

I stiffened. "Did he punish you for coming to see me?"

Momoko ignored the question. "I don't have much time—I've been out too long already. But you need to know: at the next Wizard Council session, Mason is going to request that he be made Adept of House Medeis."

"That's impossible," I said. "I'm still alive! And besides that, the council can't change who inherits the House!"

"He's going to try," Momoko said grimly. "He's trying to frame it that you abandoned House Medeis and are an unfit leader. Even if the council agrees, he can't be made Adept without the signet ring—which I assume you have now, as well as all the paperwork," Momoko said. "You need to hide it so he can't get to it."

"I don't have the ring."

"*What?*" Momoko's face turned white with fear. "Wasn't it in the vault?"

"I can't get *in* the vault," I said. "I need an ID."

Momoko released me so she could rub her eyes. "And Mason still has your stuff stashed so we can't get at it. Ugh, it is the worst possible scenario."

"Mason can't get in either, unless he convinces the council to make him Adept."

"Well, even if the ring is in the vault, at least he can't get it, and you still have the House deed," Momoko said. "I don't think they'll make him Adept without those things."

"I wouldn't be so sure about that."

Momoko's dark eyes were shiny with fear. "Why?"

"The other wizarding Houses refused to help me—our *allies* wouldn't even answer the door. I wouldn't be surprised to find that if they made a big enough show of united strength, they might convince the council." My temples pounded as I clutched my paperwork—now useless. I couldn't wait months for an appeal. I needed to get in *now*!

"But everyone heard about how you unsealed your magic," Momoko argued. "They can't see you as an unfit Adept anymore."

"Maybe, but no one is lining up outside Drake Hall to offer their support." I chewed on my lip. "We'll figure this out. Mason isn't going to win."

Momoko combed her fingers through her hair, making her silver bracelet hang from her wrist. "You're right."

I bitterly stared at the bracelet. Silver is one of the easiest metals to enchant—which is why it can be effective against werewolves and can hold a spell that cancels magic. Mason had essentially collared all the House Medeis wizards with these magic-canceling bracelets shortly after I left, making them easier to control. I briefly squeezed my eyes shut, then tried to smile. "How is everyone—and the House?"

"We're surviving," Momoko said. "It's rough—the only reason

it isn't worse is there's enough people who belong to House Medeis that he can't keep us under watch all the time."

"And the House?" I prompted again. "Is it weakening?"

Momoko hesitated.

"What is it?"

"It's stabilized," Momoko slowly said. "To the point where it's actually doing...better."

"*What?*"

Was the House accepting Mason? But it was common knowledge that if a House was passed out of the main bloodline, it went crazy and things were hard. Why, then, was House Medeis improving?

"Mr. Clark said that maybe Mason has been trying to magic the place, but it doesn't seem like it."

"Does the House obey him?"

"No. It still won't do anything any of us ask. But it's improved a lot. Mason claims it's because he's brought power back to the House—as if we're stupid enough to believe *that*." Momoko grunted.

I stared at a crack in the sidewalk, still trying to process it.

The House was doing *better*. Without me.

"Hey, don't worry about it." Momoko swept me up in another hug. "You're the Adept. House Medeis is *waiting* for you."

"Yeah, okay," I said—though I wasn't so sure anymore.

Momoko carefully studied my face. "I wish we could talk more, but I do have to go. If Mason suspects I talked to you..."

"Call me," I said. "I have a phone now." I hurriedly gave Momoko the number, which she entered in her phone.

"How did you get a phone?"

"Killian gave it to me."

Momoko paused. "Do you think it's safe to use? What if he planted a hearing device?"

"Momoko, I live in *Drake Hall*. He already hears everything I say."

Momoko gave me a wan smile. "I suppose that's true."

"I miss you. Tell everyone I miss them, too." I hugged her again, blinking back tears.

"Everyone misses you. Felix is going to be so mad that he missed seeing you—his shift is next. And Ivy asks about you all the time," Momoko said, referring to Felix's young niece.

I smiled and stepped back. "Be safe."

"You too." Momoko squeezed my hand, walked backwards a few steps so she could wave, then hurried down the sidewalk.

Killian stood directly behind me. "News from the House?"

I was tempted to back up and lean against him as I watched Momoko run. I missed my family like a hole in my heart.

But if I wanted a hug, Celestina was a much better candidate than Killian—as comfortable as it was to be near him because of the coolness he radiated.

I made myself stand tall. "Yeah. A lot of complications. Hey, Killian. Could I attend the next Regional Committee of Magic meeting with you?" I turned around to peer up at his face and gauge his reaction.

Killian narrowed his eyes. "Why?"

The news poured from my mouth as I explained everything Momoko had told me.

Killian was silent—even though he'd probably overheard everything we said. He didn't stop me even when the SUV pulled up and he opened the door for me—the back door, of course.

I slid in, finishing up as I moved to the far side of the bench seat. "Legally Mason shouldn't be able to get the position of Adept, but nothing has been going the way it should. And if my allies weren't willing to back me up when he first tried his coup, I don't think they're going to step in now."

I felt tears sting my eyes. Not tears of sadness—well, maybe a little—but mostly frustration.

I had been betrayed by a member of House Medeis, by my

own *parents*, by our allies. And I was sitting here telling this to *Killian Drake* of all people.

It was like the world had gradually turned upside down while I wasn't paying attention. *Why was* I telling Killian anyway? Even if he was invested in my training and my physical wellbeing, House Medeis was way beneath his notice.

Worried, I watched Killian slide into the SUV and shut the door.

He didn't say a word as he arranged himself in the seat, then turned to meet my gaze.

There was no sense of boredom in his eyes—and no cunning light, either.

He was just...listening.

His eyes—black with flecks of red—were fathomless, but it was obvious I had all of his attention.

I don't know if I lost my mind for a minute, or if all of the news from Momoko just broke me, but before I knew what I was doing, I scooted back across the bench seat and set my head on his chest with a thump.

I squeezed my eyes shut and almost sighed at the slight chill he radiated. I had always liked it, but today there was something extra calming about it. I breathed deeply, relaxing into Killian's welcoming coolness, and about the time I sagged against him so he took most of my weight, my brain finally caught up with my body.

I snapped my eyes open, but before I could throw myself back across the car and begin the apologies, Killian curled an arm around my shoulders.

He didn't say anything. When I risked peeking up at him, he wasn't even *looking* down at me, but out the window.

For a moment I tried to figure out if it was better for my health to stay, or lean back. Another glance at Killian revealed he still wasn't watching me, though he brushed my shoulder once or twice with his thumb.

I opted to stay.

If Killian wasn't bothered, I wasn't going to give up the comfort I had found.

I closed my eyes again and let myself rest my head on him for several long moments before I gathered up my emotions and stuffed them down again.

"I'm okay." I took a breath and nodded a few times. When I glanced at Killian, he was watching me with a curious tilt to his head. I forced myself to sit upright and scooted back to my seat to buckle myself in for the drive.

Killian and the driver exchanged looks in the rearview mirror. Killian shrugged, and the driver switched gears.

"Thank you," I said once the SUV was finally moving.

Killian had been poking around on an app on his phone, but he looked up long enough to give me a nod that I *almost* missed.

I clasped my hands and tried to forcefully pull myself together.

"Do you require another cookie?" Killian asked.

"Kitchen's out of them," I automatically replied.

"You seem to be under the mistaken belief that the kitchen staff sets the menu for us all," Killian dryly said. "The *point* of hiring such a staff is that they provide what you want."

"Chocolate chip, please."

Killian tapped away on his phone. "If I had known wizards can be easily bought with baked goods, the beginning of my political career would have been much smoother."

I laughed. "I can't see you exchanging cakes for political votes —it wouldn't match your brand."

"Yes, that is more something the Paragon would attempt," Killian admitted.

"You don't want a naked cat for yourself?"

"I don't want to even *see* that mockery of nature, but it's impossible to talk to the Paragon without him pulling out a photo of that abomination."

"I think she's actually got a pretty sweet temperament."

"Certainly—for something that looks like a hobgoblin."

I laughed, and by the time we got back to Drake Hall I was feeling a lot better.

I had learned two things on the car ride, however.

Firstly, I wasn't going to roll over and let Mason take House Medeis from me. Secondly, Killian had to have cared for me at least a little, or he wouldn't have let me throw myself at him and then trouble himself with polite niceties. He knew what he was doing when he lured me into our discussion. And that—more than the phone, my clothes, and hauling me off to see the Paragon —made me unexpectedly happy.

———

BY THE TIME the next Regional Committee of Magic meeting rolled around, I had a plan.

I'd gone through all the paperwork for my appeals to Tutu's, and discovered that if I had a notarized letter from the Wizard Council, I could skip a bunch of steps in the process—which was pretty important given that one of those steps included submitting a form to the Wizard Registration Office in Chicago for a copy of my childhood registration. That registration was going to be pretty sticky because my parents had registered me at a much lower power grade than I really was, so it wasn't even a certain thing that Tutu's would *accept* the outdated registration. (Not to mention Registration was going to get fussy when they realized my wizard mark and power level no longer matched.)

The Committee of Magic met pretty frequently, but they had official, public forums once a month, and before these special forums the subcommittees met—the Wizard Council, the Shifter Board, the Fae Ring, and the Vampire Assembly being the main ones.

That was my opportunity to present my case. Thankfully,

Killian Drake was meticulous and cutthroat, so on the days of the public forums he insisted on attending *every single* subcommittee meeting. (Back when my parents were alive, everyone said he sat in on the meetings as a form of intimidation since he was the only Committee Member who bothered to sit through meetings for a race not his own.)

So even though the Wizard Council met three hours before the actual Committee of Magic forum, Killian Drake and his guards were already there.

We had actually already been there for a while—the Shifter Board met first around noon so their Pre-Dominant—the top shifter in the region—had time to go hunt and eat before the evening meeting.

I hadn't bothered to attend that meeting—I was in the bathroom practicing my appeal with a very amused Celestina.

"The Fae Ring meeting is over," Celestina announced after her phone buzzed with a text message. "His Eminence said it's time to head to the Wizard Council."

"Okay." I tapped my papers on the fancy granite counter, then glanced in the mirror to confirm my blond hair was smooth and that my dress shirt sat right on my shoulders. I had figured it wouldn't be a good idea to wear the official Drake suit Killian had gotten for me as it would probably make the wizard leaders nervous, so I was just wearing the suit slacks with a powder blue dress shirt I had borrowed from one of the Drake Family blood donors. I had to roll up the sleeves to my elbows which gave it a more casual look. But I looked like a kid playing dress up with the sleeves down, so Casual Hazel it was!

I hurried after Celestina and slipped out of the bathroom, following her down the wide hallway, our high heels making quiet clicks on the tiled floor. (Or at least Celestina was quiet. I sounded more like a tapdancing goat.)

We wound our way through the Curia Cloisters, popping into

a hallway that ended with a T intersection, which, apparently, was where Killian was holding court.

One eyebrow was dangerously arched at an I'm-starting-to-get-annoyed angle, but the vampires lined around him didn't seem to notice.

A female vampire wearing a Victorian hoop-skirt was in the process of curtsying deeply as we approached the group. "I deeply apologize, Your Eminence, but he couldn't make it."

Killian's eyebrow twitched—not a good sign. "And what could have possibly kept Elder Aberdeen from attending and cause him to instead send one of his *underlings* in his place for the Vampire Assembly?"

"He was feeling rather melancholy, Your Eminence." The female vampire stared at the ground and still hadn't risen from her curtsy.

"Melancholy?" Killian snarled.

"Yes, Your Eminence."

Killian narrowed his eyes in a way that would have had me running for cover, but the unfortunate vampire was trapped, and shook a little in her fear.

"Fine. But inform Aberdeen that at the next assembly I will send a few of my people to the Aberdeen Family to *ready* him for the day so he will be properly inspired to attend." Killian smiled dangerously.

The female vampire audibly gulped and backed away without ever looking up. "Yes, Your Eminence."

I scratched my neck as I watched the exchange. "Does this Aberdeen guy usually skip out on meetings?" I asked Celestina.

"Many of the more prominent and respected vampire Family Elders are not often motivated to attend important meetings," Celestina said.

I furrowed my eyebrows. "Really? That seems like a pretty dangerous practice for their health. I can't imagine Killian puts up with it. Unless that's why they do it?"

Celestina shook her head. "It's not like that at all—they respect His Eminence, though perhaps grudgingly so."

"Then why wouldn't they attend? Subcommittee meetings are the biggest chance to make suggestions and lodge complaints. The wizard meetings are always packed."

"It's their state of mind," Celestina said.

I wrinkled my forehead. "What?"

Killian turned to the next vampire—a male dressed in what appeared to be Colonial American fashion with a navy jacket and breeches, a black waistcoat, and a three-cornered felt hat. "You're from?" he prompted.

The hat-wearing vampire bowed. "Lewis Family, Your Eminence. I am Elder Charity's escort for the night."

Killian fiddled with his gold cufflinks. "And what do you want?"

The vampire gulped audibly and bowed again. "If it would please Your Eminence, Elder Charity requests that a notice of Vampire Assembly meetings be sent out the week before."

Killian studied the vampire. "Reminders *are* sent out—through email."

Another bow. "Yes, Your Eminence. Lewis Family much appreciates the email; however, Elder Charity prefers a notice by mail because she—hrm—is concerned that technology may fail, leaving her uninformed."

Celestina whistled lowly. "Sacrificial lamb if there ever was one."

"I'm guessing the Elders send their underlings to Killian with all of their stupid requests?" I whispered.

"Right on."

Predictably, Killian's smile turned vicious. "I see. Please inform Elder Charity that if she is so *against* computers, I'd be happy to send out the reminder by text."

"Ah—um. Very good, Your Eminence," the male vampire said

to the floor as he bowed a third time. "Unfortunately, Elder Charity doesn't own a cellular phone of any kind."

"Then she better get one—or adopt a younger vampire into the Family to handle technology for her since it seems she'd rather rot in the past."

"Oh, no, Your Eminence, it is not that at all," the colonial-dressed vampire protested.

Killian turned away from him, his black-red eyes falling on me. "You know where the Wizard Council meeting is held?"

"I've attended a few of them with my parents." I started back up the hallway Celestina and I had walked down.

Killian caught up with me in a stride or two, the rest of the Drake Family vampires falling into position behind him.

I glanced at Killian. It seemed like he'd left his irritation behind with the crowd of vampires based on the smoothness of his face.

"Is it usually like that?" I asked.

He cut his eyes down toward me. "What?"

"Dealing with the other vampire Families?" I asked. "Is it always so…"

"Annoying?" Killian suggested. "Often times."

I was silent for a few steps as we turned a corner. "It's weird. We wizards see vampires as being one of the ultimate predators. I never imagined they'd skip meetings and complain about emails."

"We *are* one of the ultimate predators," Killian growled. "Unfortunately, the oldest of vampires are more prone to fits and bouts of stupidity."

"Sounds fun."

"You cannot imagine."

I grinned as I reached for the door to the right meeting room. "At least you have your Family!"

When I opened the door a bunch of wizards turned around to look at us, instantly turning ashen when they saw Killian. They sat in the audience seats—which were arranged in neat rows across the room.

The ten wizards who sat on the Wizard Council were already in their places at the horse-shoe shaped table. They all sank a little deeper in their chairs when they saw Killian.

I awkwardly cleared my throat and scooted to the side while Killian—flanked by Celestina and two other Drake vampires—sauntered down the aisle and chose the one row of comfortable padded chairs on the left side, leaving wizards to sit on the uncomfortable folding chairs everywhere else.

There was a podium set off to the right side, closer to the horse-shoe table. I knew from experience that was where I was supposed to be when I brought my request to the subcommittee, so I headed for the podium and found the piece of paper I needed to sign up on so I could talk.

I scratched out my name with the half-working pen and plopped down in a chair as more wizards meandered into the room.

Mason stormed in, flanked by a House Tellier wizard. He saw me seated near the podium and smiled. It was a handsome smile, but malice oozed from him like a bad smell.

I stiffened and considered tapping my magic, until the House Tellier wizard gulped and elbowed Mason.

Mason faced the wizard, who not-so-discreetly pointed out Killian and his guards.

Mason and the Tellier wizard turned white, then scooted to the right side of the room—as far away from Killian as they could get.

I stared down at my lap so I could keep my smirk to myself—though I was also a little worried by Mason's arrival. I had been hoping Momoko was wrong and that he wouldn't come to file an appeal. But I was too optimistic.

A mousy man stationed at a folding table blushed bright red when his computer blared its starting up noise. He cleared his throat and hopped to his feet. "All rise! The Wizard Council is now in session!"

The meeting progressed pretty naturally. The man with the laptop introduced the Adepts sitting on the Wizard Council for the evening—I was not super psyched to see the Adepts for House Tellier and House Rothchild there tonight.

The Houses that represented the Wizard Council rotated on a yearly basis—to keep things unbiased. In fact, our region had so embraced the impartiality design of the council that the Elite— the top wizard in our area who served on the Regional Committee of Magic—wasn't a member of the council.

The mousy guy with the laptop next read off all of the new wizards who had registered (aka been born) in the region last month, then kicked off the council's portion of the meeting with a discussion of raising the annual House fees—I swear they drone on and on about this every year—before *finally* opening the meeting up to the public.

A cheerful woman who wanted a permit to perform water magic in a park next summer as a fundraiser was denied—it was deemed too flashy and potentially disastrous—but a firefighter from Magiford was promised action when he complained that the fire department got daily calls from the public about House Chaya and the burning tree in their front yard. (A tree of fire made up the majority of House Chaya's coat of arms, and apparently their Adept had decided to bolster House pride with a life-size symbol of their House, but all it succeeded in doing was freak out the poor human neighbors.)

The mousy man with the laptop squinted. "Next, Hazel Medeis has a request regarding an appeal?"

# CHAPTER FIVE

*Hazel*

I smiled as I stood up and snagged the stepstool meant for kids with my foot, sliding it up to the podium so I could hop up on it.

"I'm Hazel Medeis, Adept of House Medeis. I inherited House Medeis this summer after the unexpected death of my parents, Rose and Rand Medeis." I rested my hands on the podium and squeezed the edge at the jab of pain that accompanied the explanation. "I'm in the process of going through my inheritance with my parents' human lawyers who have officially passed over the House Medeis deed, along with information about my parents' lockbox at Tutu's Crypta & Custodia. Due to... circumstances, I need to submit an appeal to Tutu's to access the lockbox unless I can present a notarized document from the Wizard Council. So I'm requesting the council sign this document that certifies my identity."

I opened my folder and held out the sheet of paper.

The guy with the laptop—probably a secretary of some level given that he'd been typing everything anyone had said—popped out of his chair and scurried up to me, taking the sheet from me and passing it to the nearest member of this month's Wizard Council.

An older woman with thick glasses tipped her head back so she could peer at the paper through her bifocals. "Why do you need this appeal? If you've inherited the lockbox and have the paperwork to prove it, Tutu's is legally obligated to pass the lockbox and its contents to you."

"Yes, however, they also require an official photo ID," I said. "Due to my current living arrangements, I don't have access to any IDs or official papers."

The woman frowned. "Why not?"

"It's a House inheritance issue," the Adept of House Tellier said. "Hazel Medeis was the Heir of House Medeis and inherited the House from her parents, even though she lacked the magical power to keep the House running. There's been a disagreement in who should rightfully be House Medeis's Adept as a result."

I stood up straighter—this might be my chance to throw the law at Mason if I could sway the council to my side. "It's a worry that is no longer founded," I said.

This made a few of the council members stir, and sent murmurs through the wizards in the audience.

"How can that be?" the House Rothchild Adept asked.

I smiled so big it hurt my lips. "It was discovered my magic had been sealed as a baby, and recently I've managed to unseal it. It's estimated I am almost as powerful as my father was."

The House Tellier Adept scowled. "That's impossible."

"Hardly." Another Adept—this one from House Gomez, a Michigan House—scratched his chin. "Didn't you hear? She blew the roof off a portion of the Curia Cloisters when she killed a vampire."

I was a little surprised he knew about that. While I suspected gossip had spread the news about my magic, the fight had been more common knowledge among vampires than wizards considering the reason for it.

The observation raised such a racket from the audience that the council had to wait for the murmurs to die down before they proceeded.

The House Gomez Adept studied me. "I understand you are the rightful Heir to the lockbox, but due to your sudden change in magic, it is my personal recommendation that you are re-evaluated and that you re-register as a wizard so your proper level is recorded. Tutu's will accept your registration as another method of identification, which will take care of that problem."

"Re-registering will take weeks," I said.

"Your parents died months ago, and it is only now you have a sudden need to access the lockbox?" The House Tellier Adept raised his eyebrows and made a scoffing noise as he looked at the other wizards.

That no-good hack was trying to delay me.

I snuck a glance at Mason. He was sitting a few rows behind me, leaning forward so his hands rested on his knees—his fake smile pasted across his lips.

"She inherited the lockbox, it is rightfully hers," said a female Adept. The placard in front of her said she was from House Luna, a wizard House from northern Minnesota.

"I don't think anyone can deny that," said the House Gomez Adept. "But she *needs* to prioritize getting re-tested and have her magic scores updated. We have our registration system in place for a reason. Until you re-register, I will vote against signing."

"As will I." The House Tellier Adept was quick to jump on a seemingly logical reason to deny me. He was very careful *not* to look at Mason as he tapped his fingers on the table. "This whole business seems suspicious. How could your magic have been sealed? And why?"

"The Paragon can vouch for me about the seal," I said—

hoping this was true. (If I cooed over Aphrodite enough he'd probably agree.)

"You still need to be examined," the House Tellier Adept said. "It's possible you might pose a threat to those around you."

I wanted to roll my eyes, but I knew that wouldn't buy me points with the other Adepts, so I kept a smile on my face. "And what does that have to do with giving me access to *my* lockbox?"

"I agree with Adept Medeis." The House Luna Adept narrowed her eyes at the House Tellier Adept. "So I will vote for signing the form."

"I'm afraid I must vote against it," said the Adept of House Rothchild. "I greatly respected your parents, but there must be order."

It was laughable that *Rothchild* had said this as they used to be allies. Hot anger knifed through my heart, and I wished I was wearing something with short sleeves.

I stared at Adept Rothchild until he met my gaze. "That explains it. I can see *great* order to House Rothchild's most recent actions."

He dropped my stare and looked down at the table.

The room was quiet until someone in the audience sneezed.

"I can understand your frustration, Adept Medeis," the House Gomez Adept said. "But it is my understanding that there has only been a handful of sealed wizards in the past century. You are an unusual case—which means you must be extra cautious to comply with the rules so in the future no one can claim you didn't follow them."

He had a point, and if that had been the main concern of the subcommittee I would have been annoyed, but understanding. It was clear, however, that Mason's allies were going to use it as a way to manipulate me.

Almost on cue, a gruff man with a thick beard—the Adept of House Ivanov—shifted in his chair, making it creak. "Given that my House is allied with House Medeis, I will abstain."

"Really?" I asked in a sunny voice. "I haven't counted you as an ally since the night Mason chased me out of my own House and you refused to grant me sanctuary."

The Adept of House Ivanov cleared his throat and looked away. The other Adepts eyed me and exchanged a few hushed whispers.

I should have done better at keeping my mouth shut. Thinly veiled hostility wasn't going to convince any of the Adepts to help me—they'd already proven they'd rather be passive in the matter and let me flounder than stand by their word and help.

At least it brought another unwanted revelation. I'd already been aware that I was alone in my battle for House Medeis, but today proved that I wasn't going to win a legal battle. When I tried to take House Medeis back, I'd have to physically fight Mason—and *all* his allies—for it.

But it did make me wonder...*why* were they supporting Mason like this? What were they gaining by it? Mason was charismatic, but even he wasn't charming enough to get so many Houses to let him break tradition and take a House from a direct descendant.

The five remaining Adepts argued in circles for another fifteen minutes. In the end two more sided with Tellier, Rothchild, and Gomez, and three more sided with Adept Luna.

The mousy wizard with the laptop cleared his throat. "Given that Adept Ivanov abstained, the motion fails—four to five."

My throat squeezed—as if I had swallowed a rock and got it stuck—and tears of frustration prickled my eyes.

"Come back once you have re-registered, Adept Medeis," Adept Gomez suggested.

I kept my mouth shut—though I took an inordinate amount of time to organize my papers and slip them back in my folder. I stepped off the step stool and pushed it away from the podium before I started to shuffle back to my seat.

The secretary cleared his throat and tapped a few keys on his laptop. "Next, there is a request from—"

"Hazel."

Killian had spoken my name at a normal level, but it cut off the secretary and brought silence to the room.

I slowly looked up, meeting his gaze.

Killian tilted his head back in an invitation, then pointedly looked at the seat next to him.

I keenly felt that every eye in the room was on me, but I managed to hold my head up as I passed my previous seat and made my way to Killian.

He raised one eyebrow at me, then shifted his dark eyes to the council.

I started to sit with a chair between us, then scoffed to myself.

My allies had abandoned me, and I had figured out the legal system was going to fail me, too. Seriously, what did it matter if everyone saw me sit directly next to him?

At least Killian *fed* me!

I pressed my lips into a thin line and sat down—in the seat next to Killian—with enough force to make the chair move.

One corner of Killian's mouth curled in what I recognized as a sign of amusement he was slightly stifling. "Making a point, are you?"

"Yeah—that I don't care what they think anymore."

"Good for you." Killian returned his attention to the council with pointed interest.

Silence covered the room like fog as everyone pointedly looked away from the wizard sitting with the vampires.

A few moments passed, and Adept Luna smiled. "The next request?" she prompted.

"Y-yes. R-right," the secretary squeaked.

The meeting proceeded, but I only half listened as I fiddled with my folder.

I was triple checking my paperwork when Killian casually stretched his arm across the back of my chair.

What the...?

I peered up at him—carefully studying his expression. There was no way he just *happened* to put his arm sort of/almost around me. This was calculated.

But who was he trying to swindle, and what was the message he was sending?

No one was stupid enough to mistake it as a romantic gesture —did he mean for it to show I was under his power?

"What is it?" He spoke in a husky whisper and didn't take his eyes off the meeting.

"I was wondering what your angle was."

"Aren't we jaded?"

"You're a political fiend. There's a reason behind your every move," I muttered.

"I'm honored you think so well of me."

"*Killian*."

Killian briefly glanced down at me—his eyes were for once more red than black. "I would at least hope you would know better than to expect me to tell you what the supposed angle is?"

"Yeah," I agreed. "Though I also didn't really expect you to stay for the whole meeting."

"I attend the subcommittees whenever possible," Killian said.

"*Why*? Nothing they discuss will affect vampires."

Killian shook his head. "It does, actually. It means they can't hide anything from me. I am given the opportunity to hear what each race really wants, and it gives me the chance to hear what petty disagreements they are bogged down in—as so beautifully displayed in your request."

I heaved a sigh and nodded. "Yeah, that's true."

The meeting room door creaked open. I turned back to look, and was surprised to see a werewolf Alpha shoulder his way through the door. It took me a moment to recognize him as Alpha Nash from the Flatlands Pack in Illinois.

He sat down next to Mason, his chair creaking in protest at

holding his bulk. The two exchanged whispers, and Nash looked at me.

Catching my stare, he smiled—a nasty smirk with stained teeth.

Killian twisted slightly, so his hand fell against my arm. I glanced up at him, but he was watching Mason and Nash.

"It seems a reminder is warranted," Killian said.

I looked back to Nash, who was now staring at his steel-toed boots and didn't look nearly so smug.

"Huh?" I said.

"Political maneuverings. Don't worry your pretty head."

I purposely shifted so I could "accidentally" jab Killian in the side. "Are you using me as a pawn in a scheme?"

"I would never." Killian's deceptively open voice was almost scary in its accuracy. "Although if you gave me an adoring look or two it would be useful."

I snorted. "Yeah, because having wizards think I'm besotted with you is *totally* going to convince them to support me."

"Still holding out hope that as a collective they'll suddenly pull their heads out of their posteriors? Someone is an optimist."

I grumbled as I settled back down in my chair for the remainder of the meeting. But as I sat there...it dawned on me that not only did the meeting's outcome mean I didn't legally stand a chance...but it was *never* about my magic power or lack of.

If it had been, favor should have shifted back to me.

Between that, my parents' sealing me, and Mason even attempting to betray me...all of these were things that never would have happened decades prior. What did that mean? And *why* was it happening now?

———

I LET my head fall on the leather dashboard of Celestina's car. "Life sucks."

Celestina sympathetically patted my shoulder. "I also hate life when I am forced to stand in on the Regional Committee of Magic meetings."

"That's not what I meant." I twisted my neck so I could see her, but let my head stay on her dashboard.

The meetings were over. They had gone so late, in fact, that the sky had lightened from the black of night to a deep shade of purple—pretty soon the horizon was going to glow with the rising sun. And still the Drake motorcade waited—because Killian was chatting with the supernatural elite. (I had opted to escape to the car rather than let him pull me into his politics.)

On the upside, Mason hadn't filed an appeal as Momoko said he planned to. But somehow I didn't think it was because he had abandoned the idea, and more likely because he had made other arrangements. Or maybe he was just afraid of Killian?

I sighed. "What am I supposed to do now?"

"I assume you are referring to the situation with Tutu's?" Celestina asked.

"Yeah."

The back door opened. "You'll open your lockbox of course, one way or another."

# CHAPTER SIX

*Hazel*

K illian hunched over so he could slide into the car.

I peered around my headrest. "You never ride in the car."

"If you had gotten into one of the SUVs like I *told* you to, I wouldn't have to." Killian momentarily wrinkled his nose with disgust before he nodded to Celestina. "Home."

"Yes, Your Eminence." Celestina turned on her car, which purred like a big cat, and pulled out into the street, joining the rest of the Drake motorcade.

"I didn't hear you tell me to get into one of the SUVs," I said. "You should have texted me if you wanted to chat."

"I'll remember that next time," Killian said in a dark voice that didn't bode well for me.

"Anyway, I don't know how I'm supposed to get into my lock-box. Re-registering is going to be a major pain. I don't even know if it's possible—if you ever have to register again as an adult you're supposed to have a few wizards from your House come with to vouch for you. That obviously won't be happening."

"Forget the paperwork," Killian ordered. "I'll make some calls."

"You have connections with *wizard registration*? You really do have victims everywhere."

"I have contacts, not victims." Killian smirked at me from the back seat. "And no, even I don't have anyone who owes me favors in wizard registration—not in the Midwest, anyway."

"That's shocking," I said with real honesty.

"I never saw a point in it before. You are—historically speaking—such a weak and pathetic race," Killian said, as if to explain the oversight. "I do, however, have contacts with a few dragon shifters."

I was forced to twist around in my seat so my seatbelt uncomfortably dug into my neck—I was starting to regret that I hadn't sat in the back with him, because this would have been a much easier conversation to hold. "You know *Tutu*?"

"We've been introduced." Killian stretched his arms across the back seat. "I'll see what I can do."

"...Thank you."

Killian shrugged—a small shift of his shoulders that I almost missed—then looked out the window at the brightening sky.

"Did the Night Court cause any trouble tonight?" I directed my comment to Celestina, this time. "I didn't notice anything personally, but I also skipped several of the meetings."

Celestina offered me a smile. "No. Tonight they were silent."

"Which very likely means they are planning something," Killian added, his tone bored.

I yawned as I thought of Mason and the other Houses I'd cross in the future if I wanted to get House Medeis back. "Was it worth it?"

Killian's gaze shifted from the window to me. "What are you referring to?"

"Making the Night Court your enemy to use the chaos amongst the fae to push a law through," I said. "Was it worth it?"

"At the time it was." Killian sighed and ran a hand through his artfully mussed hair. "I might have been a little more vicious and pushed to get the Night Queen deposed rather than fined if I had known what a pain Queen Nyte would be. But I thought she'd be a weak link I could press in the future—which she is. She's just an *indescribably annoying* weak link."

A question burned on the tip of my tongue—one that was rude enough it might tug on Killian's temper.

But besides getting snarly at me for facing off with the serial killer vampire, he hadn't really ever been mad at me. So I blurted out the question without stopping to reword it. "Why are you so politically pushy?"

Killian had been resting his head on his hand with his elbow propped up on the window. At my question both of his eyebrows rose. "Excuse me?"

"You're the Eminence. Most regional leaders are occupied with their specific people. But you keep an eye on *everyone*, and you manipulate and push when everyone else doesn't actually care what the others are up to as long as they are following all the regional laws. I want to know why."

The silence stretched out uncomfortably long and was on the cusp of turning oppressive.

Celestina laughed—a surprisingly natural sound even though she was obviously just breaking the tension. "Isn't it a good thing? He wouldn't have picked you up if he wasn't. Speaking of which, perhaps you'd like an update on Hazel's training, Your Eminence?"

"I push because someone among the vampires must, or we'll fade away entirely," he said.

I was shocked he answered me—Celestina was equally surprised given the weird gurgling noise she made.

I was so delirious by the very pronounced win that it took a few seconds for his words to sink in. "Fade away? You're one of the most powerful races!"

"As I have said before, our procreation rate has slowed

dramatically." Killian shrugged out of his suitcoat and tossed it onto the seat next to him. "Newly turned vampires are *rare*. We're not replacing ourselves at a sustainable rate—unlike you wizards who breed like rabbits."

"Yeah, but you live forever."

"Perhaps, but the older a vampire gets, the less they care about life," Killian grimly said. "I have to drive the vampire Elders to do anything because they no longer care about this world—or even their Family. And that is dangerous. Their jaded cynicism makes them less likely to participate in politics, which will allow other races to direct our path. I use every trick in the book to keep our power in place and to try and regain what ground we've lost."

"You could work with the other races, you know," I said. "It's not like we have to have an antagonistic relationship."

Killian laughed—a bitter sound that made me wince. "Because that has worked out so well for you with your own race, has it?" He shook his head. "There is too much bad blood between the races—too many centuries of war and history. It's a miracle we can function together, and I think it's only possible *because* we keep to our own."

He was right. *Maybe.* Those of us with magic were united because magic was dying, and we needed to stay united to keep from blowing it with humanity, or we would all suffer. It still didn't seem right, though.

"You're helping me." I spoke slowly, trying to measure my words so Killian couldn't use them against me in the future. "And it's had a positive impact on me. Celestina and the others have challenged my mindset about fighting."

"That's more a reflection on you than the ability of wizards and vampires to get along." Killian's gaze was smoldering, and it was a little uncomfortable to hold his dark eyes, so I sat back in the seat to chew on what he'd told me.

That he even admitted that vampires were in a dangerous spot was huge. He had to trust me—or trust in my virtues, as he kept calling my deep moral code—or he wouldn't have revealed the potential weakness.

The truth was, it didn't matter much. Every race had its own struggles—wizards included. Though ours was a lot more obvious, there was something about Killian's explanation that urged me to show in some way that I trusted him, too.

"We wizards might be more plentiful, but there's been a pretty steady power decline for the last few generations," I abruptly volunteered. "My grandparents' generation as a whole was almost twice as powerful as my age group. It used to be slower, but at the rate it's plummeting, wizards are going to barely be capable of more than simple magic tricks in a century."

"Magic is dying," Killian stated. "Given that it's wild and not predictable or easily manipulated, no one can forcibly revive it. Perhaps it's a sign of the times, or our punishment for the awful things we've done with it."

I twisted in my chair again to look back at him, but he was staring outside—where the horizon was now a pale shade of golden-blue.

There was something profoundly depressing about the moment—which was kind of ironic. I'd been through a lot these past few months, but it was strangely crushing to be sitting with Killian Drake and together openly acknowledge that there were some problems that were too big to be fixed. It made my unusual living situation that much more bittersweet.

My relationship with the Drake Family was an anomaly.

It was sad, because deep inside of me, I had to wonder—if we weren't the exception...how would that change our world?

———

TWO DAYS LATER, I limped into the massive dining room in Drake Hall. Several times a week, all the Drake vampires—

excluding the few on guard duty, and Killian—ate dinner together at a table that felt about as long as a hallway.

They didn't have to eat human food—usually they picked at it a bit and had a wine glass or two of blood with the snack. But I, however, was expected to eat a full meal—and attend every meal possible.

It had been super awkward the first few weeks to sit with approximately thirty strange vampires, but now I knew everyone by face and name, and it was mostly fun to see everyone. *Mostly*.

I winced as my ankle protested when I put too much weight on it as I plopped in a graceless heap on my chair.

Gavino—seated on my left, glanced at me. "Julianne got you good, did she?" He made a clicking noise that could have been mistaken for sympathy if you didn't know better—but I did. "That will teach you to be faster next time."

"I can't be faster than a vampire." I smiled at the kitchen staff member who set the last tray of food and a wine bottle of blood on the table before fleeing the room.

"You don't have to be." Julianne claimed the open seat next to me—looking irritatingly fresh and perfect. "You still beat me —Miss."

I groaned. "Don't you start, Julianne!"

"You defeated me—very resoundingly. It is a vampire practice to show the respect due to you." Julianne *sounded* both logical and sincere, but I'd seen her wrap a few of the other vampires around her little finger with ease, so that wasn't reassuring.

"If I beat you, why do I look like a train hit me, and you are perfectly fine?" I asked.

"Vampire healing," Julianne said. "Or do you *not* remember hitting me with so much electricity you made my hair start on fire?"

"You do favor lightning." Josh stood in the doorway, unloading his sai, katana, sidearm, throwing daggers, secondary sidearm, and what *looked* like a blowdart onto a sideboard placed near the room entrance. "Though I cannot blame you. It is a good match for you, and you are quite deft at using it."

"Very deft," Julianne said a little wryly. "Though I must compliment you on your shield."

"Ahh—yes!" Gavino swirled his wine glass, sniffing the blood when he finished. "It has improved a lot!"

I'd been practicing the magic shield with a diligence that comes with knowing it could save my life. Using pure magic was the right trick—there was something about its properties that could repel *anything*—including a vampire.

It was still pretty volatile, so it was difficult to keep it up and steady for any lengthy period of time. And as much as I tried, I couldn't seem to get the shield to completely encircle me. (That would have been dead useful!)

Even so, it gave me an edge up—and a way to keep my matches with the Drake vampires from being melee only so I could attack at a range, which was a lot easier since I could change the direction of my magic mid-attack.

Julianne raised her glass and winked at me. "To Miss Hazel— may you continue your way up our ranks."

"I don't know how much higher I can go," I admitted. "I seem to win each match by the skin of my teeth."

"A win is a win," Julianne said.

"Unless you are dead—then it doesn't matter if you won or not." Josh—having finally finished disarming himself—claimed the chair across from mine. "Though I suppose death on the battlefield is an honorable way to achieve the embrace of the void."

"You aren't giving yourself enough credit, Miss Hazel." Gavino said, ignoring Josh's death poetry. "You are getting better with your sword, too. I was telling Ling about your skill, and we were wondering if perhaps you had some vampire slayer blood in your family?"

While wizards were the most common kind of supernatural

humans, there were tiny subsets of humans with special powers and abilities. One of those were vampire slayers—who possessed supernatural speed and skill with weapons, making them the only kind of humans who could fight toe-to-toe with a vampire.

Because of that skill, they used to be hired out as mercenaries, or sometimes even paid to eliminate rogue, Unclaimed vampires.

Legend had it vampire slayers got their powers because there was some vampire blood in their lineage, but races hadn't intermixed like that in centuries, and the vampire slayer families in America were down to the double digits. Magic's slow death seemed to hit the rarer humans—like vampire slayers and werewolf hunters—harder, so they were dying out fast.

"No slayers. Just wizards." I made a face. "Or I wouldn't be so slow."

Before anyone could respond, Rupert slunk into the room.

Rupert was a tall, handsome, red-haired vampire I had previously crossed paths with. He wasn't my biggest fan, and had actually knocked me unconscious before I unsealed my magic.

Killian, in return, had almost killed Rupert, and the vampire had been in disgrace since then—though at least the other vampires had started talking to him again after I stole his car.

A few of the vampires nodded to Rupert as he made his way to the opposite end of the table—as far away from me as he could get.

Gavino thoughtfully rubbed his jaw. "A few more matches, and you'll be up to face Rupert again."

"Great," I said, my voice lacking any trace of enthusiasm. "I can hardly wait."

"I should get you a handgun for the occasion," Josh said. "It seems unlikely you'd be able to hit him—even though you are a fair enough shot—Rupert is far too fast for your human eyes. But it might cheer you to have certain death at your hip."

Julianne rubbed her temple. "Sir, I thought Celestina gave you a talk about appropriate ways to encourage someone."

"Was that not an encouraging thought?"

"Not even close."

"I see." Josh turned his garnet red eyes back to me. "Then please allow me to try again. If Rupert dared to seriously injure you a second time, he wouldn't survive the experience, so you can at least be comforted that he won't be attempting to inflict the *maximum* amount of pain."

Julianne sighed. "Has anyone seen Celestina?"

Sigmund—a lean vampire I'd faced previously, slightly bowed his head to me, then furrowed his forehead at Julianne. "She must not be back from her appointment. She was visiting a mankist, I think?"

Julianne blinked. "What's a mankist?"

"He means a manicurist—or a nail salon." Celestina strode into the room with long, sure strides despite her stiletto heels. "I got my first pedicure!" She stuck a foot out for us, so we could look at her pink toe nails through the peep-toe shoes.

"How pretty!" Julianne cooed.

Gavino bit into a roll as he inspected Celestina's feet. "Is the color supposed to help you in some way?"

"No—it's purely fashion." She glanced at the dining table—which was full—and closed the door shut behind her.

"Then what's the point?"

"I *said* fashion." Celestina beamed when she saw me. "There's my favorite wizard! Have you been off to see Killian today?"

"Nope," I said. "I was too busy getting beat up by Julianne and frying her in return."

Celestina nodded. "Understandable. You ought to be the one to bring him his evening blood pouch, then."

"Feeling generous tonight, are you?" Gavino asked.

"I've gotten more afternoons off since Hazel arrived than I have in the previous *decade*. If our wizard's presence encourages that behavior, I'm going to make certain His Eminence sees her as much as he wishes."

"I also was given time off." Josh tapped the rim of his empty wine glass—he'd already downed the first glass of blood. "I believe it might have been the first occasion I've ever managed to clean my entire weapon arsenal in a month."

Manjeet—one of the vampires sitting farther down the table —laughed and raised his wine glass. "To our wizard—life has gotten *so* much more interesting since you arrived."

At least a dozen of the vampires seated around the table chorused, "To our wizard!"

I grinned at the laughing Family. "Hopefully this makes my smelly blood forgivable?"

"Honey." A male vampire with a thick southern accent chuckled. "You stopped smelling bad to most of us weeks ago."

I blinked in surprise. "I did?"

Celestina daintily seated herself in the free chair next to Josh. "You've smelled neutral to the majority of us for quite some time."

I stabbed a roll—cutting a hole in the side, which I filled with soft honey butter. "Neutral—that means you don't necessarily trust me, but you don't *distrust* me, right?"

"Indeed," Josh said.

"Aww, you guys! I'm going to tear up." I played at fanning my face before I took a huge bite out of my butter-stuffed roll.

This roused another round of chuckles from the vampires— except for Rupert, who stared at his blood drink.

I started to dig into the main course that night—carbonara, one of my favorites since the head chef always added extra bacon and cheese—when a flicker of shadows caught my eye.

I glanced up, freezing when I saw Killian leaning against the frame of the doorway—which was open just wide enough to admit him.

He looked amused—or perhaps bemused—with our dinner party, and perhaps a little disheveled. His necktie was gone, and the top two buttons of his dress shirt were open. When he caught me looking, his smirk grew.

Celestina peered at me, then turned around in her chair. "Your Eminence!" She swiftly pushed back from the table and stood so she could bow to him. "Did you need something?"

Hastily, all the other vampires leaped to their feet and bowed as well.

Killian swatted his hand at them. "It's fine."

Celestina was not so easily convinced. Her shoulders were set with steely determination as she pushed on. "Did you want us to send up your blood packs early tonight?"

"No," Killian said. "I came to inform you all that we're going to have..." He tipped his head back as he thought, and his smirk turned devious. "Let's call it a *field trip*."

"Where to, Your Eminence?" Josh asked.

Killian's smirk was so wide he flashed his pronounced fangs. "Tutu's."

# CHAPTER SEVEN

*Hazel*

I dropped my fork on my plate with a loud clack. "You talked to her? What did she say?"

Killian strolled into the room, his free hand shoved in his pants pocket. "She won't bend the rules and let you skip the paperwork—particularly since the Wizard Council took such a strong stance that you need to re-register. It would be bad publicity."

That was bad news, but Killian was too *smug* for that to be the end of it. Warily, I glanced at the other Drake vampires, but none of them showed the concern I did. "What did she offer as an alternative?"

"A trade." Killian sucked his blood pouch down and tossed the garbage on the table. "Tutu has quarterly tests of her security systems at each branch location. She alternates between holding a manual employee test, and a field test where a team is hired to try and break into the building. The test for the Magiford branch location is next week. She's agreed to hire a team from the Drake Family to hold the field test."

"Let me get this straight." I set my elbows on the table and clamped my hands on the side of my head so I could be certain my head was on right. "You want us to try and break into *Tutu's*? A bank which is universally acknowledged as one of America's safest magical storage methods?"

"She's hiring us—we'll have contracts that will legally protect us *and* her," Killian said. "And if we just so happen to liberate the contents of your lockbox while we are there..." He grinned savagely.

"But would it hurt her reputation more to have something stolen from her bank?" I asked.

"Only if you plan to report that items were stolen from your lockbox," Celestina pointed out.

I blinked in surprise. That was actually a very good point. If we were hired by Tutu, and neither I nor her staff registered a complaint about my lockbox, we'd be in the clear.

"We won't take anything else," Killian continued. "And Tutu set up the contract so *when* the team makes it in and out, we have to bring proof with us. Your lockbox will be our proof."

"I think I get it." I slowly nodded. "But who is going to be on the team? I obviously can't do it by myself, and you said Tutu hired the Drake Family?"

"Precisely. So for the next week we'll be *practicing* to see who qualifies to be on the team. It will be a wonderful bonding experience." The purr in Killian's voice made me think the next week was actually going to bond us the same way childhood traumas can serve as bonding experiences for siblings.

"That sounds...great," I said.

"I'm glad you think so. Come downstairs after you finish dinner. We begin drills tonight." Killian sauntered from the room.

The second the door closed behind him, the vampires dashed to the table, downed their blood, and tore into a few snacks.

"Come downstairs as fast as you can, Hazel. Oh—but don't make yourself sick!" Celestina licked her lips after she finished off the last of her blood, then bulldozed her way past Josh—who was putting his veritable armory back on.

Julianne winked at me. "See you in the gym, Miss!" She and Gavino sprinted from the room.

I was a little confused. They seemed...excited. Which, I got that the Drake Family drilled and practiced endlessly, but that didn't explain why they'd be *excited* about breaking into a magically warded vault—even if it was legal.

I chewed a mouthful of carbonara as I thought.

And why was Killian doing this? What did he gain by potentially risking his Family? Because let me be straight, *Tutu's* was warded to the basement pipes with magical traps and wards. Even if Tutu had invited us to break in, the danger was still very real.

I doubted he'd go this far just for me, so...what was his angle? And what did he get out of this?

———

FOUR DAYS INTO OUR 'PREPARATION', I started getting worried.

Not because Killian hadn't yet announced who was on the team, but because of the *wide* variety of activities he was putting everyone through as part of the testing phase.

The night he announced the deal with Tutu, there was a weightlifting *and* flexibility competition. The following day we all went down to the pool for a demonstration of our swimming skills.

Today, we were practicing climbing on a rock wall I hadn't even known existed out by the swimming pool.

"Um, Killian." I watched Celestina rappel down the wall. "Is there something you want to tell me about what we're going to find *inside* Tutu's?"

Killian stabbed a straw in one of his blood pouches—which always reminded me of juice packs. Disgustingly, Killian's attractive looks weren't ruined by the childish picture. He made it *cool*. It was incredibly irritating. "It's fine," he said around the straw.

I stared at the climbing gear fastened around my waist and legs—which I had *no* idea of how to use. "I don't think it is, actually."

"We won't be dodging dragon shifters if that's what you're concerned about," Killian said. "Though it's pretty safe to assume there will be fire traps."

"I'll make a note to bring marshmallows."

"You never know when you'll need a snack." He grinned—the more subtle kind that actually flashed with true humor rather than vindictive cynicism like his regular smirks.

I couldn't help grinning back, until his comment about fire traps sank in. "So, we're for real trying to break into my lockbox."

"Yes."

"And Tutu is keeping her security system on, so she's not making this any easier on us."

"No."

I paused. "Killian...of the quarterly reviews that she's hired teams to try and break in...how many of them have succeeded?"

Killian checked his wristwatch. "Maybe a dozen."

"At this location?" I asked. A dozen still wasn't great odds considering Tutu's had been around in my grandparents' time. But the Drake Family was powerful.

"No, nationwide," Killian said.

"*What?*" My stomach plummeted to my toes. "How are we going to get to my lockbox if the test has only failed twelve times *ever?*"

"Getting to your lockbox alone won't work," Killian warned. "We have to successfully take something and leave. If her security team catches up with us, they'll take it back."

"How wonderful. I should have spent my mornings looking over the wizard registration paperwork," I grumbled. "Might as well prepare for the inevitable."

Killian raised an eyebrow at me. "Your lack of faith in the Drake Family's ability to break laws is upsetting."

I scrunched my eyes shut and rubbed my forehead. I needed to make some serious headway on my magic over the next few days so I could help as much as possible. Maybe we needed to visit the Paragon again so I could get another book to look at?

"It will be fine, Hazel," Killian said. "It's a challenge."

I shot him a look. "This might be fun and games for you, but I need my signet ring."

"You missed my point." Killian nodded to the vampires—who were performing all sorts of impossible athletic feats as they climbed the walls. "I train them so they can be ready for a fight to the death at any moment. They are the deadliest vampires in the area. For *them*, this will only be a challenge."

Slowly, I nodded. "You're right. They are capable." I hesitated. "I'm just afraid to hope that something will actually go *right* at this point."

"It will," Killian promised. "We will *make* it right."

We stood in silence for a few moments, until Killian added, "And I never said Tutu was the only favor I called in."

Ah, well, that explained a lot. But it also raised more questions in my mind. The top of the list still being...why?

Why was Killian going through such effort to help me?

I watched Josh shoot at a moving target while he clung to the rock wall. (No one could ever say the Drake vampires weren't enthusiastic.)

"I appreciate the help." I slowly said. "But is this really okay?"

Killian sucked on his blood pouch. "You aren't referring to the rock climbing."

"No. I'm talking about getting hired to break into Tutu's so I can grab my lockbox." I scratched my nose as I watched Rupert scale the wall with the speed of a monkey. "You're putting multiple Drake vampires at stake. And I don't think you're getting anything out of it." I watched Killian out of the corner of my eye, trying to judge his expression.

He shrugged. "It's good training for them—and it's a challenge they haven't experienced before."

His expression was too...*harmless*. Killian Drake was one of the most cunning and vicious beings in the Midwest. There was no way he was doing this because it was a good *training exercise*. "That can't be the real reason why you're doing this," I said. "Do you plan to snatch something while we're there?"

Killian snorted. "I may push for political power, but even I know when discretion is the better option. No, Tutu will gut me if she were to find anything besides contents from your lockbox missing. Dragon shifters are possessive—it's why her company was fast to take off. Everyone knew they could trust her to guard their valuables once they were put under her care."

This was a believable—and likely—answer.

But it made me want to scratch my head even more. "So what *are* you getting out of this?"

Killian finished his blood pouch and tossed it in a nearby trashcan. "You doubt I would go through all of this just for your sake?" His eyes smoldered with more hints of red than usual as he leaned in. "Don't you think I care?"

Bless my soul—I hoped he didn't. Care, that is.

His gaze was almost magnetic, and with him *this close* to me—with his arm touching mine—I couldn't miss how attractive he was, and how dangerous he could be to me.

And, no, I wasn't referring to the way he could probably kill me with a single blow.

*House Medeis.* I gulped as I forced myself to cling to that thought. *I have a duty to House Medeis.*

During my somewhat panicked thoughts, Killian pressed in closer so we were now face to face, and he rested one forearm on my shoulder. "Well?"

I patted Killian on the chest the same way I would pat a

happy dog's wriggling rear. "Please. You've taught me better than to think that."

Killian stared at me, then abruptly leaned back and laughed. "Keeping you is almost worth it for the entertainment factor alone." He shifted so he now rested both of his forearms on my shoulders in what could *maybe* be loosely interpreted as a slack hug.

"I'm going to take that as you won't tell me what you're getting in all of this," I said.

"It's the bonding," Killian said. "It's important for blending the Drake Family together."

"Yeah." I rolled my eyes. "And I'm totally naïve enough that I believe that."

Killian chuckled. Standing this close to him, I could feel it start in his chest.

I had been hot before—Celestina made me run laps before she tackled the climbing wall—but Killian oozed cool air, making him extra pleasant to stand next to. I was pretty suspicious that Killian knew this, because he was almost *too* casual in the way he draped his arms over me.

He noticed my narrowed eyes. "What?"

"You can't fool me," I declared.

"About what?"

"I don't know. But you still can't fool me."

More rich laughter. "If things don't work out with House Medeis, perhaps the Drake Family ought to officially adopt you," Killian purred.

"Is that even possible?"

"You could be our mascot. Or pet."

"Such a tempting offer." It was right about then I noticed Gavino, lingering a few feet away and staring at the ceiling in a way that communicated he'd rather be anywhere but here.

Killian didn't even have to look at him—he kept his half-lidded gaze on me. "What?"

Gavino bowed extra low. "Sorry for interrupting, Your Eminence, but everyone has completed the initial climb, except for Hazel."

Killian pulled back from me. "Fine. Come on, Wizard. You're up."

He strode for the climbing wall, and I dutifully followed—trotting to keep pace with his long legs.

He glanced down at me. "I'm impressed. I thought you'd try to get out of the climb."

I shrugged. "As long as someone checks all these ropes for me since I don't have a clue what to do, it will be fine," I said.

"You're getting braver—how commendable."

"Not really. I don't know why you think this would be such a big deal when you *chucked me off the roof* of Drake Hall!"

Killian sighed as we stopped short of the wall. "It was only the third floor."

Before I could protest, Celestina approached us with a smile. "Which part of the wall do you think she should climb, Your Eminence?"

"Hazel is extra cheeky today, so I was thinking the highest portion." Killian pointed to the one part of the wall that reached the ceiling.

He glanced at me—very obviously looking for a reaction—so I kept my expression flat just on principle.

"Or perhaps you could just yank her up and down like a pinata," Killian said.

I broke and wrinkled my nose at him. "That's so mature of you."

Killian winked, before his expression turned serious as he turned his attention to Celestina. "I wanted your observations on how everyone performed today."

I tuned out and instead scuffed my running shoe on the gym floor, producing a squeak as my thoughts returned to Killian's joking earlier.

Yeah, it'd be really bad if he actually cared about me.

Killian cared *deeply* about things that were important to him. I don't know if he loved, or was even capable of love, but between his political dabbling and public figure, it was pretty obvious he cared about the Drake Family, and it was equally obvious he'd tear the region apart if someone tried to hurt his people.

If he cared about me like that, vampire or not, there was no way I could hold out against him. And *that* was where the danger was. Because caring was definitely not the same as loving. And the last thing I needed was to have an unrequited love for Killian Drake.

# CHAPTER EIGHT

*Killian*

I sat on the windowsill of the farm house and checked my watch. 4:30 am. I needed to start the drive home soon. I was only an hour and a half away from Drake Hall, but I had to get back before Hazel woke up, or she'd ask more questions.

Questions I didn't know the answer to.

I studied the sleeping werewolf curled up on a dumpy mattress. It was Alpha Nash—leader of the Flatlands Pack and clearly one of Mason's newest co-conspirators, although obviously not a very good one.

I'd been sitting here for the better part of thirty minutes, and the overgrown mutt had yet to sense me and wake up.

*Which would be more fun—to wake Nash up with a dagger at his throat, or casually kick him awake?*

In the end I decided it was best to go with a classic, so I ghosted over to Nash's bed and set my hand against the Alpha's throat, then pressed down hard.

Nash's eyes snapped open, and he thrashed against my hold, snarling until I set my knee on the man's sternum.

Werewolves were physically stronger than vampires. But I had Nash pinned to the mattress like a bug, and based on the Alpha's eyes that were fever-bright with fear, the darkness, the throat grab, and attacking the Alpha in his own *home*—with wolves standing watch—had scared the hell out of him. And a scared enemy was never a smart enemy.

I smiled.

"Alpha Nash." I spoke in a lowered tone—one the guard were-wolves wouldn't hear, but still conveyed I wasn't afraid of Nash or any member of the Flatlands Pack. "Do you know who I am?"

Nash's eyes bulged, and with my night vision I could see the Alpha's face was turning a mottled shade of red and purple. The werewolf fought for a breath of air, then wheezed, "Killian Drake."

"Very good," I said. "You've been a bad dog, Alpha Nash. You've made an alliance with a wizard who is attempting to set himself up as the new Adept of House Medeis."

Nash tried to shake his head, but he couldn't do much more than rock his head due to the grip I had on his neck. "N-n-no. The W-wizard Council was a c-c-coincidence."

I felt Nash's throat contract with the effort it took to talk. "Really? Is that all it was? Then I suppose the legal contract of an alliance you registered with Mason at the Magiford Curia Clois-ters was also a coincidence?"

The Alpha's skin turned ashen, and sweat beaded across his forehead.

I watched him for several long moments. "Because I am gener-ous, I'm going to give you a chance to correct this miscalculation of yours. Dissolve the contract with Mason. Stay far away from House Medeis, and *never* set your eyes on Hazel. In the future, if I find so much as a tail hair from a member of your Pack around House Medeis, I'll come back with my Family. And next time *you won't wake up*."

I pushed down hard enough to make Nash gurgle, then eased

off the werewolf. I glided back to the open window. "You've been warned, Nash." I slipped out the window, landing on the front porch roof with a thump so soft it didn't make the seemingly half-deaf watch wolves twitch an ear.

It was easy enough to trace my path across the farmland that surrounded the Pack house and make my way back to the car in the darkness.

The Flatlands Pack was one of the least respected Packs in Illinois due to their lack of strength and discipline—making it child's play to enter and exit their lands without an invitation.

Regardless, Nash would have become a problem for Hazel. Already her wizard allies had abandoned her. But while I couldn't involve myself with her fight for her House, I could make sure none of the other races tried to poke a nose into her business.

I reached my car—parked on the shoulder of a country road—and slid in, turning it on.

I glanced at my wrist watch again, and tried to ignore the nagging sensation that tramping out around werewolf land for the sake of a wizard was a sign I was losing some of my famed control.

Hazel Medeis wasn't part of the Drake Family. I could pretend that if I let her rejoin her family and successfully take back House Medeis it would give me a toehold of power in wizarding society... but I knew it wasn't political maneuverings that had me away from Drake Hall and invading hostile territory without the knowledge of my own Family.

Nope, it only took a petite wizard who was equal parts saint and sass to accomplish that.

I rubbed my face and growled.

It bothered me that Hazel no longer smelled like a rotting carcass. Rather, the scent of her blood had turned intoxicating overnight, to the point where I couldn't resist purposely inhaling whenever she got close. I was barely better than one of the mutty-werewolves!

And I couldn't even answer *why*. I just knew that when I saw

Hazel relentlessly throw herself at the vampire responsible for all the killings and slayings in the vampire community...something in me changed.

Hazel had no loyalty to me—nor any of the vampire Families. But there was a stark beauty in her fierceness when she had fought Solene—because she wasn't fighting for herself, but for others.

When was the last time I had witnessed something like that?

Although, after Hazel had woken up and I had some time to think about it, it irritated me more and more to think how she had just *flung* herself into the fight with her at-the-time miniscule powers. The idiot.

I roughly slammed the car's gear into drive and stomped on the gas, trying to cut off my stupid—and disgustingly *soft*—thoughts. If I wasn't careful, I was going to sound like one of the crusty old vampire Elders who went around quoting poetry about the people they'd lost centuries ago.

The only upside in all of this, if there could truly be an upside in this power imbalance, was that she had no idea the power she held over me. She had no idea how much I trusted her. I'd have to do something about it before she—or anyone else—realized the truth.

But for now, I'd protect her where I could—even if that meant calling in favors with the dragon shifters, or visiting werewolves in the early hours of the morning. And I'd do everything I could to train her up to make her lethal—and hopefully better able to survive the fight that loomed in her future.

I didn't know what I wanted in return. Nothing, maybe?

*It would be better if I* didn't *get anything in return. It's not like she's 'the one.'*

I impatiently shoved the idea of the ridiculous, overly romanticized vampire concept of love out of my mind. I was addled, but not *that* badly.

Still. If she flung herself in harm's way again—like she had with Solene—I was going to wring her scrawny neck myself.

# CHAPTER NINE

*Hazel*

My heart thudded so painfully in my chest it made my throat ache as I walked shoulder to shoulder with Celestina, following behind Killian and Josh.

Night had long ago fallen, and we were walking up a back street that circled behind the stores that lined the block Tutu's covered. There were only a few street lights here, but it made sense that we'd approach Tutu's from the back.

In our informational meeting—after Killian had decided what ten vampires would accompany him and me—Killian said the bulk of Tutu's was underground. So even if we broke in through a back entrance, we'd still have to go down, but at least we'd avoid public notice.

Behind me, Rupert sighed in irritation.

Killian *said* he chose his team for skill alone, but I suspected he was aware that letting Rupert in on this...*challenge,* as he had called it, would restore Rupert. At the very least the rest of the Family likely wouldn't be so cold to him.

Still, I can't say I was psyched to have the red-haired vampire at my back.

Killian held up his hand to stop us when he reached the back of Tutu's.

It looked innocuous enough—a little, two-story brick building.

But when I blinked, I could see the magic wards that covered the walls. I couldn't tell everything they'd set off and do, but I was pretty confident they'd sound an alarm and hit us with some kind of pain spell if we walked through them.

Killian popped open a small mint container and carelessly flung what looked like a mint at the building.

Rather than bounce off the wall, the mint dissolved on contact, and the magic that hummed through the red wards turned a dull gray.

"What was that?" I squawked.

"The wards are down?" Killian asked.

Being the only one capable of sensing magic, I nodded. "Yeah, they're down. But what was that? It just cut off the wards. They don't have power!"

"That," Killian carefully enunciated as he turned toward me. "Was a favor." He glanced at one of the second-story windows, then barely nodded at Celestina.

Stirring only the tiniest of breezes, Celestina sprang at the window. With her vampire athleticism she easily reached it and pulled herself onto the sill, balancing with ease on the tiny spot.

She blocked the window with her body, so I couldn't see exactly what she did, but after a few muted metal clicks, she did a one-armed handstand on the windowsill and pried the window open a little, then gripped the window itself and forcibly swung it open.

Hanging from the window as if she didn't have a care in the world, Celestina gave us a thumbs up before she slipped inside.

Rupert went next, followed by Julianne. I watched them scale the wall with a slight frown.

"Wizard." Killian offered me his hand.

"No thanks," I said.

Killian raised an eyebrow. "We're going through the upstairs window. There is no other route."

"Yeah," I agreed. "But I don't need to be carried like a sack of potatoes to get in there."

I clambered onto the windowsill of the first-floor window and braced my feet on the side of the window before shimmying up.

There are certain positives to being short and slender. It's pretty hard to keep me out of places because I can fit just about anywhere, and I'm light enough that I can haul myself up. Since Gavino's been having me lift weights during my training sessions it's only gotten easier!

I wasn't as fast as the vampires—who could make it to the second-floor window with a single leap—but I was able to find toeholds in the brick and force my way up the wall. My pants, unfortunately, got stuck on the windowsill when I slithered through, so I had to wiggle my butt to get all the way in, but I hadn't torn anything, so as far as I was concerned it was a success.

The room was dark—Celestina hadn't turned on any lights—but I could make out five wooden desks topped with sleek computers.

I popped to my feet and hitched my pants up as I felt a whisper of a breeze behind me.

"Inelegant, but effective enough I suppose," Killian said.

"Yep. Two thumbs up for my new clothes, though!" I showed Killian my thumbs as I twirled around to face him. "It moves with me really well and offers a little more protection than my workout clothes!"

"I am glad you are so satisfied," Killian dryly said. "And I can see, now, why it's necessary if you plan to so artfully scale many more walls."

I shrugged. "You're just butthurt I got up here by myself."

"I'm *what*?" Killian hissed.

"I beg your pardon, Your Eminence, but might I interrupt?" Josh called in his droll, quiet voice. He was seated at a desk across the room, his face eerily lit a bright blue by the glowing computer screen positioned in front of him. "I need to speak to Hazel."

"What's up?" I asked.

"Might you remind me what your lockbox number is?" Josh asked as Celestina peered over his shoulder.

"It's in Block 45, lockbox number 45228." I drifted toward Josh and the computer as more vampires slipped in through the window.

Josh banged away on the keyboard, clicking through screens so quickly I couldn't even tell what I was seeing. "Found it," he said. "Looks like Block 45 is currently parked in the Sapphire Docking Bay."

"Let's go find it then, shall we?" Killian smirked and sauntered for the door—where Celestina was working on the office security system.

"Almost done." She had the flashlight of her cellphone turned on and had spread a dusty substance over the number pad of the system, then typed something into her cellphone.

I stood on my tiptoes to view her phone screen. "You're *googling* the security system? In the middle of a break in?"

"We didn't know for certain what the office security system is, and I need to know how many numbers are in the combo," Celestina said.

I turned to Killian, but he only shrugged. "Some things must be dealt with on-the-fly. Such is the life of a criminal."

I narrowed my eyes at him. "You sound awfully sure about that. Speaking from experience, are you?"

"Definitely not." Killian gave me his most innocent smile—which was more wolfish than angelic. "I am an honorable and upright politician. What do I know about breaking and entering?"

"Got it," Celestina said before I could respond. She typed away on the keypad, which made a little musical noise. "And we're in." She opened the door and slipped through first.

Josh flicked off the computer screen and went in after her. I poked my head into the darkened hallway—which was pitch black —and barely managed to hold in a yelp when Killian scooped me up.

"You're night blind—it will be faster this way." He soundlessly slunk down the hallway.

"You could have warned me," I hissed in his ear.

"And spared myself any amusement at your expense? No."

I rolled my eyes as I slung my arm around his shoulder and tried to peer behind him. I could hear the faint footsteps of the rest of the Drake vampires trailing behind us, but I couldn't see anything in the pervasive darkness.

Reflexively, I hunched closer to Killian.

"You are like carrying a furnace," he grumbled.

"I'm stressed," I said. "I'm hotter when stressed."

"That's a new excuse." Killian swept through a doorway. Based on the way it echoed, and its faint smell of concrete, I was guessing this was a stairway.

My suspicions were confirmed when Killian started descending—which is a pretty jarring sensation when you can't see anything and you're being carried.

I was stoked when Killian reached the first floor and slipped out of the stairway and into Tutu's ground floor.

A dim light was on in the lobby, so I could finally see my own hands—but the stairway popped us out behind some fancy iron gates that blocked the lobby from the loading station—where we were.

Tutu's wasn't like a normal bank. It didn't have stationary vaults or lockboxes. Instead, vaults and lockboxes were orga- nized in blocks. Each block moved around Tutu's various docking bays, and when a client came in the block was summoned to a viewing area—which was located behind the massive doors Celestina and Josh were working on with their high-tech gadgets.

The client was then led to the loading station—where we were. From there clients were taken to the viewing area, but *how* they were taken there varied in each branch building, and changed several times a year. Like I said, dragon shifters were both paranoid and ruthless in their protection.

In our planning and strategy meetings, Killian had explained that after lobby hours closed, the system for calling the blocks into the viewing areas also closed. The blocks still moved around —which is why Josh had to look up its location ahead of time— but they were sealed off in the docking bays.

"Done," Josh said. "The system has been disabled."

Celestina tapped her finger on the door. "The plans said there are guards behind these doors." She slipped her sidearm out of its holster. "Deadly force, Your Eminence?"

"No." Killian's breath tickled my cheek with his reply. "That will only irritate Tutu—which I'd like to avoid."

Celestina slipped her gun back in its holster and rolled up her pant legs to grab a giant syringe. "Very well. We'll use tranquilizers."

She nodded to Gavino. He stalked up to the door and grabbed it from the bottom, his muscles bulging as he pulled up on it.

I squirmed in Killian's grasp, trying to get down and lift my legs out of his grip. I only managed to make his hand slip closer to my butt which was *not* the direction I wanted to head in. This made me grumble, and I elbowed him as I tried to forcibly peel his fingers off my leg.

Killian tipped his head back to avoid my forehead smacking his jaw. "Stop wriggling."

"I can see now, and I need to be ready for a fight." I kicked my legs a little when Killian didn't let me go.

"No kicking." Killian tried to pry me from his neck, but I

didn't want to let him drop me in a heap, so I clung to his shoulders.

"Then let me go."

"Stop clinging to me like a koala and I will!"

"You're going to drop me in a pile on purpose!"

One of the vampires near us snorted in amusement. I wasn't entirely sure who it was—it *sounded* like Celestina, but she had her back to us, and no one in a ten-foot radius was even looking at us.

The noise distracted Killian long enough that I was able to climb down him, reaching the floor just when Gavino-the-beef-cake wrenched the door so it rolled up into the ceiling.

Waiting on the other side of the door were four giant were-bears in their bear forms. They snarled with a ferocity I felt in my bones, but before they could even swat a paw, Celestina, Josh, and two other vampires were on them.

One vampire headbutted his target, another punched hers. I couldn't see what Josh did—I was too distracted by Celestina *literally slinging* her werebear over her shoulder, slamming its head to the ground in a wrestling move.

The werebear instantly stilled, falling unconscious as the other vampires similarly knocked out their targets.

"I thought you were going to use tranquilizers?" I trotted through the open door and peered down at the nearest, uncon-scious werebear.

"We are, now." Celestina parted the werebear's fur and stabbed the syringe into muscle. "Tranquilizers take time to set in —at least fifteen minutes. Our initial strike will only knock them out for a few minutes. The tranquilizer contains a muscle relax-ant, so even if they wake up, they won't be able to call for help before it entirely sets in and makes them sleep again."

"Oh," I said. "So much for movie accuracy."

Killian brushed past us, moving deeper into the room—which looked similar to a giant car garage with an immense track cutting right down the center. "Keep pace, Wizard."

"There are no traps ahead," announced one of the vampires.

I frowned as I scurried after Killian. "That seems weird, considering—"

Something clicked, and I heard the roar of distant fire.

The vampires leaped back, but I lunged forward, reaching for magic as I thrust my arms out in front of me.

My face heated with my wizard mark, and I threw my shield—forged of pure magic—up just in time to block a rushing river of fire.

Flames blazed around me. My shield flickered, but held steady as I reached out with my senses.

The floral taste of magic told me the fire came from a fae-enchanted object. I followed the magic back to the source—a crystal of some sort—then held my shield in place as I loosened a bolt of blue-hued lightning at it.

My shield actually cracked due to my split attention, but my lightning bolt was accurate and powerful, blasting the crystal to smithereens so the fire sputtered out.

"Excellent reaction time." Celestina strode forward to stand just a little in front of me. "However, I am not a fan of this." She pointed to the crack in my shield.

"It's hard to keep it strengthened and use other magic," I admitted.

She pursed her lips. "It's something to work on. Perhaps you ought to start fighting two vampires at a time."

"A worthy idea." Josh joined Celestina at inspecting my fractured shield. "To ease her into it I could shoot at her while she fights."

"That's not easing me in at all," I squawked. "You're practically a sharp shooter!"

"Your reaction time is getting better." Killian sauntered forward to add to the party. "Well done."

"You *knew* the trap was there?" I asked.

He shrugged. "I was prepared to toss you if necessary. But let's not forget the task at hand. Shall we?" He motioned to the metal track, which disappeared into darkness.

Celestina led, but Josh waited this time and brought up the rear while Killian and I stayed somewhere in the middle of the group.

The ground slowly fell off as the track descended, going deeper and deeper underground. Flickering lights were soldered on every forty foot stretch of the track, dimly illuminating the way.

I craned my neck and peered over the side, trying to see the ground beneath us, but there was only darkness.

"Careful," Gavino warned from his spot behind me. "It's a deep fall."

"How far down is the ground?" I asked.

Gavino, able to see in the darkness with his vampire eyes, glanced down. "Just don't fall."

The track wound down in a corkscrew, and there was a fire trap on each level—which I destroyed with more bolts of lightning.

"It's nice having a trained wizard." Julianne patted my shoulder after I destroyed another crystal.

I snorted. "One of you would shoot these things to take it out."

"Wouldn't work," Josh said from the back. "They're enchanted against it."

When we came to the next crystal—which Celestina marked out for me with a laser pointer—I took a moment to feel the magic layered around the crystal, and was surprised to discover Josh was right.

The only easy way to destroy the crystal was with wizard magic—which fae magic was notoriously weak against—or with another fae spell.

"It does seem like an architectural weakness." Killian smirked as we walked over one of the lights embedded on the track. "One Tutu will be highly aggravated to learn of."

"I can understand why it escaped her notice," Rupert muttered. "Thinking to ward against wizards is like thinking to ward off rats."

"Clearly not, or Hazel's magic wouldn't be nearly so useful. You can't let your prejudices get in the way of strategy, Rupert, or you'll end up dead." Julianne's voice was extra sweet, and when I glanced back at her she gave me a cheeky smile.

"Wizards are generally regarded as weak," Killian said. "Mostly because they are unoriginal and fussy. Hazel, however, is proving what they could be. And while it is unlikely a House of similarly trained wizards will suddenly pop up, it is something Tutu should guard against in case of rogues."

Killian's observation silenced everyone, until the track came to an end, cut off by another giant door that was supposed to roll up into the ceiling like a garage entrance.

"A viewing area?" I asked.

"Precisely," Josh said from the back.

"Expect enemies again," Celestina warned. She peered up at the ceiling and shot at what looked like a locking mechanism, then savagely ripped the door up.

The viewing area was pitch black—not a single light. Knowing I wasn't going to be any help, I crouched down, letting the vampires leapfrog over me. A few roars, the clang of swords, and all was silent.

"Clear!" Celestina called.

I stretched my hand above me and activated my blood, pulling magic from the air and transforming it into a big ball of blue light, casting a blue hue on the viewing area.

Celestina and the other vampires were busy tranquilizing the passed-out defenders—four werewolves, two fae, and two vampires—as I cautiously hopped off the track. At the far side of the garage-like structure was another track—this one wasn't flat and train-like, but constructed by metal pipes. Clearly, it was the track the blocks were transported on.

Josh joined me, staring intently at his cellphone. "According to the schedule we saw on the office computer, the necessary block is still located in the Sapphire Bay, which is...this path." He pointed to the metal tube on the far left.

"We're going to walk to it?" I asked. "On a *pipe*?"

Josh adjusted his glasses. "The software used for controlling the blocks is highly sophisticated and imbedded with magic. Strictly speaking, it's not possible for a vampire to run, and while you might be able to power it, the security to crack into it is beyond my rudimentary skills."

I eyed the pipe—which was perhaps about a foot wide, but still circular, which meant it was going to be a heck of a lot easier to pitch over the sides. "Great."

"You didn't want to be carried," Killian reminded me.

I rolled my shoulders back. "And I still don't."

"If you slip, there is a fairly good chance one of us will catch you," Josh said.

I wasn't sure if he was trying to be encouraging, or realistic, but the thought still wasn't a happy one.

Killian smirked and motioned to the pipe. "After you, Wizard."

Josh and a few other vampires hopped on the pipe with ease, starting down the path. I shot Killian a glare, but marched after them, my ball of light lagging behind me like a pet on a leash.

The walk was pretty uneventful, but only because Killian flung mints at three different sets of wards. Since I hadn't seen much dragon magic before—though I was coming to recognize its sooty, brimstone-like flavor—I couldn't tell exactly what they were for, but I was almost certain one of the wards caused instant death.

The pipe split, with the main path continuing on into darkness while a smaller pipe led to a docking bay dimly lit with red-hued lights. Even I could read the sign that said "Ruby Bay" from our pipe, so I was surprised when Josh and the leading vampires hopped onto the smaller pipe.

"This isn't the Sapphire Bay," I said. "Don't we need to keep going?"

"We will," Killian said. "But first we have an insignificant side task."

I suspiciously peered at him over my shoulder—because nothing Killian labeled as 'insignificant' in the current circumstances could actually be a small matter—but fell in line behind Josh. My stride was a little wobblier since the pipe was much smaller. I clambered the last few steps and leaped onto the bay when I felt my feet starting to slip. I rolled on my shoulder and popped to my feet—a testament to all my new training—and brushed my clothes off.

Killian leisurely climbed onto the docking bay and sauntered up to the rows and rows of lockboxes. He meandered through them for a minute, then stopped and tapped a desk sized lockbox. "This one."

I scratched my neck. "This one what?"

Celestina set a glittering gem on the lockbox, where it sparkled and gleamed. Unfamiliar magic pinged like ripples in a pond—it was so swift and sudden reacting I didn't even have time to process what it smelled or tasted like—and the lockbox lock clicked before the door swung open, revealing a box stuffed with glittering jewels, a few gold figurines, and what I thought looked like a magic sword.

"What are you doing?" I hissed. "You said we weren't taking anything besides the contents of *my* lockbox! You swore to Tutu you wouldn't take anything else!"

"I said I wouldn't take anything." Killian reached into his tailored suitcoat and pulled out a cream-colored envelope sealed with a dollop of red wax. "I never said I wouldn't put anything inside."

# CHAPTER TEN

*Hazel*

He set the letter on a stack of sparkling jewels, then turned his back to the lockbox and glided off.

Celestina shut the lockbox, nodding when the lock clicked, and all the vampires made for the small pipe.

"Come along, Hazel," Killian called. "Don't dawdle."

I grumbled under my breath as I hurried to follow, slowing down as soon as I hit the smaller pipe. My skin was clammy from my rush of anxiety by the time we picked our way back to the main pipeline. "That was the Night Court's lockbox, wasn't it?" I asked.

Killian, now in front of me, paused long enough to smirk back at me. "I wonder..."

"I would have thought a fae Court would need a bigger lockbox," I said.

"Fae Courts traditionally store their wealth in their realms," Celestina explained. "The Midwest Courts only keep their truly priceless magical tools here. Supposedly."

"It's all guesswork," Killian said. "Because *we* certainly haven't seen the insides of a Court lockbox."

I wanted to rub my forehead and squeeze the bridge of my nose, but I wasn't going to do anything that compromised my balance at the moment, so I dutifully followed after Killian. "I bet your letter said something along the lines of 'I was in here, guess what I stole', right?"

Killian actually chuckled. "I don't know if I should be proud that your intellect has clearly improved as a result of training with us, or concerned that you believe I am that predictable."

I grunted, but some suspicious part inside of me finally relaxed. I *knew* there was no way he was doing this just for me— or to provide his Family with a good training experience.

We walked in darkness—except for my ball of light—for a few minutes, until the big pipe split again, this time leading to a bay lit with purple-y-blue lights. The sign read "Sapphire Bay".

"This is our stop," Josh announced.

Killian held his hand out to me, helping me make the jump to the smaller pipe. "I suggest you take only what you need from your lockbox," he said. "Carrying a lot while we flee would be a pain."

"Yeah, I just want the ring." I inched along the smaller pipe, a drop of sweat dripping down my spine when my balance wobbled for a moment. "I can come back for everything else."

The pipe connected about three feet below the bay rim, so I had to heft myself up over the edge of it. Most of the vampires jumped over my head and landed on the Sapphire Bay with hushed taps when their boots touched down on the metal floor. I brushed my hands off on my thighs, and I swear I felt my heart throb all the way down in my toes as I carefully zigzagged back and forth in front of the lockboxes.

It took me a few minutes to find the right block of lockboxes —it was located at the very back of the bay—and then another long minute to find my parents' lockbox, tagged with a metal plate numbered 45228. Their lockbox was about the size of a shoebox—which was what I expected. We wizards did all right when it came to money, but very few wizard Houses managed to build enough wealth to rival vampires or fae.

My hands shook as I pulled the lockbox key out of a pocket in my jacket, and I could barely manage to turn the darn thing.

Finally. I was finally going to get the signet ring that proved I was the Adept of House Medeis. No matter how much the other Houses backed Mason, if I had the ring, they couldn't take House Medeis from me.

I held my breath as the lock clicked and the small door swung open. The lockbox was stuffed. There were a bunch of documents —old letters and communications between wizards whose names I didn't recognize—a pouch of gold coins that was so heavy I almost dropped it, and, pushed in the far back, a small velvet covered jewelry box. I pulled the box to the front and anchored my hands on the rim of the lockbox as I flicked the jewelry box open.

Inside, nestled in a velvet pillow, was a silver banded ring topped with a blue sapphire. The House Medeis coat of arms was etched into the rock, the symbolic unicorn and leopard curling protectively around it. This was it, the signet ring. My dad wore it a lot when I was a kid—he was the last Medeis, before me anyway. My mom had a matching silver band, but Dad always flashed the signet ring around for official occasions.

I rested a fingertip on the ring's gem and felt the quiet throb of magic.

Killian loomed behind me. "That's it?"

I sucked in a deep breath. "Yeah."

"Then take it and lock up." He turned, his arm brushing my back. "We'll be making a fast exit."

I snapped the jewelry box shut and put it in a zippered pouch secured to my belt. "I'm actually kind of surprised. I thought it would be way more intense to break in." I closed the lockbox and pulled the key out.

Something rumbled deep in the ground, rattling the blocks and rows of lockboxes and making dust bunnies fall off the ceiling support beams. I cautiously looked around, and a few of the Drake vampires pulled out weapons—both blades and handguns.

"Tutu takes precautions to keep out potential thieves," Killian said. "But the real crux of her security is the secondary layer of magic, enchantments, and wards...which drops the moment an unauthorized withdrawal is made."

"Is that your hint that we better run?"

"Yes."

I sprinted across the bay, skidding to a stop at the lip that dropped off into nothingness. It took me an extra moment to lower myself to the smaller pipe, and it was around then that I realized I didn't need my magic light anymore. A hot, orange light sliced through the darkness of Tutu's cavernous insides. The light brought with it the scent of ash and brimstone.

"Speed it up, Wizard." Killian was already standing on the main pipeline, a slight frown marring his face as he stared into the ever-brightening light.

I hurriedly picked my way across the smaller pipe, but the light made my head spin. Not because of any magical properties— if only! But because it lit up the vampires, me, the pipes we crawled across, and the gorge the pipes traversed, letting me see the simmering pits of tarry magic at the bottom. Scorpions —*giant* scorpions that even I could see from this distance—scut- tled across the top of the tar, their exoskeletons veined with threads of orange magic.

The drop was deep enough that it wasn't likely I'd survive it if I did fall, but even if I did, there was no way I'd make it through those pits and the scorpions.

I tried to hurry, but the pipes had misted over with the heat the light brought, and my foot slipped twice.

Killian tilted his head as he studied me. "Gavino."

"Your Eminence?"

"Assist the wizard in picking up the pace."

"Sorry, Miss." Gavino grabbed me from behind and tossed me over his shoulder so my belly hit his unfortunately tough shoulder muscles.

I first felt to make sure my pouch was still attached to my belt, then grabbed the back of his suitcoat and held on so I didn't flop so badly as he leaped to the big pipe, then joined the others in *sprinting* down it.

Killian ran just behind Gavino and watched me with glittering eyes. "What, you're not going to complain?"

"I'm smart enough to know I can't keep up at this pace." I spoke through gritted teeth so I didn't bite my tongue. Gavino ran smoothly, but when you're thrown over someone's shoulder, you feel every stride. "And," I added, "his hand isn't anywhere near my butt."

"I thought you would appreciate being carried like a princess instead of a bag of cat food."

"Is this really a conversation to hold *now*?" I squinted into the light—which had started dim like a sunrise, but was now about as bright as the late morning sun.

Killian smirked. "You were the one to bring your butt into it."

I was going to reply, but Gavino abruptly jumped, jabbing his shoulder into my stomach, so I wheezed instead.

The vampires covered the ground a lot more quickly, so only a short time passed before we reached the viewing station, where all the guards were still knocked out cold.

The orange light was now accompanied by a faint roar—which was fast growing louder—and a general rattle that made everything sway. "Does anyone know what magic that is?" I asked as Gavino jumped into the viewing area.

"We don't have to." Celestina yanked on the door, slamming it shut and temporarily blocking the light. "We can tell it will bring death."

Gavino hustled across the viewing area—jumping over one of the snoring werewolf guards.

Uneasily, I smelled the floral scent of fae magic. "Gavino, wait."

Gavino jumped out of the viewing station onto the much wider track. "I can't put you down. You won't run fast enough."

"That's not what I was going to ask—but we have to stop for a second." I tried to brace myself so I could sit up, but he was going too fast for me to get the necessary momentum.

"Can't."

The rest of the vampires clumped behind us, increasing my worry.

"Wait—you don't get it—*stop*!"

Something clicked, and I felt the fae magic burst to life.

I reached behind me and grabbed Gavino by the neck, half-choking him as I yanked myself upright and simultaneously opened myself to magic, which flooded my blood. Black-colored electricity shot across the track in sizzling volts that would fry anyone—wizard *or* vampire.

I threw my shaking shield up just in time to block the attack. The blue light of my magic shield absorbed the attack, and the black lightning disappeared as abruptly as it had come.

My shoulders heaved, and I let go of Gavino's neck. "All I was going to say was you better give me a piggy-back ride so I can use my magic while you run," I snapped.

A vampire behind us coughed in the awkward silence, but Gavino knelt down for me, making it a lot easier to slip off his shoulder and hop on his back instead.

I had to dig my heels into his side so I was tall enough to peer over his shoulder so I could see what was coming. "Sorry," I said when I thought I kicked his rib.

"If you can keep us safe, this is nothing," Gavino said.

I let more magic float through my blood as the rattling and rumbling increased, shaking the solid track we stood on.

"Move out!" Killian snapped.

Gavino and the vampires ran so fast I could barely see. I had to operate mostly on feeling. Whenever the taste of rosewater teased my tongue or my nose itched with the scent of soot, I shrieked for them to stop and tossed out one of my shields.

I think the vampires would have gone even faster, but the second time I had to warn them to stop, Julianne almost didn't freeze in time, and nearly pitched over the side in her effort to avoid a molten ball of magma. Fortunately, Celestina managed to grab her by the wrist and throw her back on the track.

Killian had to use his mints a few more times—which worried me, but not as much as the orange light which had burst through the viewing area and crawled down the track after us, rapidly gaining speed.

I was hot and sweaty—for once not just from my magic or adrenaline, but because the fierce light was close enough to slather us in its brutal heat. My grip on Gavino slipped, and I would have fallen off him if he hadn't been holding on to my legs. I grabbed the back of his shirt and threw a shield above us when I felt fae magic.

It blocked a hazy, *green* rain that dropped from the ceiling and hissed and sizzled when it hit my shield.

"Hurry!" Celestina jumped into the loading area and started tugging on the door.

Gavino and the others hustled through, rushing across the garage-like floor without stopping. Gavino nearly skidded out when we hit the lobby area, and for a moment the room spun as he tried to regain his footing.

"Out the doors," Killian snapped. The bright light had reached the loading area, its pulse of magic as bright as the sun as it mercilessly descended on us.

"We'll set off the security systems I couldn't shut down," Josh piped in.

"It's a little late for an *alarm* system," I sourly said, squeaking when Gavino rammed the metal gate that divided the lobby at full speed.

Two other vampires sliced straight through the gate bolts with glowing swords, making the massive structure fall. Julianne grabbed a chair and flung it at the front window—it bounced off without so much as chipping the surface.

Julianne said a very naughty word from modern slang I was pretty surprised she had learned.

Behind us, the magic light reached the far end of the lobby, cutting us off from the stairway we'd taken down from the second floor.

"Stand back!" I leaned over Gavino's shoulder and rammed the window with magic, cracking it. The second blow punched a head sized hole through, and my third try blew the window out with a bang that made my ears ring.

The light was close enough that the rumble made Gavino stagger a few steps, and the heat was almost unbearable.

"Out!" Killian snarled.

The vampires whisked outside. Celestina was last, jumping through the window with the light so close behind her it brushed the lock of her hair that was the last to pass through the window, making it bright gold before it disintegrated into ash.

Celestina glared at her ruined hair, then glanced at Killian. "I thought you said Tutu lowers the strength of her defenses on test nights so instead of auto-killing her contracted thieves it stuns them."

Killian shrugged. "She must have forgotten to do it."

"Likely story," Gavino muttered.

"Any bets that she was mad he called in this favor?" I slid off Gavino's back, landing on the ground with a stagger I felt from my heels to my knees.

"On the best of days dragons don't like giving up treasure under their protection," Julianne said.

I unzipped my pouch, confirming the jewelry box was still there. "Even though it belongs to me?"

"Even then."

I clutched the velvet box in one hand and used the other to tug at my black jacket, trying to peel it off my sweaty skin.

The deadly orange light still flooded the lobby at Tutu's, and I could feel its malevolent intention straining against the building.

Sirens wailed—it sounded like a police car, but it was pretty likely the Curia Cloisters were sending someone out to investigate, too. (There was no way we hadn't just alerted all of those with magic in the mile radius—Tutu's defensive spell was too overpowering to even think about cloaking.)

"Check in with the First and Second Knight," Killian declared. "Then prepare to leave—we're pulling out before those guards wake up."

Gavino frowned. "They survived *that*?" He beckoned back at the still-glowing lobby.

"Tutu's people are all granted immunity to her spells during their shifts," Killian said.

The vampires meandered toward the knights. I, however, stepped closer to the street. There was a faint magical signal. It was nearly unnoticeable thanks to the blazing sun of magic behind me, but it was a faint itch I couldn't scratch.

I closed my eyes as I tried to isolate the feeling. Was it wizard magic? Dragon shifter magic? Or something else...

I wouldn't have known Killian came to stand by me, except that he sighed slightly.

"There's something out there," I said. "I think it's fae magic." I peeled my eyes open and squinted into the darkness.

"There." Killian pointed to an alleyway.

I saw a flash of light—the fae magic I think—that briefly illuminated a willowy figure as it retreated.

"The Night Court?" I asked.

"Most likely," Killian said.

I clutched my jewelry box. "They sure are obsessed with you."

Killian turned to address his underlings. "Rupert," he said. "You're with me. The rest of you, go. We'll meet back at Drake Hall once we finish here."

I thought I kept my mouth shut tight enough, but Killian must have heard my noise of protest. He swung back around to face me. "We'll need a way to get back, and Rupert drove here."

"So did Celestina and Josh."

"They need to watch over the others." Killian didn't even look both ways before he strode across the street. "Keep up, Hazel."

"Didn't we already have enough fun for one night?" I pointedly looked up and down the street, then jogged after him.

Rupert trailed behind me, his expression watchful as he joined us at the mouth of the alleyway.

"Fae scout," Killian told Rupert. "We'll follow it for a little while, but keep our distance—it could be an ambush."

"The Night Court needs hobbies. Or something more to do." I picked my way through the alleyway trash—which reeked of dirty diapers. "How can they possibly have this much time on their hands?"

"Poor rulers who lack ambition but have ample amounts of pride," Killian answered.

We popped out of the alley and followed the fae's trail—or what Killian assured me was the fae's trail—through a zigzag of blocks, until we came to a small courtyard.

"I feel magic again," I announced as I stood at the courtyard edge.

"Fae?" Killian asked.

"No. Wizard magic?" I scrunched my nose as I tried to pin down the feeling.

"Are you sure you aren't sensing your own magic?" Rupert asked.

I frowned at him. "How would that even be possible?"

"Inferior skills."

"Could the two of you stop shouting like angry seagulls?" Killian sauntered into the courtyard and turned in a slow circle, inspecting the area.

Not quite able to let it go I whispered, "Sensing magic isn't a skill, but a sensitivity." I stalked after Killian. "And whatever this faint whiff is, it isn't—fae magic!"

Light blasted the courtyard, and the overwhelming scent of rosewater filled my nose and mouth so it felt like I was drowning in a bath. Vines made of light unfurled and curled across the stone courtyard, a visible representation of the fae spell.

Only certain kinds of fae magic affected wizards, so even though I felt the ground spell pull at me, I staggered back to the edge of the courtyard, coughing.

Killian was stuck in the center with Rupert a few feet behind me.

I hadn't brought my sword to break into Tutu's—Killian told me it would only get in the way—so I gathered lightning in the palms of my hands as I tried to find the fae responsible for the trap.

"It's so good to see you again, Hazel. It's been too long."

My heart fell into my stomach at the familiar, charming voice.

# CHAPTER ELEVEN

*Hazel*

Mason stepped out of the shadows, his face illuminated by the silver of the moon in the sky, and the glowing fae spell. He smiled at me and nodded to Killian and Rupert. "I didn't think you'd be keeping such illustrious company."

"Let them go, Mason." My voice was so harsh I almost didn't recognize it, and I let my magic pool at my feet so lightning ringed around me.

"Certainly." Mason held his hand out. "Once you pass over the signet ring."

Something twisted in my chest, but I managed to screw my face into a look of confusion. "What? Do you think the ring appeared to me in a vision from my parents or something and now I magically have it? No!"

"I have recently made ties with a very powerful new ally. They happen to have an interest in the Drake Family, so I know you broke into Tutu's." Mason bowed his head to Killian.

The Night Court. Mason made an alliance with the *Night Court*. It wasn't shocking—the Night Court hated Killian, and

Mason wanted me dead. Why not team up to get us both? Except...

"Exactly how debt-strapped have you made House Medeis?" I prodded a light vine with a toe. "You must owe nearly every House in the city a favor or two already. Can you really pay this back?"

"That's no concern to you," Mason said. "Hand over the signet ring you just retrieved from Tutu's, or Killian Drake will die."

I laughed. "You think you can kill Killian Drake? Even when he's caught in the fae spell he's probably one eyebrow-twitch away from killing you."

Killian appeared almost bored by our conversation and quirked an eyebrow when I mentioned his name.

I had to wonder for a moment—did he have a way out? I could feel the binding of the fae spell. His mint tin could dissolve the magic, but he couldn't move to get it.

"It is likely if I approached Killian he'd break free somehow," Mason said. "But that's why I have this."

Mason dropped what looked like a gob of ruby red slime on the ground. It bubbled and frothed until it expanded so it was about the size of a bathtub and sank beneath the fae spell holding Killian and Rupert in place. It circled the courtyard, slowly closing around Killian.

It radiated an ancient, wild magic. I had no idea what had created this...*thing*. It didn't smell like fae or dragon shifter magic. It might be wizard magic, but the spell was so old and twisted I couldn't tell. I could feel ancient magic radiating from it, peppered with a deep, soulless hunger.

A tiny bolt of my magic leaped into the fae circle, and the ancient magic snapped on it, greedily swallowing it.

"Vampires don't use magic, but it's still in them," Mason said. "Soon, the spell will latch on to your friends and eat them whole. Unless you give me the signet ring."

"You're crazy," I said. "The Drake Family will track you until the end of time and make you suffer so much you'll *break*!"

"No they won't." Mason's smile was affectionate as he studied me. "Because you won't let him die."

I stared at the ground and watched the deadly spell lurk a few feet away. It hadn't moved beyond the bounds of the fae spell—it looked like it was stuck there. I inched the toe of my boot into the circle the fae spell made.

Immediately the red glob shot in my direction, slamming to a halt when it reached the boundary of the spell.

It seemed it was attracted to the biggest magical signature. Given my ability to wield magic, mine was obviously stronger than Killian's or Rupert's. It would know the instant I stepped inside the fae spell. I couldn't rescue them—not without a distraction.

"Hazel." Mason's voice started to harden. "Stop stalling, and give me the ring."

I swallowed hard, my hands turning clammy as I fished the jewelry box out of my pouch with shaking hands. It was my birthright, a centuries old treasure of House Medeis, and a symbol of my position. Without it, the fight to take back my House was going to be a lot harder.

I licked my dry lips. "Can't you do anything, Killian?"

Killian watched the red spell circle around him—it was about a car length away—with a disinterested look. "I'm sure I'll figure something out," he said.

What was that supposed to mean?

"You're running out of time, Hazel." Mason brushed off his suitcoat—which had the House Medeis coat of arms on it.

My hands shook with my anger. "How can I trust you to let them go once you have the ring?"

Both Rupert and Killian twisted their necks uncomfortably so they could look back at me. Killian briefly furrowed his brow, but

I was more consumed with watching Mason for any sign of treachery.

My fellow wizard smiled. "I'm a wizard of my word. The signet ring for their lives. Besides—I'm not *that* anxious to kill the Midwest Eminence. It would bring a lot of...complications to my life."

He meant the rest of the Drake Family would hunt him for sport.

But letting us go would bring similar consequences anyway.

Unless...was he planning to kill all of us, and hope the Drake Family never figured out who had done it? (Or maybe he thought Celestina and the others would assume it was the work of the Night Court? It was, in a way.)

I couldn't give him the signet ring. It was my only bargaining chip. But I couldn't save Killian either from the ancient magic. Could I fight Mason and get control over the magic?

No. Whatever the dark, powerful magic was, it was now close enough that it almost brushed against Killian. Another few seconds and it'd be over.

I thought I could hear the ancient magic hiss and pop, but I really hoped that was just my imagination. If it wasn't, it was possible this spell was strong enough to rival the wards on Tutu's. And Mason had gotten it from the fae?

"*Hazel.*" Mason's voice was sharp. "Stop screwing around and hand the ring over."

I tightened my hold on the jewelry box and stared at the spell.

There was a way I could save Killian and Rupert without playing Mason's game. But I'd lose what I had fought so hard for.

*They'll die.*

Even as my eyes stung, I lifted my chin and met Mason's gaze. "You want the signet?"

Mason's cheek twitched in his irritation. "*Yes.*"

I flicked the jewelry box open, waiting so he could see the gem-studded ring. And then I tossed it.

The ring box landed inside the circle made by the fae spell; not far away from me, but about as far away from both Mason and the ancient spell as it could get.

"NO!" Mason shouted.

The red magic froze, then streaked across the ground, closing in on the ring.

I sprinted past the red spell, slamming into Killian when I couldn't stop fast enough. I dug into his coat pocket and grabbed his mint tin, ripping it open as the ancient magic reached the House Medeis signet ring.

Mason had tried to make a run for it, but the magic beat him by a long shot. It bubbled underneath the ring, its ooze growing until it piled above the ring box and snapped shut around it.

A sob caught in my throat, and I dropped a few mints before I smeared one on Killian and a second on Rupert.

The courtyard glowed red while the slime spat hot sparks, and the center of it lit up as if a roaring fire crackled at its center.

"You idiot! What have you done?" Mason shouted.

Killian scooped me up and ran.

I clung to his neck, flinching when a large bubble on the ooze popped, releasing a cloud of black smoke and what felt like a sonic boom that rocked the street block.

"You destroyed the signet ring! How could you!" Mason howled.

Killian set me down safely at the edge of the courtyard, Rupert right behind him. In movements so smooth they could only be the result of years of practice, Killian pulled out his handgun, racked it to load a bullet into the chamber, flicked the safety off, and spun around to face Mason in the time span of an eye blink.

Mason swore and almost tripped as he scrambled backwards, darting behind a stone planter.

Killian still shot at him, riddling the planter with holes.

There was a roar of magic, and the fae spell and ruby red magic that had consumed the signet ring slowly faded.

Rupert ghosted across the courtyard and knelt at the planter. "He's gone, Your Eminence." He delicately sniffed the air. "I think he escaped into the Night Court's realm."

Killian lowered his gun. "Call Celestina." He abruptly turned toward me. "Was that really the signet ring that *thing* destroyed?"

"Yeah." My voice cracked.

"Why." Killian didn't so much ask for an explanation as demand one as he studied me.

I rubbed at my face, fighting back the prickly feeling in my eyes. "I needed something with a stronger magical signature to distract it, or it would have gone for me."

"You didn't want to make the trade?"

"Once he had the ring, he would have killed us all," I said. "It was the only way to save you two."

Killian didn't say anything more. He holstered his weapon and looked around.

Across the courtyard Rupert exchanged a hushed conversation over the phone.

"So the Night Court and Mason are allies now," I glumly said.

"It seems the Night Court is convinced you are a bigger threat than they first thought," Killian said.

I glanced up at him. "What do you mean?"

Killian shrugged. "If they believed you were beneath their notice, they wouldn't have approached Mason."

"You think they were the ones who offered the alliance?"

"Do you think Mason bought that spell from a store—or off the internet?" Killian scoffed.

"No. That was old magic. *Really* old magic."

"Fae are almost as bad as vampires at squirreling old things away. They likely provided it to him, knowing it was the only thing strong enough to hold me and force your hand." Killian wrinkled his forehead.

It was pretty odd, because he looked, I don't know, *concerned?* His eyes were tight, and there was a slight downturn to his lips. I would have bet for sure he was furious about being held captive by Mason. So that meant this new alliance was even worse than I thought, or he was worried about something else layered in all of this.

My hands automatically crept to my belt pouch, to check for the jewelry box that was no longer there. My shoulders slumped, and I clamped my eyes shut.

Not here.

"Come on, Hazel." Killian ambled out of the courtyard, rejoining one of the city streets.

"Where are we going?" I asked as we backtracked in Tutu's direction.

"To get the car," Killian said. "And if you try to sit up front, I will stab you."

I forced a smile and skipped along behind him, pausing only long enough to make sure Rupert—still on the phone—trailed behind us. "Touchy tonight, are we?"

Killian made a noise in the back of his throat. "Your dramatics over sitting next to me are unwanted."

I laughed because he seemed to expect it, even though my whole body ached.

The signet ring was gone. I had destroyed it. How was I supposed to rescue House Medeis now?

———

I SMILED and held in the desire to cry once we reached the car, and even the whole drive back.

Gavino insisted on inspecting me once we arrived, though I suspected his bigger purpose was to serve as a distraction for me as Killian and Rupert swept off to the big vampire meeting room.

Obviously, since the Night Court was allied with Mason, this was going to bring a new dimension into their fight.

"Go take a shower and make sure you get some rest," Gavino ordered.

I stretched my arms above my head. "I feel fine."

"It doesn't matter. It was a rough day." Gavino shook a finger in my direction. "And this is a late night—for you."

"Okay," I agreed only because it would make him leave me alone. "I'm still hopped up on adrenaline, so I'm going to take a walk first, and then turn in."

"Call if you need anything," Gavino said.

"Sure!" I chirped. I made my jog light and purposely picked my feet up as I followed a path around the exterior of Drake Hall. When I reached one of the gardens I slowed to a walk and wove my way through it, reaching one of the patches of woods in the surrounding acreage.

I passed the pool, and gave the rock wall a wide berth, stopping when I was fairly certain the vampires couldn't hear me anymore unless I screamed at the top of my lungs.

It was still dark outside—I think it was about three in the morning. Usually I went to bed way before this, but unfortunately the bulk of the vampires stayed up until dawn. Thankfully, most of them were probably at whatever meeting Killian had called.

So when I finally collapsed in a heap and pressed my hands against my mouth to keep from screaming my heartbreak, I was pretty confident that no one would hear me or look for me— particularly not with Celestina still poking around the 'crime scene' and Josh—and most likely Gavino—attending the meeting.

My lungs twisted in my chest.

Had I just irrevocably given away my House? For *Killian Drake*?

The signet ring was gone. Centuries of tradition destroyed. My *Dad* had worn that ring. And now it was gone...just like him.

My grief was a mountain that collapsed on me.

It was too much—my parents' betrayal, the loss of my House, and now the ring.

Couldn't I do anything right? I should have been more aware while following the fae, then Killian never would have stepped in that trap.

Wild magic swirled around me. I felt my wizard mark burn on my cheek as the magic filtered through my blood.

I cried as if I were being torn in two and dropped my hands, digging them into the dirt. Blue lightning sizzled around me—a sign of my leaking emotions.

I tried to breathe, but it hurt too much. I couldn't even *think*. The knowledge that the signet ring was destroyed was a bitter taste in my mouth. Felix, Momoko—I had let everyone down.

The one solace was that Mason didn't have the ring either, so he couldn't claim the House. But what could I do now?

Signet rings weren't easy things to replace. They required ancient magic that was rare—and even more rarely mastered these days. Was it even *possible* to remake it?

More lightning crackled around me as I sobbed, drowning in my own misery.

"You regret it."

I screamed, startled. I shivered uncontrollably as I wiped my face on my sleeve and glanced over at Killian, who was crouched on the ground next to me.

"W-what?" I cleared my throat and tried to stifle my magic, wincing when I accidentally produced a lightning bolt that struck the nearest tree with a deafening rumble and split the trunk in two.

"You regret sacrificing your ring for me." He shrugged a little. "It's understandable."

"I regret that I had to sacrifice the signet ring, yeah." I spread my fingers wide and stared at them. "The signet ring is precious to the House. It's been passed down for generations, and now it's gone. It also would have made things a lot easier. Without the ring, Mason couldn't become Adept, and no one could say House Medeis wasn't mine. But since it's destroyed..." I trailed off. Feeling wet and miserable from my cry, I added, "I don't regret saving you, though."

"You're lying." Killian stood. I think he wanted the even-greater-than-normal height-advantage. He glowered down at me, the rims of his black eyes glowing red. "*How* can you not regret it?"

I sighed and rested my chin on my chest. "Because I like you," I said. "You, Celestina, Gavino—you're all important to me. I'd never regret saving any of you."

He crouched again, this time his expression more thoughtful as he studied me. "That's what drove you to attack Solene."

I sniffed, and closed my eyes in concentration as I stuffed the magic down when it tried to leak out through my pores. "I thought we weren't talking about that?"

"We are now." Killian sat down next to me, folding one long leg underneath him and stretching the other out. "You were an idiot for that attack, too."

"Why are you so snippy about it?"

"Snippy?"

"When I first woke up after the accident, you seemed pleased I had unlocked my magic." I sat on my rear and pulled my legs flush against my chest so I could rest my chin on my knees. "It wasn't until later that day that you were irritated with me for doing it."

"Let's just say I had a slow, dawning realization," Killian drawled.

"About what?"

"Your special brand of idiocy that drives you to put too much on the line for others. Hazel, you didn't have to save me."

His voice was dark and deep, naturally drawing me to look at him. He looked again like a stinkin' model in a night garden photo shoot. I was reeeaaalllyyy tempted to kick him and maybe knock him over and ruin that perfect confidence and unshakable attractiveness, but I was more likely to injure my foot than actually knock him off balance. "You could have gotten free?" My voice was scratchy still from crying.

Killian shrugged. "Most likely. But no one would have expected you to sacrifice the ring. You could have run."

I huddled in a miserable ball. "No, I couldn't have. I have to do what I can live with."

"And *this* you can live with?" Killian waved a hand at me.

I drew in a ragged breath. "It hurts right now, but yeah. Maybe I'm not fit to be a leader. We're supposed to sacrifice everything for the House, but I just can't ignore people."

"I am well aware of the veneration wizards have for Houses," Killian dryly said.

There was something extra sarcastic in the way he said it. "You don't think it's a good focus to have?"

"Your magical Houses? Not particularly." He set his hands behind him and leaned back on them, the most relaxed I'd ever seen him besides the time he let me pull him into the pool. "I find it shocking that *I* am saying this out of all people, but shouldn't it be the reverse? The House should exist for the wizards, not the wizards for the House."

His observation shouldn't have been shocking. It should have been obvious. But there was still something about it that rattled me. "I...what?"

"Wizards didn't have this unhealthy obsession with their Houses until it became clear that magic was dying and that our society would fade away with it," Killian said. "It was around then that everyone—wizards included—rallied to their power base in a hope to preserve it for as long as possible. For wizards, that meant protecting their House. As decades passed, it seems it's been taken to an extreme so the House has precedence over the wizards themselves."

I stared at Killian. "Exactly *how old* are you?"

Killian smirked. "Old enough to know it hasn't always been like this. Old enough to know we're all a product of desperation."

"And by all your political maneuvering and—as you called it—rallying your power base, it seems you don't think there's another way?"

Killian stared at me for several long moments, which made me realize exactly how prying the question was.

I had asked in a strange twist of hope and worry. Was there another way? Killian didn't think there was or he wouldn't be so—

Killian took my hand in his and raised it to his mouth. His black eyes glittered with extra chips of red. "A year ago I would have said no."

My throat was embarrassingly tight—let's face it, even if you had great survival instincts like me, when you were staring at a face like Killian's and he was gently holding your hand like you *mattered*, well, there was no resisting that. "And now?" I managed to squeak out.

I pretty much expected Killian to grin at me because, like I said before, he knew he was attractive, so I was extra shocked when he gently kissed the top of my hand, his breath cool against my skin. "I don't know."

I stared at my knees with great interest when he dropped my hand. *Don't look at him, don't look at him, it will be over if I look at him.*

"I'm sorry, Hazel."

I dumbly turned to him. "Huh?" Shock and confusion fought in my brain—shock because I had *never* heard Killian say he was sorry before. Killian never said anything that could possibly put him in debt with anyone. (He didn't even thank me when I killed Solene!) And confusion because what did he have to be sorry about?

Killian held my gaze until my lungs twisted in my chest. "I'm sorry about the signet ring."

"Oh," I said in a small voice. I tried to force a smile, but I could already feel the sting of tears in my eyes. "It's not your fault.

Mason is a crooked wizard, obviously. He was the one who threatened you. He deserves a good smack in the face and to be tossed in jail—even if the Wizard Council doesn't see it that way. But you don't have to be sorry about it because it was my choice, too, and I—"

Killian grabbed my wrist again—cutting off my uncontrollable babble—and tugged on me, tipping me over so I toppled against his chest.

He gently curled his arms around me, his coolness comforting against the heat of my tears and sadness.

It was a rare kindness from the usually hardened vampire, and it was too much to take.

My face crumpled, and I couldn't hold in my sob. I shoved my face against his chest—hoping to muffle myself even just a little—and latched my arms around his waist.

Killian maneuvered me into a more comfortable position that had me sprawled against him, then wrapped his arms around me again, his thumbs gently caressing my shoulders.

For a moment I wondered if this was okay. Was I an idiot for crying my eyes out and snotting all over Killian Drake's shirt?

"Don't think our discussion about the Unclaimed vampire is over." Killian's voice cut through my cloud of confusion.

"Why *do* we have to talk about it?" I rested my cheek against his chest.

"Because you're an idiot." Killian sounded resigned.

"What else is there to say?" I asked. "We figured out the motive and everything. My magic was unlocked. Isn't it case closed?"

"Your behavior is the problem," Killian said. "Specifically, your tendency to throw yourself head first into danger."

"You didn't seem too upset with me right after the fight."

"The more time passes, the longer I've had to dwell upon your special brand of idiotic justice." Killian's chest rumbled against my cheek as he talked.

I tried to discreetly push a little closer to him—his coolness was a lot more comfortable than the moist heat I'd stirred in myself between the crying and my magic. "What happened to being virtuous?"

Killian tightened his arm around me in response to my movement. "I called you a virtuous idiot. That is still an excellent description."

"So is that the reason why Solene suddenly became a forbidden topic?" I asked. "You were mad at me for going in without backup?"

"Yes," Killian growled.

I stared at the soft fabric of Killian's dress shirt, a little confused.

What was so taboo about that? Yeah, I had been brash, but it turned out okay. If it upset him that much why didn't he just tell me and move on instead of growling about it for months afterward? "You are surprisingly petty about weird things."

"And if you weren't half as amusing as you are, you'd be dead by now," Killian drolly said.

The underlying threat didn't bother me. I lifted my head off his soft shirt just long enough to smooth the fabric before I let my head fall back on his chest with a thump. "If you meant to put me in my place, you should have done that *before* I used your shirt as a giant tissue."

"No longer afraid of me?"

"Not for me, no. Though I am mighty aware that you wouldn't be nearly so long-suffering with anyone outside Drake Hall," I said. "I'm plenty certain in your skills of intimidation and terror."

There were a lot of possible responses I expected from that—playfulness, maybe. Agreement. Perhaps smugness because I was sort of praising him.

I did *not* expect him to rest his chin on my head and let the comfortable silence stretch on.

Exhausted, I let my eyes drift shut, and let Killian bear my full weight. (I was pretty small, he had vampire strength, he could manage as far as I was concerned.)

I was vaguely aware my breath was deepening and I was about to fall asleep, when Killian abruptly spoke.

"You'll get your House back."

I snorted awake. "Huh?"

"You're the Adept of House Medeis, with or without the signet ring," Killian said. "You'll get it back."

"Yeah," I agreed as I shut my eyes. "I won't give up until I have it back."

I fell asleep under the night sky, leaning into Killian Drake.

A year ago, if someone had told me that would happen, I would have laughed until I puked. But having lived through everything I had...that time with Killian was one of the most peaceful moments I'd had all summer, and I was glad he chose to share it with me.

# CHAPTER TWELVE

*Killian*

Which one was Adept Fayette?
I'd only glanced at a picture of him on my phone before coming out here. I should have done more research, but since living with Hazel I'd forgotten how *similar* humans looked. I sighed in irritation and dug my phone out of my pocket, bringing up the image before peering down at the humans milling about on the main floor like a bunch of ants.

It was good luck that Fayette and a select group of wizard Houses were in attendance at this dinner reception held at an upper scale, Magiford hotel restaurant, Jolie Fleur, because I wasn't thrilled at the idea of...*talking* to him in his own House.

I would have survived such an encounter and gotten my message across, but this took a lot less effort. Which was always an important measurement to take into account.

The stuffed laughter of the pompous wizards floated up to where I stood, leaning against a stairway banister. They clinked champagne glasses and congratulated themselves on successfully manipulating wizard politics for the first time in decades.

Idiots. They had no idea how little they mattered, and how easily things could change if any of the more apathetic or selfish wizard Houses woke up and realized what was going on. Or even if the Regional Committee of Magic got a hint. Elite Bellus was not among those in attendance, which meant thus far the group was still relatively small, but it was growing.

I'd received word that Mason was gathering allies. Obviously, becoming Adept had always been his goal, but it seemed since Hazel's magic had fully unsealed and I'd made it fairly public that she was not to be trifled with, he'd changed tactics and decided that he could politically make his coup rather than attempting to kill her or manipulate her.

It was a tactic I might have admired—if it hadn't involved Hazel and that wretched House she was forever fretting over.

I still didn't understand what possessed her to throw away the House Medeis signet ring to save me. Though I'm intelligent enough to admit I was, perhaps…. *upset* with her for even doing that.

I didn't care about the ring—or the blasted House.

But she did. And it greatly irritated me that she threw something away for me—particularly because I probably could have gotten out of the trap with some effort, but I was curious. I wanted to see what would happen if I didn't try, and I wanted to get a proper measure of her runty cousin.

I was regretting that impulse—another thing that irritated me because I *don't* like second-guessing myself.

I frowned as I watched Adept Fayette linger around the edge of the party and make his way through a door that opened up into a hallway.

"That one." I pointed Fayette out to Rupert—my sole guard for this excursion.

Since my goal was information and intimidation, Fayette would be more frightened if I had other vampires with me, so I'd reluctantly chosen Rupert.

It was his chance to make up for his mistake in attacking Hazel, and he was already low enough in my esteem that he knew not to try to needle me as Celestina would, or list the many reasons this was a dangerous plan, like Josh would.

"I believe the restrooms are located down that hallway. He's likely going there. We could nab him after he comes out," Rupert suggested.

"Fair enough."

Rupert ghosted behind me as we left the banister and moved through the second floor of the hotel, finding the correct hallway and a stairway that would let us intersect with Fayette.

I lingered in the shadows just outside the restrooms, while Rupert investigated the patio through an outside exit.

As expected, Adept Fayette—a short, thin man who vaguely reminded me of a worried spider—exited the restrooms, twitching his jacket into place.

"Adept Fayette." I stepped out of the shadows and smiled. "We should talk."

Fayette scowled at me and opened his mouth to speak, but froze when he got a good look. His skin turned an ashy pale white color, and he audibly gulped. "Y-y-your Eminence?" he said.

"Precisely."

Rupert made his appearance. He rested a hand on Fayette's shoulder and marched him through the glass door to the patio.

I rolled my neck as I strolled after them, more comfortable outside than I had been in a hotel restaurant full of wizards. It was an uncharacteristically cool night for August—though if Hazel were here she'd undoubtedly be grumbling about heat and sweat.

"W-what, what's going on?" Adept Fayette asked in a shaking voice.

"I don't know." I strolled closer, tilting my head so I knew my dark eyes caught the moonlight and reflected more red than normal. "That's why we're here—so you can *share* with us."

"I have nothing to do with vampires," Adept Fayette blurted. "I don't know any regional politics!"

"Now that is a lie." I folded my hands behind me. "Rupert, why don't you invite our guest to sit down? It seems this will take some discussion."

Adept Fayette whimpered as Rupert marched him over to a plastic set of patio furniture and shoved him down in a seat.

"You see, Adept Fayette, you *do* have something to do with vampires. You were invited to this dinner tonight by Mason of House Medeis. Mason was very open in his invitation, describing the gathering as a group of individuals seeking to change the path of wizard politics, specifically in changing the House Medeis leadership. Do you deny this?"

Adept Fayette sank lower in his chair and pulled his hands to his chest in a worried and defensive gesture. "No."

"Then surely you must know that the *true* Adept of House Medeis is Hazel Medeis, and she is currently living in Drake Hall under my protection, and the protection of the Drake Family. So." I pulled a dagger from my left sleeve and stood close to Adept Fayette so my hand was just about level with his throat. "How is it, then, that you say you have nothing to do with vampires, when you are actively moving against a wizard under *my* protection?"

"I, I, I thought she was a mere blood donor!" Fayette squeaked. "House Tellier promised you weren't interested in the girl. I assumed she was a staff member or someone unimportant."

I frowned as I studied the small, sweating man—his heat only amplifying the dead fish smell of his blood.

For a very stupid moment of weakness, I wanted Hazel and her fresh smell and bright grin.

I pushed the thought away and focused on the main point. "You thought she was *unimportant*?"

Rupert stirred at the deep growl in my voice, and even I was a little surprised with myself.

"It was my mistake!" Fayette babbled, his mouth loosened by

fear. "My mistake entirely! She's obviously very strong, very charming, very important to you and your Family—perhaps even all wizards and all of mankind."

He'd brought up an important point—though he didn't know it. I thought I'd been fairly vocal with my support of Hazel. But were there still werewolf Packs, fae Courts, and particular wizard Houses that didn't know?

How was that possible? Fayette claimed a House Tellier wizard had misled him, but I'd nearly killed a Tellier months ago for making a similar mistake.

Did House Tellier just not *care* if I killed a few of them, or was there something bigger than I thought at play?

But even if Tellier didn't mind a few sacrifices, the other Houses would. It seemed I would have to go through greater efforts to prove Hazel's and my...whatever. But what more could I do besides parade her around town and smile disgustingly out of character? Which would certainly worry everyone and make them take notice, but for different reasons.

I turned my back to Fayette, only half listening as he continued railing.

"I obviously won't join Mason—it's wrong of him to go against Adept Medeis! I hadn't officially accepted his invite, yet, anyway! I'll refuse to join him, and I won't say a word to the other Houses he is recruiting."

"Simply apologizing isn't enough, Adept Fayette," I said.

"It's not?" the Adept weakly asked.

"No." I crouched down next to the chair, fiddling with my dagger so it glinted—an unspoken promise. "I want you to give me the names of *every* House you know of that he's tried recruiting. And when we're finished with our conversation here you won't tell anyone that we chatted. However, you will tell *everyone* that Hazel Medeis is backed by Killian Drake and the Drake Family—not as a blood donor or a servant, but as one of their own. Understood?"

Adept Fayette nodded violently. "Absolutely! I will tell everyone at the dinner before I leave!"

"Good. I'm glad you are so *understanding*," I said. "Now, tell us everything."

Adept Fayette gave us a list of names I only vaguely recognized. Rupert recorded it on his phone, and we sent the deeply terrified and thoroughly sweaty man on his way once it became clear he knew very little about Mason besides Mason's goal and the dinner guests.

"Do you mean to take him out, Your Eminence?" Rupert asked once Fayette disappeared back inside and the patio door swung shut behind him.

I glanced at my underling. "Mason?"

"Yes."

I stared into the sky as I considered the question. "No."

"He tried to kill you." Rupert's voice was hardened with hate—a reminder that I'd need to give notice to all the vampires in Drake Hall that Mason was to be left alone.

"He did," I agreed. "Under different circumstances that would be enough motive for me to wipe him and his family line from the earth. However..." I paused, wondering if I should *really* tell this part to the impatient vampire. "Hazel needs to face him," I finally said.

Rupert's face scrunched up as he struggled to understand. "You won't kill a rat-blood who deserves it because the wizard needs practice?"

"No." Yes. I shouldn't have bothered telling him—but it was too late to walk back the decision now. "Hazel needs to fight Mason to remove all doubts that she isn't fit to be Adept. If I kill Mason and she returns to House Medeis, all her life she'll face talk that she isn't a good enough Adept—at *best*. At worst, most will think I took the House back and installed her as my puppet."

"You're right, Your Eminence." Rupert bowed slightly. "It is better if others do not suspect the power you have over her."

There was something in that statement that made me want to grimace—and that was enough to make me freeze.

When had she changed from being a pawn I could use for my ends, to being *Hazel?*

Never mind—I knew the answer to that question. It was when she had stopped smelling so foul to me.

But Rupert was wrong. I wasn't intending to secretly control Medeis from the shadows. I didn't intend to have anything to do with that wretched House in the future besides visiting Hazel—and perhaps watching her kinsmen turn pale whenever they saw me for the entertainment value.

Oh—I'd try to influence Hazel, but it was more likely she'd give me that fake smile of hers that said she was grimacing so hard her teeth might crack and tell me to buzz off.

And that was very out of character for me.

Essentially, unlike everything else in my life, I wanted Hazel free to do what she wanted.

Right now what she wanted was that stupid House. But she'd also want to get it her way—up front with all the right paperwork and by justly following the process, the boring and thankless things I tended to bypass with my particular politics.

The only thing I could do was try to limit Mason and block him from gathering more allies. The Night Court was going to be an unwanted irritation, but they were easy enough to manipulate. The real danger of the Night Court was the impulsive hatred of the queen and her consort. I could easily provoke her, which would bring out a very predictable fight.

I sighed and rubbed the back of my neck. "You will not tell Hazel of this."

"Yes, Your Eminence. What of the First Knight and the others?" Rupert asked.

How much of a pain would it be if the others found out?

Probably more trouble than I wanted.

"Keep quiet on the matter for now," I said. "In a few weeks, when I have finished hunting the false Adept, you can tell them."

Rupert puffed up his chest—likely he was smug that he'd get to know something Celestina and the rest of the Family did not.

He still acted appallingly young at times, but he'd keep learning—he had already.

"We have the targets, I think we're done here for tonight," I said.

Rupert bowed again. "Yes, Your Eminence. I'll pull the car around?"

"Yes."

Rupert melted into the shadows and disappeared, heading off in the direction of the parking garage.

I glanced back at the hotel, contemplating my options.

Nope—it smelled too bad with all those wizards in there.

I jumped a bush and landed on the sidewalk that wove around the hotel's exterior, and swiveled so I faced the direction of the front entrance.

*What am I doing?*

It wasn't like me to interfere when I didn't expect a payoff. Rather—I'd *never* do something like this if there wasn't a payoff.

Hazel was making me soft.

The one consolation was that at least it wasn't without its benefits. She was amusing, not only to me but my Family as well; she had the Night Court scared, as they wouldn't have bothered to make an alliance with Mason if they didn't see her as a real threat; and I'd shoot myself in the arm before I admitted it, but it was pretty addicting to sit with her.

I'd forgotten what warmth felt like. But whenever she leaned against me, she radiated a soft heat that sank all the way to my bones.

Her smell was becoming more addicting with each week—which was actually troubling, but she smelled too good for me to seriously consider reversing the effect.

The one downside to that smell was I was fairly certain her blood would still taste as sour and foul as ever if I happened to lose my mind and bite her, given that she was rightfully suspicious of my motivations.

It wouldn't happen—I didn't care *how* amazing she smelled, I would never trust a human enough to feed off them. Even if that person was Hazel.

But it rankled me to know she didn't trust me the same way I, apparently, trusted her.

Maybe one day that would be useful—it seemed like the sort of thing I could twist for my own purposes.

For now it was enough to take action against Mason and go home and pull Hazel's proverbial tail to see if I could get her to produce those funny squawking noises she made when outraged.

And at least I had one move I needed to analyze: what was the easiest way to broadcast to the region that I was serious in my protection of Hazel, so the small fish like Adept Fayette stayed out of the fight?

I suspected the solution was going to be quite a bit of fun, and lots of delightful squawking from Hazel...

# CHAPTER THIRTEEN

*Hazel*

"Attack him, Hazel. Stop retreating!" Celestina shouted.

It was a nice sentiment, but Rupert was so *fast* I couldn't do anything except block.

I threw a shield up in front of me and switched my sword stance.

As expected, Rupert zipped around my shield, but I was prepared for that and stabbed my chisa katana behind me.

He had to veer backwards to avoid being stabbed, but by the time I tried to follow it up with a lightning bolt, he was already gone, back around to the front.

I backed up, trying to get some space between us so I actually had room to maneuver, but Rupert followed so close his clothes flicked my shield.

*He's almost got me—if I don't wing him soon he's going to corner me!*

I planted my feet and stabbed forward, taking my shield down at the last moment so my sword could pass through.

Rupert ducked the sword, slugged me with enough force that I felt it all the way back in my *spine*, and when I sagged forward he ruthlessly grabbed me by the neck and threw me to the ground, planting his foot on my throat.

I tried to gasp for air, but it wasn't easy with Rupert's shoe pressing down on my windpipe.

"We're finished here," he sneered down at me.

I nodded—my lungs burning like a wild fire—and coughed with a strangled gasp when Rupert removed his foot and prowled off.

I was going to be so bruised when I woke up tomorrow. I groaned and tried to stand, but my muscles wouldn't listen to me —they were too sore and jelly-like.

Obviously, Rupert still hated me—he was brutally ruthless, and based on his freaky smile he *enjoyed* throwing me around. Equally obvious, however, was that he had learned his lesson. The first time I'd faced him he made me black out. Killian hadn't taken kindly to Rupert damaging his wizard-in-training, and had just about killed Rupert proving that point.

I'd faced Rupert twice in the past week during my training sessions, and he'd been very careful to take me to the brink of pain but never push me into unconsciousness.

Celestina's face veered into view. She'd braided her thick hair in a single braid today, which dangled over her shoulder as she peered down at me. "You could beat him if you stopped defending."

"You say that, but if I didn't defend, he'd take me down in one hint," I groaned.

She offered out her hand, which I took, and peeled me off the ground, helping me stand. "You have magic, *Wizard*. But you don't use it much besides making that beloved shield of yours."

"I've attacked him with lightning bolts and fire," I protested.

"Blast him with your magic," Celestina advised. "You'll never match his speed in defending—you're only fighting the inevitable. Your best bet is to push him straight off and take him down with as much magic in as short an amount of time as possible."

I set my hand on my aching lower back and peered in Josh's direction. "You have anything to add, Josh?"

The dark-haired vampire was sharpening a sword, though when I spoke he paused. "Death is inevitable; by facing Rupert you are only learning how to prolong your miserable end. Strength is nothing when we jump off this mortal coil, and offers no sweet solace when it is over," he said.

"See?" Celestina planted her hands on her hips. "He also thinks you need to attack more."

"How on earth did you get 'attack more' out of that?" I pointed to Josh.

"Celestina does speak the truth," Josh added. "One can never take a castle solely by defending their own, nor can you beat an enemy of superior size, strength, speed, and strategic intellect by hiding behind a shield."

I scowled at my trainer. "Hey, that was a little too personal—and hurtful!"

"Try again," Celestina firmly said. "This time use more of your magic. You have a greater capacity for magic than most in your generation, and magic is a vampire's greatest weakness. Use it."

I sagged, but I didn't bother protesting because Celestina was already marching across the gym.

"Rupert!" Celestina barked. "You're fighting again."

"I do not wish to," Rupert said in a stiff tone.

"Your wishes don't matter, get back to the mats."

I circled the thickly padded area and tried to sort through my options.

Celestina and Josh were obviously right, I needed to attack. But in facing the vampires below Rupert's skill level, all I had needed was my shield to keep them back long enough that I could prepare an attack.

Rupert, however, was too fast, and commonly circled around me or went for one of my open sides.

So far I was only good at keeping a shield up directly in front of or behind me, and though I could make it bigger, I still couldn't get it to encircle me.

And even if I did, all I'd be doing is sealing myself inside, leaving Rupert to hammer at the shield until fatigue got to me and I collapsed. I needed to be able to attack all around me...

I nibbled my lip as Rupert strode onto the mats, meeting me at the center.

"Listen, *Wizard*," he snarled. "I don't have the time to baby you like Ling and Julianne did. If you don't try a new trick this time I'll subdue you with enough force that you won't be able to fight any more this week. *Do something*, or prepare to incur a lot of pain."

I wasn't exactly scared by his threat—he couldn't hurt me too badly, or Celestina would make herself an instrument out of his ribcage for daring to harm Killian's hobby that kept him occupied.

But I didn't particularly like aching like an arthritic grandma, so I shook my arms out and eyed Rupert. "What's got your fangs extra sharp today?"

"Your idiocy. All of this fuss for a smelly wizard, even—" He cut himself off and shook his head. "Prepare yourself, Wizard."

"Awww, the way you keep spitting my title it's going to make me think you don't like me," I said.

"I *don't* like you!"

I grinned cheekily, but I didn't get a chance to tweak him farther.

"Hazel, stop baiting and get ready," Celestina ordered.

"It is a skill worth honing at another time," Josh added. "A frustrated enemy is easier to entrap. You are almost there with Rupert already."

Rupert scowled, but didn't dare glance at the Second Knight, who had pulled a dagger seemingly from thin air to sharpen since he had finished his sword.

I squared my shoulders and opened myself to magic, blinking when my wizard mark scrawled a hot path up and down my face.

"Begin!" Josh declared.

Instead of following my usual tactics against Rupert and creating a shield—or even adopting my usual method of lunging forward with my sword—I funneled magic through my blood and pushed out an arcing wave of blue fire that covered both my sides and curved out in front of me.

I gritted my teeth with effort and pushed, making the wave expand and roll across the mats like a crest, driving Rupert around the side.

"Yes, yes!" Celestina shouted. "Now follow it up with another attack, and don't let him get close!"

Her warning was too late. Rupert became a blur as he evaded the fire, leaving a breeze in his wake.

But it *did* give me an idea.

I let the blue fire collapse in on itself and built a circle of dagger-sharp ice shards about waist high—on me, anyway—in a circle around me.

Rupert skidded to a stop just shy of the wall and looked from it to me. "Seriously?" He fluffed his bright red hair. "I tell you to try something new, so you build a snow fort?"

I didn't mind his snark. It told me I was on the right path since he bothered to stop and say something instead of beat me senseless. (He'd have to break through my blue ice to get to me; I had made my barrier over two feet thick so he couldn't grab me over the top and yank me free.)

I flexed my fingers as I considered my ice wall.

While it was impossible to keep my shield stable and circle it around me, maybe a magic attack would be different.

The Paragon's book had pictures that showed wizards standing at the center of circles of fire and electricity. Wouldn't an attack be easier to push out than my shield—which I had to maintain even when Rupert rammed into it?

I flooded my blood with magic and stabbed my katana at Rupert above the ice wall, making him take a step back.

Using a fraction of the magic hoarded in my blood, I melted my magic ice, turning it to water, then transformed it into sparking, hissing electricity.

Rupert tried to circle behind me, but the electricity was still there. When he paused, I let the surplus of magic floating in my blood free, funneling it into the electricity.

The blue sparks blew up into thick bolts that leaped high above my head, tripled the area my attack covered, and were so bright I couldn't see past them.

I did hear, however, three bolts strike Rupert—who was stuck in the expanded area covered by my attack—in quick succession and shake the gym with the accompanying peals of thunder as Rupert shouted.

I cut off my magic—killing the lightning—and had to rapidly blink a few times before I could actually view my results.

Rupert was flat on the ground, his clothes smoldering as his muscles and limbs twitched.

"*Excellent!*" Celestina clapped loudly, her smile almost as dazzling as my lightning had been. "That's exactly what I meant! Well done. When you throw an avalanche of magic like that around, a vampire at Rupert's level won't be left standing."

"I might have gone a bit overboard." I teetered on my feet for a moment—the rush that magic always left behind was almost enough to make me silly.

Josh slightly bowed his head, as though finishing a deep meditation. "One must grow used to handling greater power so that they may face greater opponents in the never-ending fight that will eventually consume our world." He blinked as he studied me. "That is to say, you can blow Rupert up, he is expendable. But you must learn the flow of your magic so you don't injure yourself in the process."

Celestina nodded in agreement as she approached the mats.

"Josh is right! It's all about learning your limits." She stopped just short of Rupert and peered down at him.

"Is he going to be okay?" I asked.

Celestina laughed. "He'll be fine. I think he's just shocked a wizard knocked him down."

Rupert growled at her feet, but he seemed incapable of proper speech—or even more than pained wheezes.

Josh appeared at my shoulder and joined Celestina in gawking at the red-haired vampire. "It seems congratulations are in order. With this win you have surpassed Rupert. Well done." He nodded approvingly at me.

"You won? Way to go, Miss Hazel!" Julianne cheered from where she was practicing with throwing knives.

"We knew you could do it," Gavino chimed in.

"But does this really count?" I asked. "He's beaten me a bunch of times. Winning once hardly feels like I'm really at his level."

"You may fry him with a few more oversized bolts of lightning if that would convince you," Josh said.

Rupert made a strangled noise.

"I'm sure Rupert would say you have surpassed him," Celestina added.

I waited for more growling noises, but it seemed Rupert was too occupied trying to get his legs to stop jumping.

"I don't know about that," I slowly said.

"I'll have to get my checkboard to see who you face next, but first I think you ought to practice that neat trick you used on Rupert," Celestina said.

"You mean making the area attack with lightning?" I asked.

"Yes." Celestina slung her braid over her shoulder as she furrowed her eyebrows in thought. "I wonder if you could make your magic spiral out, or more thinly cover a larger area. The three lightning bolts would have killed a vampire less powerful than Rupert, so depending on your foe you may need a bigger area to attack rather than a higher potency of lightning."

Before she could pursue this thought, the gym doors swung open.

Killian strolled in, once again missing his perfectly pressed suitcoat and tie, and instead wearing a smug smirk.

"Your Eminence!" Celestina, Josh, and all the vampires in the gym bowed to Killian—except Rupert. He struggled to stand, but could only get onto his knees.

"What's up…" I paused, trying to think of a nickname that wouldn't end up with me getting maimed. "…Sunshine?" I suggested.

Killian stared at me.

"Well, you get to call me 'Wizard' all the time," I grumbled.

"What brings you here, Your Eminence? Do you wish to observe Hazel's training?" Celestina asked.

"No. Rather, I'm here to give future orders."

"And that would be?" Josh asked.

"The annual Summer's End Ball is in one week," Killian said. "We're going."

The ball was a big deal for the Midwest's supernatural community. It gave everyone a chance to mingle, network, and make observations about the community as a whole. New alliances were usually started at the ball, and attendance was somewhat choosy—invitations were usually only extended to leaders of Houses, Packs, etc. The higher ups like Killian would be allowed to bring a guard with them, but when my parents attended they were the only ones from House Medeis allowed to go.

Based on Celestina's and Josh's expressions, I didn't think that was unexpected, until Killian swiveled in my direction.

"And this year I'll bring Hazel as my plus one," he said.

I rolled my eyes. "You're just going to take me so you can use me to bait the Night Court, aren't you?"

"In a way," he acknowledged.

"Look." I ambled across the mats and snatched up my scabbard so I could sheath my chisa katana. "Just because you have a twisted sense of humor…"

I trailed off when I noticed Julianne was staring at Killian with huge moon-like eyes.

I twisted around, my worry building when I saw open shock on Celestina's and even Josh's face.

"You've never taken a date to the ball before, Your Eminence," Celestina said, her perfect composure shaken. "*Ever.*"

"I'm well aware of my past habits," Killian said dryly.

"Then you are aware how some might interpret Hazel's position?" Celestina asked. "Given that she would be the first you take to a public event?"

Josh tilted his head back. "You mean to say everyone will assume Hazel and His Eminence are romantically involved?"

My sword slipped from limp fingers and fell on the mats with a muffled thump. "Pardon?"

Celestina shot Josh a look. "Yes."

I shuffled back to Killian. "*Why?*"

"Must I have a reason?" Killian asked.

"Yes, because you have a reason for everything!"

"I told you my reason for breaking into Tutu's, and you weren't satisfied with it," Killian said.

"Because you *lied*! You obviously agreed to break in so you could deliver that letter to the Night Court's vault."

"I didn't lie," Killian said. "I hadn't yet decided if I was going to leave the letter or not."

"You are unbelievable," I grumbled. "And I don't think you've thought this through."

Both of Killian's eyebrows went up. "You think I haven't deeply considered my strategy?" His voice was just the tiniest bit frosty, but I didn't care—I already knew it was unlikely he'd actually kill me.

"I think you impulsively want something and have decided to

use me to get it, but you haven't realized the long-lasting effects," I said. "Killian, you're *infamous* in our society."

"You think going with me will tarnish your reputation?" Killian wryly asked.

"No! I mean—it will, but *your* reputation is the bigger thing! People aren't going to dismiss me as being your pet or just a fad. They'll think we're...they'll believe we're an item," I said. "It's going to take you months—possibly years—to shake the idea from the public mind."

Killian scoffed. "The public mind is far easier to manipulate than you think."

"Fine." I folded my arms across my chest. "Then tell me why we have to manipulate it in the first place."

Killian sighed as he ran a hand through his hair, mussing it slightly. "Isn't it enough to know we'll both benefit from this?"

"Then it has something to do with the alliance between the Night Court and Mason?"

"Yes."

I narrowed my eyes as I carefully studied the set of his eyebrows and mouth, and finally peered up into his dark eyes.

Disbelief nipped at me—Killian was perfectly capable of lying, but he was probably more skilled in deception and distraction. He still hadn't come out and exactly said *why* this was necessary— even though I bet there were multiple layered reasons for it.

But besides the Spring Summons and the Snow Ball, this was the event of the year.

I might have an opportunity to talk to the wizards serving on the Wizard Council about my position, and the House Medeis signet ring. Especially if I got Killian to vouch for me that Mason had attacked me.

Killian was absolutely using me—it was only natural I was allowed to use his reputation to my advantage, too.

"Okay..." I slowly started. "I'll go as your date. But I have a question. When we went out to eat together we acted as more of a boss-servant relationship. How did you plan we would appear at the ball?"

Killian grinned, and suddenly I regretted agreeing without ironing out this *very* important detail first.

"Hazel," Killian purred. "I'm so glad you asked..."

# CHAPTER FOURTEEN

*Hazel*

I was shocked by the sheer amount of preparation that went into getting ready for the Summer's End Ball. But I also wasn't quite prepared for the enthusiasm Celestina attacked it with.

Actually, Celestina was why preparations were so...intense. She cut my training schedule in half so I could only train in the late evenings and nights, which left my early afternoons open for things like manicures, pedicures, dress fittings, facials, a massage, and a haircut.

I would have felt guilty—Killian was footing the bill for everything—except Celestina came with me for all of that and was clearly having the time of her life, and I figured Killian probably owed his First Knight a few pedicures for everything he put her through, so it balanced out.

"I have always wanted this." Celestina smoothed out a wrinkle in her gorgeous crimson dress—which brought out warmer hues in her tawny-brown skin.

"You do look drop-dead gorgeous in that dress," I acknowledged as I tried to wriggle into my dress.

"No, no—I have a hundred dresses." Celestina swatted her hand through the air, brushing off the idea that she could easily switch places with a model for the night and no one would notice. "I meant *this*." She gestured back and forth between us. "Girl time! This week has been so *fun*!"

"I've really enjoyed it, too." I grinned at her when I finally got the waist of my dress in place. "And I'm glad you did all of this with me. But can't you have girl talk with Julianne?"

Celestina's silky hair tumbled over her shoulder in perfect curls I honestly didn't know were possible outside of Hollywood. "Not entirely. I'm His Eminence's First Knight. That puts me in a position of power and respect, so it is difficult to be truly friends with those under my command." Celestina's clear red eyes looked distant as she stared unseeingly at the mirror. "We're comrades— we'll live and die together. But although we may train together, doing things like this..."

"Selfishly, I'm glad you're so happy. I had fun with you this week, too—thank you." I smiled at the vampire when she came to help me with my dress.

The design was pretty simplistic—off-the-shoulder sleeves, a fitted bust and waist, and long skirts that had a bit of a ruffle to give it some poof. What made the dress remarkable, however, was the fabric. Simultaneously shimmery and glossy, the silvery fabric seemed to glow with the faint light of a full moon. White embroidered swirls covered the three-quarter-length sleeves and traced the neckline in shapes that looked remarkably similar to my wizard's mark.

I couldn't help but smile at my reflection as Celestina zipped me up, but I shook my head and tried to pick up the thread of our conversation.

"But about being friends with other Drake vampires...Julianne hero-worships you," I said. "I think she'd probably die of glee if you invited her to get a manicure with you."

There was a tap on the door, and Josh poked his head in. "Are preparations complete?"

"Almost." Celestina applied another layer of lipstick, then circled around me, inspecting my carefully applied makeup—which we had seen a stylist for that afternoon.

Josh straightened and slipped into the room—Celestina had taken over an upstairs drawing room and had rows of mirrors put up to make it easier to get ready today. Since he was going with us as part of Killian's guard escort, Josh wore a tuxedo that fit so well, I couldn't even pick out where he had holstered his sidearms or throwing knives.

"Looking good, Josh!" I winked at him.

Josh looked down at his tuxedo and shrugged. "It is appropriate attire."

I studied Josh for a moment, then turned back to Celestina. "Okay, I get it. I think you *can* be friends with her—or anyone from the Drake Family—but I can see how it would be difficult. You guys don't really do anything besides train, guard, and have your Family dinners." I waved at Josh to illustrate my point. "It's not like Killian gives you gobs of time to play a team sport, or have sleepovers and watch movies or something." I paused and curiously peered at Josh. "And now I'm stuck thinking what a sleepover with you would be like."

Josh sniffed. "I can do girl talk."

I arched an eyebrow at the vampire. "Try it."

Everything in Josh lifted *up*—his mouth, his height, and his voice. "Hazel, you look so *cute* in your dress! Killian is going to *die* when he sees you. Celestina, that lipgloss is fabulous."

"Lipstick," Celestina corrected.

Josh slightly pursed his lips. "Close enough. Should we talk boys now? Or do you want to tell me where you have all your weapons hidden? Hazel—you have *at least* one sidearm, right?"

I laughed. "I have a dagger, but no gun," I said. "Though I do have my clutch."

Josh briefly tapped his foot on the floor, then nodded. "Considering you knocked out a wizard last time with your clutch, that is acceptable."

"What did you stuff it with this time?" Celestina asked.

"Rocks." I held up my clutch—made of the same silver material as my dress. "They filled it up better and gave it a rounder appearance. You're sure there aren't going to be guards who ask to inspect it?"

"Nah." Celestina shook her head, making her glossy hair shine. "The place is warded and shielded to the teeth. It's pretty much impossible for a fight to break out inside the actual ball. Traditionally skirmishes and assassination attempts happen on the way in or out—outside the Curia Cloisters, of course. That's neutral territory that can't be fought in."

I made a face. "Have there really been that many fights that it's a tradition?"

"No. Only a few times over the past century," Josh said. "Your clutch will be plenty. Now, did I not do a sufficient job at girl talk?"

I laughed. "You did great—better than I thought!"

He straightened his tux jacket. "Excellent. Now, if you both would come downstairs as swiftly as possible, His Eminence is waiting at the front entrance."

"We'll be there shortly. Now off you go." Celestina shooed him from the room while I plopped down on a well-padded chair and put on my shoes—a pair of surprisingly comfortable heels that gave me an extra three inches of height, elevating me into loftiness. Or at least what passed for loftiness for me.

"You've reviewed your conduct with His Eminence?" Celestina asked.

"Yeah, I know how we're going to act," I glumly said.

Celestina chuckled. "Cheer up. You're dressed beautifully, and you're going to a ball with the most powerful vampire in the region. And, they serve delicious food."

"That last one is probably the most tempting part, though hopefully I'll be able to make my case with a few of the wizards who are a bit higher up and might be able to help me out." I slipped the strap of my clutch over my wrist and checked my hair —the stylist had curled it and sprayed it within an inch of its life so it sat demurely on my shoulders. My hair wasn't as thick or luxurious as Celestina's, but the stylist had managed to make it gleam like spun gold, and I shoved it back in braids and ponytails so much these days—so it wouldn't get in my face during a fight— it was kind of shocking to have it down again.

Celestina slipped on her own shoes and grabbed her clutch. "Shall we?"

I followed her when she swept out of the sitting room, playing with the clasp of my purse as I tried to push my nerves down.

The concept of being Killian's date made my head explode, but I was pretty sure he'd keep the night entertaining at least, and I had to use this opportunity to speak to the other wizards. I had gotten a start on the re-registration papers this week, and it was abundantly clear it was going to take me days to get through it all. I needed the subcommittee to officially acknowledge me and block Mason while I screwed around with their stupid paperwork.

My thoughts buzzed in my brain as I obediently trailed behind Celestina, who led us down to the second floor and through the maze-like innards of Drake Hall, all the way to the giant sweeping staircase that would dump us right out at the doors.

I almost rammed into Celestina when she stopped at the top step and loudly cleared her throat.

Killian stood near the double door entrance, talking to Josh and Gavino—our other guard for the night. When Celestina coughed, Killian looked up at us as he finished placing his second cufflink on.

Celestina pointedly stepped aside so she no longer stood in front of me, then beamed as she elegantly swept down the stairs.

I was a lot slower. I had to pick my way down—between my heels and the long skirts of my dress I wasn't going to risk falling face first down the stairs.

Killian stared at me, but wandered closer to the staircase, so he was waiting for me at the bottom by the time I reached it. His eyes traced my dress and my hair. "You look lovely," he said with no embarrassment or reluctance. (I wondered if that was a Killian thing, or if all vampires were capable of that because once you got old enough you just never. Ever. Cared.)

Because I'm me, I couldn't help the blush that heated my cheeks. "Thank you. And thanks for everything—the dress and hair, and all of that."

Killian nodded, then leaned over so his lips hovered *just* above my bare shoulder, and sniffed my skin.

It was about then I really wished he still had some shame left in him so I wouldn't feel quite so alone as I felt my blush burn even brighter on my cheeks.

To make it worse, he threaded his hands through my hair and raised his head so his mouth brushed my ear. "You're quite worth it. Shall we leave, my date for the evening?"

"Yep, let's go!" I grabbed fistfuls of my skirt and yanked myself from his grasp before marching to the front door, his laugh curling around me like smoke.

I grumbled under my breath about inappropriate vampires having twisted senses of humor—but just loud enough that I was certain he, Celestina, Josh, and Gavino could all hear.

I heard Celestina's throaty chuckle and Gavino's guffaw even after I popped outside. I gleefully cast a smirk over my shoulder, then hurried down the stairs and to the SUV with the vampire driver waiting just in front of it. "Open the door, open the door!" I pointed to the front passenger's seat as I hopped down the last step.

The driver sucked his neck into his shoulders, then looked to the drivers of the cars directly in front and behind him.

"Don't," Killian ordered, his voice cutting through the cool evening air.

The driver quickly moved to stand in front of the passenger door, blocking me from it.

I turned around and scowled at Killian. "Spoilsport."

Killian quirked an eyebrow at me. "If you are my date for the evening, wouldn't it be ridiculous for us to arrive sitting apart?"

"You just don't like getting left out."

Killian heaved his eyes up at the sky. "Yes, because you and the day's driver can exchange secretive information in the open cab." He opened the back door and gestured for me to climb in.

"Whatever, Mr. I-can't-sit-alone." I eyed the SUV seats and struggled to properly gather up my skirts and clutch so I could heft myself up.

I must have taken too long, because Killian took it upon himself to scoop me up.

"Thanks—but watch where that hand is going," I warned him as he twisted at an odd angle to set me inside.

Killian raised an amused eyebrow at me. "Where do you *think* it's going?"

"Just keep it away from my butt!"

"You are wearing yards of fabric. I don't think I could feel your butt even if I tried." He set me down, his hand trailing across my lower back as he stepped back.

I scooted farther down the bench seat to give him space to cram his long frame in. "Doesn't matter. It's the thought that counts."

"Why are you so protective of your butt anyway?" Killian speculatively looked at my seat as he slid in.

"It's inappropriate."

It was, but I was neglecting to add that Killian was too hot to go around touching my butt without taking a few years off my life. Such a shame.

Killian sighed. "Wizards." He shifted his gaze to the driver. "Move out when the rest of the motorcade is ready."

"Yes, Your Eminence," the driver said.

The car was silent for a few seconds as the SUV slowly rolled forward.

"Since you're my date, does that mean if someone else touches your butt at the Summer's End Ball, I am allowed to maim them?" Killian abruptly asked.

"It shouldn't be a problem. You are the first person I've met in my entire adult life who picks me up bridal style," I said.

"What is that supposed to mean?"

"You're either super old, or you have a hidden romantic streak."

"If I say the latter does that mean I can kill any potential butt-touchers?"

"I told you it wasn't going to be a problem. And can we stop talking about my butt?"

"You are the one who is so insistent it be guarded and left alone."

"*Killian!*"

———

KILLIAN HAD a good laugh at my squawks of outrage, but I was just glad we finally dropped the subject of butts by the time we arrived at the Curia Cloisters.

The ball was held in a small piece of the fae realm—not unlike the Paragon's pocket realm—that was owned by the Regional Committee of Magic. Fae Courts and fae nobles were the only ones who could afford to have a place in the fae realm, given how toxic it was and all the spells and magic required to keep a space clean and safe over there. But smaller slivers were sometimes gifted to political organizations, like the Committee.

The doors to the realm were set up in the Curia Cloisters, so the drivers dropped us off at the doors. Celestina, Josh, and Gavino ringed around us as Killian led me to the front doors, but I paused when I recognized a suitcoat with House Medeis piping.

I froze mid-step and convulsively squeezed Killian's arm when the wizard I was studying turned around.

It was Felix—you couldn't miss his shiny hair or dazzling beauty even without vampire sight. But he looked *awful*. The circles under his eyes were so dark, I thought for a moment they might be bruises. Even standing up he just seemed...*bent* and tired—as if every muscle in his body was so exhausted he couldn't really stand.

He was surrounded by a few House Tellier wizards, his expression stony even as they nudged him and laughed at him.

Mason must have made him come—though I have no idea why. He had that awful magic-canceling bracelet on, so it wasn't like Mason could make him use magic.

Our gazes met, and Felix's eyes widened fractionally before he pointedly looked away, and then turned his back to me. He tucked his hands behind his back so the House Tellier wizards couldn't see, then made a shooing motion.

He wanted me to go inside...

"Is everything all right?" Killian asked.

I tried to speak, but something was wedged in my throat. "Yeah." I peeled my gaze off Felix and smiled weakly at Killian.

He glanced at Felix, then pulled his arm from my grasp so he could curl it around my waist. "He is from Medeis?"

"Yeah."

Killian cocked his head as he listened, though he nudged me toward the door. "It sounds like he was dragged along. They are discussing the horde of House Tellier wizards that are back at House Medeis. Perhaps he's collateral?"

"Or they're using him to say House Medeis supports Mason, and everyone else is collateral," I whispered.

Killian rubbed my shoulder. "There's nothing you can do about it right now."

"Yeah, but it shows that I have to do something," I said. "I need to talk with the wizards on the Wizard Council."

We strolled down the hallway, passing the visitors' desk. There were signs that pointed out the directions to the realm gate, and when we reached the entrances—wooden doors surrounded by fog and placed in the middle of the hallway—Celestina produced our invitation for inspection.

A werewolf—obvious by the golden gaze and muscled arms—took the paper and glanced it over before she bowed to Killian. "Welcome, Your Eminence Killian Drake and Adept Hazel of House Medeis. Please, enter." She pulled one of the wooden doors open, and motioned for us to step through the fog.

Killian led with me right behind him.

It was a different feeling from getting sucked into the Paragon's pocket realm. The fog left a strange, mist-kissed feeling on my skin and seemed more gel-like. The floor seemed to spin under my feet, and the next step I took I left the carpeted rug of the Curia Cloisters and stepped onto marble flooring, my heels producing a quiet tap on the rock.

The world was muffled, and then music broke through—the sweet song of stringed instruments combined with the soothing tones of a piano.

We had stepped into a ballroom—like, a *legit* ballroom. It was two stories tall with Grecian columns that bled up into sculptures of fae, wizards, vampires, werewolves, werecats, and what I *thought* was a pair of elves popping out of the ceiling as if they were coming to join in the festivities. There were three massive chandeliers that were bigger than me, but the room's exterior was lit by bobbing lights that emitted the faint buzz of wizard magic, and the tables—bursting with so much food I was surprised they hadn't collapsed—had glowing crystals that gave off a whiff of floral fae magic.

I slightly shook my head, trying to adjust to my new surroundings, and let Killian lead me farther in.

Already there were crowds—one large crowd was clustered around the tables of food. Another much smaller group was dancing to the music, but lots of people milled about, too.

The vampires were easy to recognize—they all seemed drawn to Killian the moment he entered, and all of them were wearing formal clothing that was at least fifty years out of style.

When they noticed that he had his arm curled around me, their pale faces and red eyes all shifted to me.

Killian tapped my lower back with his thumb. Was I ready?

I drew in a breath and put on a smile, then tried to laugh without sounding like an idiot as Killian lifted his arm to drape it over my shoulder.

"It's all so beautiful here!" I reached up and entangled my fingers with his hand that cupped my bare shoulder. "Thank you for bringing me!"

Killian smiled down at me, multiplying his attractive factor by ten. "Of course. Anything you wish for will be yours, Hazel."

I think the most impressive actors of our bunch were actually Celestina, Josh, and Gavino. They didn't even blink at our disgusting exchange. (I was also soooo glad Killian had decided against bringing Rupert. I don't know that the red-haired vampire could have kept himself from looking disgusted.)

A woman dressed in what appeared to be a renaissance-era gown edged closer to us. "Your Eminence." She glanced curiously at me. "And...?"

"Adept Hazel—of House Medeis," I said.

"You are accompanying His Eminence today?" the vampire asked. I admired her guts—she certainly wasn't wasting any time!

"Rather, I am accompanying her." Killian played with the sleeve of my gown and smirked down at me.

The woman gaped at the pair of us, her head slowly swiveling to look from Killian to me.

"I'm sorry," I said. "I'm afraid I don't know your name. You are...?" I held out my hand, expecting to shake hers and hopefully hint that she was supposed to supply a name, but I was shocked when she took my hand and bent over, touching my fingers to her forehead.

"I beg your pardon for the intrusion. Enjoy your evening, Your Eminence, Adept Medeis." She tottered off without saying anything more, and even though she didn't speak a word, enough supernaturals were gifted with extra strong senses and hearing, so whispers rippled out around us in waves.

Two female vampires flicked fans open and whispered to each other behind their painted surfaces. A ring of three Alphas rumbled to each other in lowered voices as they watched us, and based on the faint "*what?*" and the gaping looks, a whole set of Adepts had just found out.

Killian tugged a little on my arm, scooping me closer to his side. "It seems we've made a splash, my Wizard. Where should we go first?"

I craned my head out past his arm to peer around, then looked up at him. "Food?"

Killian stared down at me.

"What? It took a long time to get ready. I didn't even get lunch!"

Killian made a soft exhale of laughter that I doubt many heard. "Fine. I'll get you fed."

I slipped out from underneath his arm so I could tuck mine in his. "It's an investment. This way I don't get hangry on anyone."

"What a terrifying thought."

We made it to the tables of food—which cleared of party-goers like magic. I was starting to see the unexpected benefits of coming with Killian; this just might make the night even more fun than I hoped!

I took a plate and filled it at the first table—various cheeses and special smoked meats that the werewolves had been chowing down on—when I saw the dessert table where I *thought* I saw my favorite dessert ever, tiramisu. I shoved my cheese and meat plate into Killian's hands for safekeeping, then hustled my way over to the desserts.

China cups of chocolate mousse, squares of delectable tiramisu, pyramids of macaroons, and ramekins of creme brulee filled the table. I took one of each, then made my way back to Killian with my sweet treasures.

"You're going to begin with dessert?" Killian asked when I took a forkful of my tiramisu.

"Sure," I said. "You only live once!" I popped my tiramisu in my mouth, and it took a lot of effort not to hum with happiness. It was so rich and creamy, and the faint coffee flavor was amazing!

I took another forkful, and noticed Killian watching. "Want a bite?"

He blinked down at me.

If we had been at Drake Hall I would have rolled my eyes and said something about getting him a juice pouch, but given that we were actively trying to encourage the image that we were romantically involved, I didn't think that would really help our case.

So instead I put on my brightest smile and shoved the fork into his mouth.

That got a reaction out of everyone around us—including Celestina, Gavino, and even Josh. The trio guarding us tensed, and slowly raised their gazes to Killian, fear crackling in the set of their shoulders. Someone in the crowd audibly gasped, and the dinner crowd stepped back even farther away from us.

For a moment I froze. Had I gone too far? I mean, I had pulled him into the freaking *pool* earlier that summer. I didn't think force-feeding him a bite of tiramisu was that terrible of a deed. I slowly looked up, fearing what expression I'd see as I pulled the fork from his mouth.

Killian licked his lips, his expression thoughtful. "It's not bad," he finally said. "It's not disgustingly sweet like most human desserts."

"That's because it has coffee in it." I was pretty impressed that my voice didn't shake as I got another forkful of the dessert for myself. I glanced up at him again, trying to discern if he was going to make me run miles after the ball out of spite, but he wasn't looking down at me with the promise of death.

He held my plate out with one hand and rested the other hand on my hip as he studied the other guests—giving me the kind of casual mindfulness you only show people you inherently trust.

*I have to take it back. He's by far the best actor here. Way better than Celestina and the others.* I finished my tiramisu and other desserts and tried tugging my cheese and meat plate from Killian's hands.

Killian, not quite relenting, took my empty plate and handed me my full one. "I see someone I need to talk to," he said. "Will you be fine by yourself?"

"Of course!" I chirped like a good little idiot. "Enjoy."

Killian gave me that slick smile of his, forged especially for those standing in a fifteen-foot diameter around us. "You too." He leaned over and kissed me on the cheek, then prowled off.

Gavino and Josh followed him, though Celestina stayed with me.

"Hey, Celestina, want some cheese?" I asked. "It's really good."

Celestina laughed and smiled, then leaned closer and whispered under her breath. "I don't know whether to compliment you for your nerves of steel, or call you an idiot."

"I didn't think it would be a big deal," I whispered back. "I've seen everyone from Drake Hall eat human food." I'd sat with them and watched while they ate and laughed and drank at the required dinners.

"Except for His Eminence," Celestina reminded me, shattering the memory.

I winced. "Will he get sick?"

"No. It's a personal preference. But his reaction explained a few things I've wondered about," Celestina said.

"Huh?" Clueless, I turned around to properly face her, but I was too late.

A slender woman built like a gymnast and a gorgeous buxom woman who appeared to be approximately in her late forties were hustling in my direction. Going by her eyes, the gymnast had to be a werewolf—her eyes were a piercing shade of blue found only in wolves. The buxom woman's dress had a wizard coat of arms stitched in the fabric so she was probably a wizard—even though I would have thought she was too beautiful to be just a human.

The wizard stopped short of me and tapped her clutch on the thigh of her well-fitted, mermaid-style gown. "So," she said. "You are the little Adept who has captured the best of the vampires. Impressive!"

The werewolf delicately wrinkled her nose and shoved her hands in the pockets of her pantsuit. "Personally, I wouldn't have believed ol' Rock Face ever deigned to love a woman, but he positively *reeks* of your scent, and his smell is plastered all over you. The nose doesn't lie." She winked, then tapped her nose.

The wizard set her hand on the werewolf's shoulders. "He let her *feed* him. Have you ever seen Killian Drake eat or drink in public before?"

"Not in the Regional Committee of Magic meetings," the werewolf said.

Both women swung their gazes back to me and studied me intently.

I fidgeted. "Um...I'm sorry, who are you?"

"I apologize—where are our manners?" the wizard laughed.

"I guess we were too excited," the werewolf grinned. "Oh, hello, Celestina."

Celestina bowed her head slightly and moved to stand just behind my shoulder. "Adept Medeis, please allow me the honor of introducing you to Pre-Dominant Harka and Adept Bellus."

Now it was my turn to gawk at the pair. Pre-Dominant Harka was the top werewolf in the Midwest, and served on the Regional Committee of Magic as the werewolf representative. Pre-Dominants came directly under the Dominant—the highest-ranking werewolf in North America. And Adept Bellus was—obviously—the Adept of House Bellus, but I knew her name because her husband was the Elite—the top wizard in the region.

I was basically rubbing elbows with political royalty.

"The honor is all mine," I faintly said.

"Committee meetings are going to be *so much* more fun now," Pre-Dominant Harka said.

"You can sit with Beta Colton and I—he's Pre-Dominant Harka's very recently announced fiancé." Adept Bellus winked and nudged Pre-Dominant Harka, who had turned a lovely shade of crimson.

"Killian and I—that is to say the Eminence and I—are still... sorting our relationship out," I evasively explained. "I don't know that we're at the point, yet, where I feel like I could attend the meetings."

"Don't be silly, dear," Adept Bellus said. "He brought you *here*. We may as well begin ringing wedding bells."

I laughed, but internally I hoped Killian knew what he was doing with this little act of ours.

"I should introduce you to my husband," Adept Bellus said. "I'm sure he'll be very keen to meet you."

"You mean he'll hope she could tame Killian's ruthlessness?" Pre-Dominant Harka suggested.

Adept Bellus laughed. "I never said that!"

"I don't think Killian could ever truly be...er...tamed," I said. (The trick to making our little play believable was to inject just enough realism in it to make it realistic.)

Pre-Dominant Harka nodded. "He must be strong to remain the Eminence of the Midwest."

We all nodded wisely—as if repeating folksy wisdom—until Gavino skidded to a stop next to me.

"Miss—that is—please excuse me, Pre-Dominant Harka, Adept Bellus." Gavino bowed politely. "But His Eminence has need of Adept Medeis." Gavino refrained from touching me, but he herded me away from the ladies and off in the direction Killian had gone.

"Excuse us, ladies!" I called to the pair.

They looked amused as they waved farewell, and Gavino and Celestina herded me away.

"I was doing fine," I muttered to Gavino. "Killian doesn't need to worry."

"His Eminence is not worrying," Gavino hissed. "Rather, *we're* worrying about His Eminence, and we need you to stop it!"

"Stop what?"

Gavino stopped edging me forward when we reached a cleared section of the ballroom dance floor. "Oh, boy," I whispered, my lips numb.

# CHAPTER FIFTEEN

*Hazel*

In the center of the open space was Killian, his eyes extra black and his expression murderous as Josh stood at his back, guarding him.

Standing just in front of Killian was a beautiful woman in a big skirted black dress, wearing a black crown that was so large I wondered if it made her neck hurt. Between the black dress and the glowing diamond necklace she wore—and paired with her coppery skin tone and slightly tapered fae ears—I was willing to bet my week's desserts that she was the Night Court Queen, particularly given that Consort Ira stood just behind her shoulder.

I stepped into the empty circle around them, wincing at the sensation of palpable tension and hatred that crawled up my spine. But Killian's hand lingered near his hip where I *knew* he had a gun holstered. And while Celestina might have said it was impossible to fight here in the Regional Committee of Magic's realm, she didn't say what the consequences were for attempting it. I was betting it was not pretty—even for a Committee member and the Eminence of the vampires.

I was aware of the stares drilling in my back as I approached the standoff. "Killian," I called out to him to warn that I had arrived. (The last thing I needed was for him to think I was one of the Night Court's minions and accidentally deck me.)

I touched his hand when I reached him—it was icy cold, but at least he didn't withdraw. "Are you enjoying yourself?" I leaned into his arm and glanced at the Night Court Queen and Consort, then made a show of tapping my cheek for a few moments before brightening. "Consort Ira, is that you?"

"Killian," the queen of the Night Court snarled—I think Killian and the Paragon had called her Queen Nyte. "This is a discussion for the important. Send your dog away."

The muscles in Killian's arms hardened. "You insult Hazel?"

"You care?" Consort Ira sneered. "Is she not a mere human? Your play may work against the stupid and the idyllic, but we know to you humans are only for food and servants."

"You weave an impressive web of lies." Queen Nyte smiled. "But it will not delay your destruction. I can only imagine the squeals your dog will make as it dies." The queen gave me a look seeped in hatred. My instincts screamed at me to step back and retreat, but I placidly forced myself to stand my ground.

Killian's smile was terrifying. "Are you proposing all-out war?" Killian started to move his free hand under his jacket, probably reaching for his gun.

Ohhhh boy. We were escalating fast—I had to throw on the brakes somehow because Queen Nyte clearly had no idea what danger she was in.

I sighed and briefly leaned my arm against his shoulder. "I honestly would have expected a higher quality of insult. Calling me a dog is so easy it borders on overdone." I mournfully gazed at the queen as if she had let me down. I then purposely turned my back to her and stood directly in front of Killian. Thankful for my high heels that made me a bit taller, I linked my arms around his neck. "Killian, this is *boring* and so predictable it takes all the fun out of it. Why can't you introduce me to Elite Bellus?" The final touch in communicating my utter disregard for the queen had me more nervous than Queen Nyte herself. I tugged Killian down a bit and stood on my tiptoes to kiss his cheek.

Killian settled both of his hands on my waist. I held my breath for a moment, until he broke eye contact with the rulers of the Night Court and looked down at me. He didn't quite soften his expression—I could still feel the tense set of his shoulders—but when he looked at me I saw more glimmers of red in his black eyes, which was a good enough start.

He leaned over—I thought to return the cheek kiss, but he kept going down. I almost jumped out of my skin when he kissed my neck—slowly, as if he reveled in it. His lips were a brush of coolness in the heat my magic—and worry—produced, and matched with the way his hands crept up my back, it felt a thousand times more intimate than my cheek kiss.

It took every ounce of control I had to stay in place as he sighed against my neck, and I was so grateful for my skirts, which hid my wobbling knees. There was something about having an apex predator so close to my neck that made my instincts scream, but my brain was pretty confused because it also recognized Killian as an oversized tissue I had recently spent the night slumped against.

*What was going on?!* My body howled at me—trying to decide if adrenaline or a blush was necessary.

Killian straightened. "If that's what you want."

"What?" I intelligently asked.

He let me go long enough to take my hand and led me away from the fuming monarchs at a slow walk, Josh right behind us.

"Eminence," Queen Nyte hissed.

Killian ignored her, and together we rejoined the rest of the attendees, seemingly breaking the spell on the area so everyone returned to chattering—overly bright this time. When I caught a few people still staring at us, they sheepishly looked away, as if to show they hadn't all been gawking moments ago.

I let out a whoosh of air and craned my neck, trying to see through all the tall werewolves and vampires. It took me a moment, but I saw Celestina and Gavino. Gavino gave me a discreet thumbs up while Celestina winked at me before they both skirted around us to join Josh at our backs.

I finally let myself relax, all the tension leaking from my frame. "Well, that was something."

Killian didn't respond. He seemed to be purposefully guiding me through the crowds—maybe to drop me back off at the dessert table? (Even with my heels I was too short to get a good look at where we were going.)

He stopped for a moment, and a server with a tray full of champagne paused.

"Would the lady or sir like a refreshment?" The server offered out his tray.

Killian shook his head, his dark eyes combing our surroundings, but I was thirsty after all my treats, and having to soothe a murderous Killian had only made it worse, so I took a champagne flute with a smile. "Yes, thank you!"

The server bowed and headed to the next cluster of attendees.

I sipped at the bubbly drink—which had a faint trace of sweetness that was almost completely overwhelmed by the bubbles.

"There," Killian said.

"There what?" I admired my champagne flute before taking another sip.

Killian nodded. "There's Elite Bellus."

I almost spat out my drink when he tugged on my arm, pulling me along with him. Bubbles went up my nose when I finally managed to swallow. "You're really introducing me?"

Killian raised both of his eyebrows at a slant that conveyed he was considering my mental health. "You *asked* for an introduction."

"It was an excuse!"

"Ahhh, Eminence Drake! Fancy seeing you here, eh?" An older gentleman I recognized as Elite Bellus laughed at his own joke as he approached us. Elite Bellus was perhaps a decade older than his wife, but he wore his age well with deep smile lines, a noble sort of profile, and a well-groomed goatee that matched his slicked back, silvery hair. He winked at me when he caught my stare. "Care to introduce me to your lady?"

I tried not to look too star-struck. Elite Bellus had represented the wizards on the Regional Committee of Magic for a while, and just about every wizard idolized him for his kindness and quick wit.

"Elite Bellus." Killian released my hand long enough to shake Bellus's, then rested his hand on my lower back. "This is Adept Hazel of House Medeis."

"Adept Medeis, it is a pleasure." Bellus shook my hand with a firm grasp. "I was sorry to hear of your parents' deaths."

I bowed my head. "Thank you, Elite."

He nodded. "So what—"

He didn't get a chance to continue as the Paragon almost bowled him over while careening into the conversation.

"Merely training her to get the maximum benefit, was it?" The Paragon scoffed and shook a finger at Killian. "I *knew* it! I knew you had a thing for her!"

When Killian, Elite Bellus, and I all stared at him, the Paragon coughed. "That is to say," he amended, "I knew you cared deeply for her." He peered from Killian to me. "Are congratulations in order, then? This is all consensual?" He studied me, as if looking for signs that I was being forced into this supposed relationship.

Killian gave the Paragon a smile sharp enough he could have

eaten glass. "I am well aware of my reputation, *Paragon*, but I have to ask if you really think I'm *that* sort of monster."

The Paragon folded his arms across his chest and squinted at Killian. "Well, you can be possessive."

I scooted closer to Killian—if I got in the way he wouldn't have a clear shot of throttling the Paragon—and patted his chest. "Paragon, you've met Elite Bellus, I assume?"

The Paragon shook himself. "Oh, yes, of course. How is your evening, Bellus?"

"Rather more eventful than I imagined." Elite Bellus smiled politely, then nodded to me. "My wife announced her intention to meet you. Did she get the chance to?"

"Yes," I said. "She is a beautiful and lovely woman."

Elite Bellus's smile turned warm, and he seemed to relax slightly. "She is my heart."

The Paragon turned to Killian. "So, is Hazel your—"

"Finish that question, and it will be the last thing you say," Killian stated. His expression was stoic, but there was an extra coat of ice to his voice.

"Touchy," the Paragon grumbled.

When a server bearing a tray of wine glasses passed him, the Paragon plucked two off and offered one to Elite Bellus, who took it.

I shrugged out of Killian's arm, which made him look down at me with raised eyebrows, until I took his newly freed hand in both of mine and leaned against his arm, half shielding our joint hands so no one saw me squeeze his fingers in warning.

"It's okay, Killian," I said in a lowered tone—my attempt at reminding him we were *supposed* to appear loving. (He was so used to bickering with the Paragon he probably replied on sheer instinct. I thought.)

Killian stared at me for a few heartbeats, then nodded.

Elite Bellus and the Paragon exchanged looks—of what I couldn't quite say.

Killian returned his attention to the Paragon. "Have you come any closer to finding what you're looking for?"

The Paragon sighed. "Not really, no."

"Excellent, then you are free to help," Killian said.

"What? No, I'm not." The Paragon straightened and looked slightly alarmed.

"You don't have to do anything. I'll simply use your name now when I speak to the fae Queen of Spring."

"No, no, no," the Paragon said. "You can't do that."

"I would like to see you stop me." Killian pulled his hand from mine so he could brush a lock of my blond hair. "Enjoy your conversation with the Elite. Celestina will know where I am."

I nodded and tried to think of mournful puppies or sad baby seals so I didn't blush like an idiot. "Okay."

Killian swept off, a protesting Paragon on his heels. Gavino and Josh moved so naturally with the crowd, I didn't actually see them leave with the two as much as I noticed they weren't standing with Celestina.

I took a deep breath and tried to mentally prepare myself. This was an excellent opportunity to bring up Mason. I probably took too long—or my nerves were super obvious, because Elite Bellus spoke first.

He took a sip from his wine glass and peered at me over the rim. "I'd heard you were staying at Drake Hall."

"Yes," I said. "Killian offered me safe haven after Mason—a senior wizard from my House—attempted a coup, and I was forced to flee for my life."

"I'll be blunt. I thought it was political maneuvering on Killian's end. He always sees ten years ahead of the rest of us and blocks us before we can even move." Elite Bellus swirled his wine glass. "All supernaturals know this."

"...Yes."

"Which is why it's shocked us all that his usual rules don't seem to apply to you." Elite Bellus studied me. "But I feel that I must give my due diligence, and I've heard you're an intelligent girl, so I will warn you. You're a wizard, Adept Medeis. Killian Drake's priority has always been and will always be vampires. He's ruthless, paranoid, and I don't entirely know that he can love like the rest of us."

I blinked at the harsh observation. It was true—or at least true-ish. But it seemed almost cruel the way he painted Killian. "I understand where you're coming from," I said slowly. "And perhaps you are right about some things. But I can promise you that Killian does love."

It was obvious he loved the Drake Family. Yeah, he wasn't open or doting like some vampires were with their underlings, but I knew he'd sacrifice a lot for his Family.

Elite Bellus, however, interpreted my statement in an entirely different way. "I've never seen him the way he is with you. However, Adept, he is manipulative. It *suits* him to let everyone else believe he's fallen for you."

I tried to keep my facial expression as "slightly confused" and hoped that the Elite didn't realize how right he was.

"And I will give it to you—he gives you freedoms with him that he wouldn't allow with anyone else. But there is no possible way he holds true love in his heart for you."

"Actually, I wasn't referring to—"

"Has he drunk from you?"

"What?"

"Has he fed off you and drunk your blood?"

I blinked hard, barely able to believe Elite Bellus was actually asking that personal a question in the middle of the Summer's End Ball. "I. Beg. Your. Pardon?" My frustration started to leak through as I wasn't able to keep all the gruffness out of my voice.

"He hasn't," Elite Bellus said. "And he won't, ever. Killian Drake only drinks from blood pouches. I don't rightly know the reason why—it's certainly a personal choice given that he keeps blood donors on staff for his underlings. But he won't ever drink from you, Hazel. There's not a clearer sign in the world that he also won't ever fully love you."

I sucked a breath in. "I'm surprised."

"That I know this?"

"No. That you are *so rude*," I said. "What does it matter to you —or to anyone—how Killian eats? It's not my business, and it's certainly not yours. And yeah, maybe he is cunning, ruthless, manipulative, and a total ass."

"I didn't actually say that," Elite Bellus muttered.

"But whatever Killian and I have between us is exactly that, between us! And you know what? I'm calling you out on *your* issues! When I ran from my own House—scared for the lives of my family—not a single wizard House would help me. All of House Medeis's allies abandoned me. Killian took me in, trained me, and protected me when other wizards attacked me. So, yeah. When I finally get House Medeis back—and I say when because I *will*—if Killian asks for a favor or two, I'm going to help him, because he's shown more care for me than anyone in the *wizarding* community has!"

I was starting to attract some attention, but I didn't care. This was stupid—how could Elite Bellus sweat over my personal life when I met Killian BECAUSE OF A COUP ON MY HOUSE?

"Another thing." I held up a finger, my smile more savage now. "Don't you try to give me this 'I'm concerned for you' stuff. Neither you nor *anyone* among the Houses cared enough about me to see if I was even okay until I came in here with Killian, because it finally occurred to you that in your rejection of me you might have given him a foothold in wizard politics. He's manipulative, but you are obviously just as bad!"

I was pretty sure I'd just bid my opportunity to ask for help a very permanent farewell, but I was so mad I couldn't see straight.

I mean, really? Was he really going to try and 'warn' me when the entire community was so set against me—or so selfish they just didn't care?

Adept Bellus appeared, a breath of fresh air with her kind smile. "Darling," she said. "Why are you upsetting Adept Medeis?" Her smile turned apologetic when she turned to me. "Please forgive him, Adept Medeis. His heart is in the right place, but he can be blind at times. I'm sorry for any careless words he might have spoken."

Elite Bellus stared at his wineglass for a moment, then looked at his wife. "I think I made some improper assumptions and gravely misread the situation."

"My love," Adept Bellus smoothly said. "You weren't even looking in the same direction as the situation."

Elite Bellus looked past me and paled slightly. "Ah."

Curious, I twisted around.

Killian was on the other side of the room, but his eyes were almost pitch black as he stared at us. I don't know that he heard exactly what I had said—there were so many people crammed into the room that even though I had shocked the gossips around me into silence, the rest of the ballroom buzzed with conversation and laughter.

But he must have realized I was upset, because he narrowed his eyes and took a step in my direction.

*Shoot*! Our act was going to fall to pieces if politics became the main point, or people thought he was using me. I had to stop him.

I gave him my sappiest smile, touched my fingers to my lips, and threw him a kiss.

Killian stared at me—I think he thought I had reached a new level of stupidity.

I batted my eyelashes and emphasized my grin.

His expression finally broke, and he laughed. I couldn't hear it, but the way he tipped his head back was an undeniable tell.

Phew. Danger over. Relieved, I turned back to Elite Bellus, wondering how I was going to clean up this mess.

Adept Bellus elbowed her husband several times.

He bowed to me. "Adept Medeis, I apologize," he said. "It was my error. I hope you can find it in your heart to forgive this old man, and perhaps wipe this conversation from your memory."

I awkwardly cleared my throat. "I have to give my own apology—I perhaps was...overly blunt and curt with you."

The Elite shook his head. "You pointed out the fault in my thinking. Thank you."

"Excellent." Adept Bellus smiled, her charm almost dazzling. "With that ugly incident behind us, perhaps you could tell us a little more about the situation with House Medeis? I haven't heard all the details, but it has become clear to me that was a mistake."

I guardedly explained it to them—reciting how I had fled and gone to Killian. I touched briefly on the inaction of my allies, and on the subject of my sealed magic, before I presented the crux of the issue: my position as Adept.

"The Wizard Council refused to step in and officially recognize me as Adept," I said. "They require I re-register due to the new strength of my magic. With the signet ring gone, the application is my only hope—which has put me in a dire position given that Mason is doing his best to block me."

The Elite smoothed his goatee. "I had heard Mason was attempting to rally allies, but I think his progress has screeched to a halt. Everyone abruptly lost interest."

"Was there any word on why?" I asked.

The Elite gazed past me, again looking at Killian. "I'm sure I have no idea," he mildly said.

*That's a logical conclusion for him to jump to, but I know Killian isn't helping me. So what made the change?*

"I have the deed to House Medeis," I continued. "I was the Heir, and according to my parents' will and our traditions I am Adept of House Medeis." I paused, my voice hitching slightly. "A part of me understood when my magical abilities were so poor, but that's no longer the case."

The Elite sighed. "Mason's backers made their choice. If they tried to retreat now and let you reclaim what is rightfully yours, not only would they lose face, but their Houses would drop in esteem and trust."

Adept Bellus set her hand on her husband's shoulder. "Could you interfere? All of this is surely against committee rules and regulations."

"I can try," the Elite said. "I'll tug some strings, and I'm sure eventually I can knock something loose. The problem is that it seems time is of the essence, and as the Elite I am not a voting member of the Wizard Council, or even allowed to sit on it."

"Any help would make a difference to me," I said.

The Elite rubbed the back of his head. "I'll give orders for an investigation—that much I can do. And I'll make some calls. Unfortunately, it seems Mason planned his attack well. There aren't many regulations on House inheritance because it's so ingrained in our society. As a general rule, House inheritance is a House matter, and the law shouldn't interfere."

I tried to smile. "Even if it was believed I was too weak to make a good Adept?"

"It's a House matter," the Elite firmly repeated.

"It's likely an unfortunate reflection of our society's morale." Adept Bellus sighed. "We are too scared about losing magic. It makes us meddle where we shouldn't."

"Yes," I slowly agreed. "Thank you for the help. I appreciate it —as does my family."

The Elite nodded. "Of course. You were right—I should have sought you out at Drake Hall once I'd heard you'd been run out."

"I thought we agreed to forget that conversation."

"Forgetting doesn't remove the truth of your words. Which I ought to begin working on." He offered out his hand. "Good luck, Adept Medeis. You'll get your House back, and you'll make a fine leader."

I shook his hand. "I hope so."

"I'm sure your relationship with His Eminence won't hurt

your chances. I'd say at least half of everyone here tonight believes you must be his *one*. But it seems to me that even without Killian, you've got the necessary fire to take back what's yours," he wryly said. Adept Bellus scolded him, but he ignored it and gave me a wink, clicked his heels together, and was off.

I frowned a little as I mulled over his words. The other supernaturals would think I was Killian's *one*? I'd heard the phrase once or twice, but I didn't remember any exact specifics. (Before I ended up in a mansion full of vampire housemates, I can't say I had ever paid a lot of attention to vampire habits and politics.)

Adept Bellus shook her head as she watched her husband leave. "He is a dear man—opinionated, but still dear."

"Yes?" I said—I wasn't 100% sure I was supposed to even respond to that.

"Now that you're free, I have so many people I'd like to introduce you to—or rather they would like me to introduce you to them! Come along, Adept Medeis. This way!" Adept Bellus glided off without checking after me.

I glanced back at Celestina, who grinned at me, then followed the older woman, feeling hopeful for the first time in a long time.

————

HOURS PASSED. I talked to so many people I could no longer distinguish faces (I also ate so much I was pretty certain that if I had even one more piece of tiramisu I wasn't going to fit in my dress anymore). It was late—past 3 AM—and with all the people crammed inside the ballroom the place had become stifling hot.

Like, I was seriously baking, and was starting to wonder if I was overheating.

"Celestina, are they serving ice water anywhere?" I peered up and down the tables of food—which were still being replenished —and tried to spy out the servers wandering around with drinks, but it seemed there were only alcoholic beverages—no cool, sweet water.

"I don't believe so, no." Celestina pulled her phone out of her pocket. "Do you want me to text Gavino and ask him to get some?"

I grimaced—I hated the idea of asking my friend to fetch something I was perfectly capable of getting. But sweat was starting to drip down my spine, and it was getting hard to breathe in the heat. "Maybe—"

"No need." Killian appeared at my side, pressing a tall glass of ice water into my hands. He, of course, looked as cool and crisp as ever. No heat stroke for Mr. Breezy.

I took a big gulp of the water, then held the cold glass to my forehead. "You're magic," I mumbled, feeling a little better.

Killian took the glass from me, then captured my right wrist. "Come."

I staggered after him, hoping he would lead me to more water. "Where are we going?"

"To cool you off." Killian led me past the musicians and beyond a set of ridged columns, to the glass windows that lined one side of the room.

There were a few doors that opened out into a walled in garden area. The doors were already wide open—trying to get a breeze in, probably—and none of the staff protested when Killian tugged me outside.

It wasn't much cooler outside—apparently it was still in the heat of summer in the Committee's piece of the fae realm. But it wasn't as oppressively hot, and there was a slight breeze. Even better, it was *quiet*. So quiet my ears were ringing in the silence.

I slipped past Killian and crossed the patio, hopping onto one of the cobblestone paths that led into the gardens—which were full of fragrant fae flowers, some of which glowed in the dark blanket of the night. There was a thick stone wall that stretched between the gardens and the patio of the building. I dusted it off then boosted myself onto it. The instant relief to my aching feet made me groan.

Killian gave me my water, and I sipped at it, closing my eyes when I finally heard frogs croak and crickets chirp.

Killian and Celestina exchanged a murmured conversation, then Celestina slipped past me—patting me on the shoulder as she swept by—and her gun appeared in her hands as she headed into the gardens, probably checking for any potential attackers.

Josh and Gavino remained by the patio doors, their gazes watchful as they slowly inspected the area.

"Did you make any headway with your House?" Killian asked. Even though he wore his suitcoat still, not even a bead of sweat dared to dew on his forehead. Given his usual body temperature, he was probably the coolest thing around after my ice.

"I think so." I shook my glass, rattling the ice cubes. "I talked to the Elite about it. He said he'd start looking into it for me." I twitched the long skirts of my dress, trying to get a little more air.

Between my natural heat as a wizard and overheating from the oven-like room, I was finding it hard to cool off. I took my last gulp of water, finishing it. "Have you talked with everyone you wanted to? Has our...*relationship* played its part?"

"Yes," Killian said with great satisfaction. "Now it's just a waiting game, to make certain the warning was received."

"Warning?" I asked.

"It's nothing."

# CHAPTER SIXTEEN

*Hazel*

I set my glass down on the stone wall with me and shrugged. I stared at Killian for a moment or two, debating the genius of my plan, before I decided I was too hot to care. I held out my arms and made a grasping motion with my hands. "Gimme."

Killian raised an eyebrow. "You want my suitcoat?" He took a step closer, getting in my range, so I latched on to his coat and pulled him in.

"Nope. I want you." I plastered myself against his chest as if he were a wall of ice. Instantly the cooler temperature of his body permeated the cloth of his shirt and knifed through the heat of my face and arms. I heaved a deep sigh of contentment.

"Are you using me as your personal air conditioner?" Killian's voice sounded a little incredulous, but I couldn't be bothered to open my eyes and check his expression.

"Yes. Ahhh, this is heaven." I turned my head, pressing my other cheek to his chest. "It's not fair that you get to be so cool all the time," I grumbled into his shirt.

Killian didn't reply, but he stepped a little closer so I didn't have to lean precariously over and risk falling off my seat.

I don't know how much time passed—a few seconds or a few minutes—but when I no longer felt like an inferno, I yawned. "How much longer are we staying?"

"Getting tired?" I didn't know if it was because he was relaxing, or he'd had enough of people as well, but his ever-so-faint British accent was a little stronger than usual.

"Yeah, a little."

"I intend to stay until dawn—but that's expected given my position." Killian bumped me a little as he shifted, pulling his tuxedo jacket off.

I peeled my eyes open—because, yeah, I wanted to make sure he wasn't going to take his heavenly coolness away and leave me alone to bake. To my delight, once he was free of the jacket, he slid his arms down my back, the coolness of his skin seeping through his sleeves.

"You, however," he continued, "can return home. Unless you wished to speak to anyone else?"

"Not really," I said. "I think I'll need the Elite's help to change the Wizard Council's stance."

"Many of the wizards tend to retire from the ball around this time. You wouldn't have much longer to speak to them anyway," Killian noted.

"Yeah. I haven't seen Mason," I said.

Killian patted my back. "Did you *want* to see him?"

"Not really, but Felix is here, so I thought Mason would be, too. Though that would be pretty insane—how would he get an invite when he's not the Adept?"

"Don't doubt the pettiness of our society." I would have thought it was a joke, except Killian's voice was cold and grim.

I pulled back so I could crank my neck to peer up at him. "Thank you for introducing me to the Elite."

Killian shrugged. "It would have been expected, anyway, given how closely I work with him." He paused. "What did he say to upset you?"

"Hm?"

"Before his wife arrived, you were clearly aggravated and talking louder."

I pressed my head against his chest to hide my face again. How much should I tell him? Or how much did he need to know? The Elite said he regretted his words, and I was sure it wasn't anything that Killian hadn't heard before.

"I was surprised," Killian continued. "I knew you planned to ask him for help. For you to yell at him, I thought something must have gone wrong."

He wasn't going to drop it, was he? Well, I may as well summarize it—Celestina would spill everything when I left for home anyway. "He was warning me off you. His wizardly duty or something." I leaned back so I could watch his face—or specifically the slant of his eyebrows.

"Warned you off?" Killian asked.

"You know, gave me the fatherly talk—you're just using me, blah, blah, blah," I said. "Although at the end he changed his mind and said I might be your *one*. What did he mean by that?" I asked, hoping to distract him.

Killian's expression didn't shift as he stared out into the gardens. "It's what a vampire calls the person they choose forever. A particularly playful vampire might marry multiple times as they outlive their spouse, but *the one* comes only once in a vampire's very long lifetime, and they love *the one* forever."

"I see." I wanted to ask how on earth Elite Bellus could even imagine Killian would ever have a *one*, but that seemed kind of mean to say, so I kept my mouth shut.

"It's practically a myth," Killian continued. "Or a fairytale, really. Most vampires never experience it. A few Elders claim they have. However, given that they are the same Elders who are prone to skulking around their homes at night and reciting excessively long and melodramatic poetry, I can't say I'm inclined to believe them."

"You don't think it's real, then?"

Killian shrugged. "I think it is far rarer than most of my kind thinks. There is only one vampire I have met that I truly believe found his *one*."

"Really?"

"Yes, Rupert."

"*Rupert?*" My voice hitched up with disbelief. "Sour-puss Rupert the party-pooper?"

"Obviously, Elite Bellus was speaking foolish drabble." Killian ignored my less-than-stellar nickname for his underling and pushed on. "But I suppose his warning is the sign of a righteous soul."

I considered pressing the Rupert matter for a moment. But as nosy as I was, it wasn't really my business, so I let him change the discussion topic. "You know, considering how much you like to scheme, I find it interesting you like labeling people righteous or virtuous," I said.

"Why would that make you mad?"

"I'm not mad, I just think it says something about you."

"I was referring to your reaction to the Elite's warning."

"Ooooh. Yeah." I wondered if I could get out of answering again by mashing my face on his shirt. "Well...he was being kind of hypocritical."

"He most likely wasn't wrong."

"Most likely," I blithely agreed. "But it's still an unfair thing to say when you've done as much for me as you have."

Killian's expression was unreadable. "Perhaps I am merely swindling you into a place of complacence before I ask you to do something as shadowy as the Elite fears."

I snorted. "And you should know me well enough to know by now that if you *did* ask me to do something like that, I'd probably pull you in a pool again."

His lips twitched in a smirk. "It would be a waste of time to ask you," he admitted—which was about as close as he was ever going to come to outright saying he didn't plan on asking me to participate in the seedy side of politics.

"Yep!" I stared at his shirt and wondered if I was still hot enough that it was acceptable to lean into him again. (Forget his model face, his lower body temperature was soooo dreamy!)

A few moments passed. "You would believe me over the Elite?" he asked.

"Killian, I've lived off you like a tapeworm for weeks, and I hang out with the Drake Family every day." I finally lifted my gaze, meeting his red eyes. "I *know* you."

"And it doesn't scare you," Killian mused. I could tell he was more speaking an observation than asking me a question.

But there was something about the moment that made me squirm.

"Well." I paused for comedic effect. "It's pretty scary when Celestina has made me face off with Josh and he comes running at me with those giant swords."

Killian didn't acknowledge my attempt at humor. He drew closer still so my legs brushed his. He leaned over and planted his hands on the stone wall. We were practically nose to nose. The red flints in his eyes seemed to gleam in the moonlight.

"If I attempted to lock you up in Drake Hall like the treasure you are, you would probably kick me," he said.

"No." I tried to smile, but my voice cracked a little. "I'd try to fry you with a lightning bolt first."

Killian laughed—his whispery exhale one that wasn't a true chuckle, but one he used whenever something particularly struck him. And then, as naturally as he laughed, he leaned in and kissed me.

It was shocking—not that he did it, but I swear I could feel the same electric pulse I sometimes felt when magic swept through me. Something about that made it natural. By all rights, kissing a vampire was generally one of the last things a wizard should want to do, but I leaned into Killian, slowly raising my hands to link together behind the back of his neck.

When Killian moved his mouth in response, I was pretty sure I felt the faint prickle of his pronounced fang teeth on my bottom lip.

It could have been a few minutes or an hour before I pulled back for air, still feeling that electric tingle in my veins. "That was...wow." I let my arms stay ringed around his neck as I sucked in a breath.

Killian leaned in, his lips grazing my neck in a smirk I could feel. "Note how I am taking special care to keep my hands off your butt."

I couldn't help but laugh, and I rested my forehead on his shoulder.

We stayed like that for a few moments, until Killian pulled back and nudged my head up again. Our lips were a hair's width apart when I heard voices.

Killian sighed with enough force to move a tendril of my hair. He left his hands where they were, but twisted his neck to look back at the patio. I had to poke over his shoulder like a prairie dog, but was rewarded with the sight of two different vampires—likely Family Elders—standing in the patio doorways with dropped jaws.

Gavino was bodily shoving them back in the ballroom, but I don't know if they were resisting, or if they were so shocked over the unexpected show they weren't capable of movement.

Killian growled, then turned to face me. "Go back to Drake Hall. It's only going to get more boring from here on. Celestina will go with you—you won't have any training tomorrow." He grabbed his tuxedo coat from where he'd tossed it.

I kicked my feet and self-consciously cleared my throat. "Okay." I thought I sounded pretty normal—I mean, normal considering I'd just locked lips with Killian Drake.

Killian smirked. "Sleep. I'll see you tomorrow."

I held a finger up. "Technically, you'll see me today since it's already so early—"

Killian cut me off with another kiss—this one was barely more than a quick touching of the lips—but it was just as magnetic as the first.

I blinked, and he was gone—halfway across the patio.

I sucked in enough air to make my cheeks puff, and then let it go with one slow, long breath.

What just happened?

Wait, no, I knew what just happened…but…why? What did it mean?

"Hazel?"

I was in the process of trying to get off the wall without ripping my dress, but Celestina's sudden appearance caught me off-guard, so I almost fell on my face and barely managed to catch myself in time.

"Heeeeeey, Celestina," I said.

A slow smile spread across Celestina's lips—one that was a thousand times smugger than anything I'd ever seen Killian wear. "His Eminence said I should take you back to one of the cars and go home."

I coughed and grabbed my clutch. "Yeah, that'd be great. Thanks."

Her smirk grew. "Yes. You must be so *exhausted*."

I bumped my hip into her. "Shut up." I could feel my ears burning red as my friend laughed at me.

Celestina led me through the patio door Josh guarded, avoiding Killian and the other vampires entirely.

The ballroom had emptied some—it looked like some of the wizards had left as Killian predicted. It was still stiflingly hot, so I gratefully trooped behind Celestina and wheezed with relief when we stepped through a foggy wooden door and set foot back in the Curia Cloisters.

"I'm sorry you didn't get to talk to anyone. You still look gorgeous." I gave Celestina a side-eyed look of admiration.

Celestina laughed. "I didn't attend to chatter, but to protect. I am *greatly* satisfied with the night, and everything I witnessed." She wriggled her eyebrows at me.

I groaned. "Can we not? I don't even know—that was. Ugh."

Our heels clicked on the flooring as we made our way through the hallways, nodding to the few party attendees lingering to finish conversations.

"Do you regret it?" Celestina asked.

"No, but I have no idea what the takeaway is."

Celestina was so amused she actually snorted a laugh as we passed through the Curia Cloisters' entrance.

Once she had recovered, she snapped open her red clutch and pulled out her phone. "I'm texting one of the drivers. It will take them a minute to pull around."

I made a noise of understanding. "I need to get better about carrying my phone," I said.

Celestina's mirth left her, and she frowned at me. "You didn't bring it?"

"I didn't want it getting crushed by the rocks if I had to take a swing at someone."

Celestina's lips warred between a frown and a grin for a moment before she gave in and smiled. "I guess that's fine for tonight. You were always going to be guarded anyway. But in the future, you need to bring it."

"Okay, Mom."

I expected Celestina to laugh—or maybe poke me. At the very least I thought she'd grin.

Instead, her gun appeared in her hands, and she glared at something over my shoulder.

I turned around, and all the loose, happy feelings that had been bumping around inside of me froze. "Hello, Mason."

Mason looked handsome in his tuxedo, which had a House

Medeis coat of arms pin stuck into one lapel. His hair was slicked back, and he had that calm, tempered smile he wore as a mask. "Hazel, I didn't expect to see you here."

"I could say the same."

I passed my clutch to my throwing hand—preparation is key in launching surprise attacks. "What do you want?"

"Nothing," Mason said with too much innocence. "I just want to express my well wishes to you."

"Hah!" I laughed. "Why are you bothering to act when there's no one around?" I jerked my thumb to gesture over my shoulder. "Celestina already hates you because you threatened Killian. Or are you unaware she's part of the Drake Family?"

Mason nodded very politely to the gorgeous, gun-wielding vampire. "Good evening."

Celestina racked her gun, pulling back the slide to load a bullet in the chamber with a metallic click.

"That seems to be a pretty clear message." I idly swung my clutch by its strap. "Get lost."

Mason slightly bowed his head. "Very well, but since we *were* family—"

"HAH!"

"I'd like to share my news with you." Mason held out his wizard ID registration card.

I raised my eyebrow and was about to ask what the point was, when I glanced at the fine print—which was readable only because of the street light near us.

There, by the coat of arms for House Medeis engraved on the plastic ID card, was his title. Adept Mason of House Medeis.

The world slammed to a halt, and I couldn't believe what I was seeing. "...How?"

"It's all thanks to you, Hazel." Mason's eyes crinkled with his smile. "You helped me a great deal when you destroyed the House Medeis signet ring."

I frowned. "*You* destroyed it! It was your spell, and you broke at least a dozen laws threatening Killian Drake!"

"The Wizard Council didn't see it that way." Mason's smile had an edge now. "When I told them how you willfully destroyed it, they decided that until you show the maturity necessary to lead that *I* will be the Adept of House Medeis."

*How could they?*

I was so shocked, so appalled, I couldn't feel anything. It felt like a haze had settled over my mind.

"Though you may have successfully saved yourself by running to the Drake Family, it ultimately will be your undoing," Mason said. "Did you *really* think you'd be trusted when you're living with vampires and conveniently had your magic sealed?"

"I won't let this go," I snarled. "I'm not giving my family over!"

Mason slightly shook his head. "You've already lost, Hazel. House Medeis is mine."

"I have the deed!"

"You do. But you don't have the leadership. You don't have the signet ring, or even the support of other wizards." Mason's smile deepened. "And you don't have the resources to fight me."

"Killian does."

"But you won't let him go after me." He laughed, a sound I felt in my toes. "Not when some of your beloved family could get caught in the crossfire. Besides, didn't you see?" Mason brandished his ID card again. "Since I've taken leadership, House Medeis has moved up in ranking of respect. And as you know...the House comes before *everything*."

He reached out, extending his hand. I don't know if he was going to touch my cheek or hit me, but the quiet click of a gun's safety flicking off broke the silence.

# CHAPTER SEVENTEEN

*Hazel*

M ason froze, and gave a sheepish smile as he raised his hands. "Come now, First Knight. You can hardly kill me on Curia Cloisters lands."

For the first time since knowing Celestina, I felt the predator hiding under her skin.

She'd never trotted it out before—even in training, she was so much stronger than everyone else she didn't have to bother. But now, facing Mason, her eyes were flinty and glowed red, and she peeled her lips back in a snarl that displayed her white fangs.

There was a pressure to the air that hadn't been there before, and her usual elegance was razor sharp.

"I think you'd be surprised just how easy it would be for me to kill you, wizard." Celestina's usually beautiful voice was so cold it made my heart twist. "Unless you'd like to discover just how fragile the human throat is, *leave*." She licked her lips as she stepped in front of me, almost blocking my view so I had to peer around her.

Mason's smile dropped. His eyes flickered in my direction, but he must have realized Celestina wasn't playing around because he slowly backed up and didn't say anything else.

Celestina stood there—her teeth bared and gun out—until Mason disappeared inside. Then she sighed, flipped the safety back on her gun, and all the deadliness seemed to drain from her, leaving her as beautiful and warm as she had been before.

She scowled, and thankfully one of the Drake SUVs pulled up.

"Come on, let's go home." I tugged on her elbow. "He's not worth it."

That got Celestina loose. She twirled around to complain to me —while herding me to the car. "He's not, but the act of *killing him* would be worth it! *So* worth it! And so incredibly satisfying. I wouldn't even have to use my gun—no, I wouldn't want to." Her voice was dreamy as she pictured the many ways she could maim Mason.

"Thanks," I said to the driver when he opened the door. I scrambled inside, Celestina right behind me.

I stared at my hands as the car rolled forward. Darkness threatened to press in on the corners of my mind.

They'd made Mason Adept.

*How could they?*

My hands shook, and I recognized if I didn't do something I was going to dissolve in a puddle of goo. And I couldn't, because this wasn't over. It felt like it, but I couldn't give up. Even if the Wizard Council improved House Medeis's rank—even if the House had turned apathetic like Momoko had told me and didn't hate Mason as I thought it would.

None of that mattered.

Mason thought the House came before everything, but I was more concerned about my family and how they'd survive under him. For them, I'd fight until the end.

So I couldn't break down. I had to keep going. I squeezed my eyes shut, then forced myself to look at Celestina. "I'm surprised you seem to hate him so much. I didn't think anyone from the

Drake Family had much of an opinion about Mason and House Medeis."

"We have opinions," Celestina said. "*Very strong* and *very violent* opinions. But that is a discussion for a different day. Tonight you should dwell on what fun you had at the party—you know, chatting with everyone, greeting leaders, kissing His Eminence."

"Celestina!" I groaned as I buckled myself in.

Celestina's laugh was so gleeful I couldn't resist joining her, and we spent the rest of the ride in barely contained laughter.

———

KILLIAN HAD SAID there would be no training the following day. I kind of assumed that meant I'd get to bum around the house, sleep in, maybe raid the kitchen or something.

Instead Celestina roused me in the early afternoon and dragged Josh and me out to the mall for some shopping.

This mostly involved clothes shopping for Celestina, but she bought me some really nice steel toed boots that I was pretty sure I could do some serious damage with—hopefully to Mason, one day—so I wasn't inclined to complain.

It wasn't until I was sitting in a booth at the food court with Josh and Celestina, sipping the iced coffee Celestina had bought for me, that I realized this wasn't about Celestina wanting the chance to be out and about, but probably for me.

They were trying to distract me from the bomb that Mason was officially considered Adept of House Medeis.

"So, Celestina." I set my coffee on the table and folded my hands together. "Do you want to tell me what the Drake Family's strong and violent opinions about Mason are?"

Celestina sighed and slumped a little in her spot next to me. "I was hoping you would forget that."

"Your mistake." Josh took a sip of his chai latte—he sat across from me—as he carefully scanned the food court.

Celestina drummed her fingers on the table. "We Drake vampires would like nothing more than to end Mason's miserable existence."

"Violently," Josh piped in. "Preferably death will not warmly embrace him, but instead eviscerate him."

"However, His Eminence has warned us off killing Mason, specifically," Celestina continued.

"Why?" I asked. "I got the feeling he didn't care a ton about him, and I would have thought that Mason threatening him would be an instant death warrant."

"It would," Josh agreed.

"Except if Mason were to perish at the hands of the Drake Family, it would make your position as Adept of House Medeis even more unstable," Celestina said.

I cupped my hands around my iced drink and took another sip as I thought.

I would have scoffed at her excuse last night, but after seeing the way Elite Bellus *leaped* into assumptions, perhaps she was right.

Killian Drake was famous for his manipulations, under-handed maneuverings, and pushing to get what he wanted—politically speaking. Before I'd come to stay at Drake Hall, I probably also would have made the assumption that he would kill Mason and use me as a plant among the Adepts to give him information and spy.

I was certain Killian would eventually call in some favors when I finally did get my position back. But given his tendency to call me a virtuous idiot, I knew he'd never be asking me for anything...seedy. (He'd probably tell me to join fights or something given my magic powers, and leave my House out of it entirely. He'd made it clear that he considered me a decent fighter, but he still considered traditionally trained wizards useless anyway.)

"He's not moving because he thinks I'll eventually be able to take House Medeis back, and I'll take care of Mason myself, which will re-establish me as the legitimate Adept."

Celestina made a noise of disgust. "I still fail to understand how Mason could have been made Adept."

I pressed my lips together. "He said the Wizard Council decided to do it once they found out the signet ring was destroyed. I guess I can kind of understand—I don't think a signet ring has ever been destroyed. Not in the past century for certain."

"It's still doltish of them," Josh said. "They believe they can justify a dramatic switch in leadership—for a *House*, which bonds with its family line—over a mere ring?"

"It's a bigger deal than that," I said. "The signet ring helps establish an Adept's initial connection to the House. You need it for the ceremony that officially ties you to the House, and it's necessary to wear for at least the first five to ten years, until you have a good enough connection with the House that it's no longer needed."

My iced coffee was sweating all over the table, so I absently wiped it up with a napkin. "They're made with really old magic, too. I don't actually know if there's anyone around who can make them. Mom used to say they were forged by the elves...and they're all gone now."

Josh set his latte down. "It's been hypothesized that their death is what kicked off the steady downward spiral of magic and it's slow—but inevitable—death. Perhaps this is another example of why the loss of the elves hit our world so badly."

Celestina tapped the lid of her coffee drink with a manicured nail. "Perhaps, but this is the reality we live in. We will have to learn to cope with our situation."

"Perhaps this *is* the wizards' attempt at coping," I said. "House inheritance should *never* be taken public, unless the Adept and Heir die and a new family line has to be declared, but they went ahead and did it anyway. Killian said they can't back down since no one tried to help me when Mason first came after me, and given that we wizards usually are a little more passive, I can see that. And I think they chose to back Mason because they didn't want an Adept with so little power in place."

"Why do you believe that?" Josh asked.

"The ranking of House Medeis jumped up." I pursed my lips as I tried to remember exactly what Mason's ID card had shown. "I think the wizards are seeing what has happened and realizing we will become irrelevant in a few generations. In day to day life, a local House with a weak Adept isn't a big deal. If we look at the long-lasting effects, however, there could be repercussions in my family line, it would maybe permanently weaken House Medeis unless I married someone with enough magic power to counteract what we thought was my lack of magical ability."

"Naturally, the best way to face this fear is to throw a coup and deal in underhanded politics," Celestina grumbled.

I nodded. "No matter their motivation, they were wrong. Most obvious is the fact that Mason is Adept."

Josh glanced curiously at me. "Are you talking about the blatant stupidity in ignoring that you are still alive, or...?"

"Nah—though that is a big deal too. No, I mean that Mason was made Adept when the Wizard Council hasn't met since the last monthly meeting when they told me to get re-registered. That means they approved Mason *out of session*."

Celestina snapped. "I wonder if all the wizards sitting on the council are even aware. It's possible Mason could have privately approached some of them, and skipped over the Adepts who supported your case."

"Probably. That's totally illegal, but given that the council didn't care I was being hunted like an animal and my allies couldn't be bothered to keep their word, it's not out of character."

I narrowed my eyes. "So much bloodshed and manipulation...all because my parents chose to block me from my *real* abilities."

A sour taste flooded my mouth—one that even the bitterness of my iced coffee couldn't wash away.

One day I could hopefully think of my parents and feel peace. But now, while I was still trying to deal with the aftermath of what *their* manipulations had done, it wasn't coming.

Celestina gave me a side hug, then stood up and took my trash. "We should probably head out soon."

Josh checked his cellphone. "Yes. I assume His Eminence will rise, soon. I imagine he will want us back by the time he finishes his morning reports."

Celestina walked the trash to the trash can, and I took the last few noisy sips of my coffee as Josh slid out of the booth.

"Sorry, finished." I slid along the bench seat, but there was a soft pop, and something spattered by my head.

In an instant Celestina was by my side, gun out, and Josh had pulled out a handful of throwing knives that he layered between his fingers.

People screamed, and Celestina shoved me under the table. "Josh."

"I smell it." I saw Josh's dress shoes disappear as he ran off.

"Celestina?" I asked, huddled under the table. "What happened?"

"Someone shot at you."

I froze under the table, my throat squeezing painfully. "*What?*"

"It appears to be a paint ball. Do you detect any magic?"

"No, none." Just in case, I opened myself up to magic, letting it swim through my blood. "I can't sense anyone using any kind of spell or enchantment."

Celestina paced back and forth in front of me. Even from my low vantage point, I could see her pull her cellphone out of her pocket. "Bring the car around, there's been an incident—come to the food court," she barked.

I shifted under the table, breathing a little easier with magic surrounding me.

A paint ball? Why would someone shoot at me with a paint ball? Was Mason trying to make a point? If so he was a total idiot to attack me with Killian's First and Second Knights sitting with me.

"Hazel?" Celestina slowly turned in a circle. "We're going to move. I want your shield up at all times. Do you understand?"

"Yes."

"Good, then let's go."

I scrambled out from under the table, my blue shield flickering to life at my back.

It was much steadier and more stable—I'd been practicing with it and area attacks since fighting Rupert—so I moved confidently with it at my back, and I stretched it a bit to cover Celestina as well.

Celestina led the way outside. The set of her mouth was a grim slant, and she almost wrenched one of the exit doors off its hinges with her excessive vampire strength.

A Drake car was idling just outside.

I reached it first as Celestina swung around to watch our backs. I climbed in, my heart racing as Celestina jumped in after me and slammed the door shut.

"Go!" she barked.

The car tires squealed, and I was thrown back against my seat when it shot forward.

I opened my mouth, intending to start a rant, but I noticed Celestina's pinched expression.

She didn't know what was going on either. That meant she probably didn't know if it was Mason, or the Night Court, and she obviously hadn't sensed them or she would have blocked the paint ball.

And that, more than the actual experience, terrified me.

———

WHEN WE ARRIVED BACK at Drake Hall, things were in an uproar. Like, Killian must have called in the rest of the Drake Family because vampires I had never seen before walked the hallways with flinty expressions.

Training was still canceled—we didn't even have the regular dinner that night—so I spent most of my time hanging around the kitchen talking to the staff I knew and attempting to pry news from any familiar vampires who passed through.

Apparently—from the little pieces of news I managed to get —the shooter was a Night Court fae who *had* been caught, but then killed himself with a magic ring before he could be questioned.

The identity of the paint ball shooter didn't shock anyone, but the entire situation made all the vampires jumpy, and I can't say I liked it much more. I mean...why would you try to shoot me with a paint ball?

The vampires ran a sample of the paint ball through a lab, and it was exactly that—*paint*. Queen Nyte sent one of her fae in— and he *died*—just to shoot me with a paint ball?

Killian summoned me to his office with a text around noon the following day. For a vampire that was an almost ungodly hour to rise, but I didn't think anything about it as I impatiently yanked the door open, until I saw him.

Between the crumpled blood pouches on his desk, his lack of his black suitcoat and perfect tie, and the way his skin seemed extra pale, I was almost positive Killian hadn't slept since the paint ball incident—maybe not even since before the Summer's End Ball.

I hesitated in the doorway. "Killian, are you okay?"

Killian glanced at me, and the blackness of his eyes felt sharp like a sword. "Come in."

I slipped inside and noticed Josh standing just inside the door.

The weapon-loving vampire's eyes were fixated on some point across the room, and he didn't blink when I passed in front of him.

Was he sleeping while standing upright or something?

I approached Killian's desk, my eyebrows furrowed in concern. "I heard about the confirmed attacker—and his... demise," I said.

Killian shrugged and stared at what looked like a fancy, hand-written letter based on the creamy color and thickness of the paper.

"Did Queen Nyte send you a nastygram about that?" I asked.

Killian stood so fast he knocked his chair back. "*What*?"

"I asked if Queen Nyte sent you a nastygram—a letter of complaint," I carefully said.

It was unlike Killian to not know modern slang—even if he didn't use it. But it was probably just another sign of how tired he was.

The door clicked, and I twisted around just long enough to see that it was Celestina before Killian walked around his desk, redrawing my attention.

He stopped just short of invading my space. When he raised his hands and reached in my direction I thought he meant to drape them over my shoulders or something, but instead he folded his arms across his chest and narrowed his eyes.

I kind of wanted to smack him. The last time I saw him we'd kissed, and now he was acting like a caged animal. "Killian, what is it?"

Killian glanced at the letter he'd left facedown on his desk, then he returned his eyes to mine. "Leave."

I let out a nasally sigh. "Did you seriously call me all the way to your office just to send me right back out?"

"No." Killian smirked—the one he used when closing a trap on someone. "I called you here to banish you from Drake Hall."

# CHAPTER EIGHTEEN

*Hazel*

I blinked as I tried to process what he had said. "Did you fall on your head after I left the ball yesterday?"

"We're finished." Killian's smirk had an edge of smugness to it. "You are no longer allowed in Drake Hall, nor are you to be treated like a member of the Drake Family. You will leave the premise immediately." His voice was the dangerously-charming voice I'd heard him use when meeting politicians and people he didn't like—it held more raw vampire power than usual.

*What is he trying to do?*

I pressed my lips together. "Killian, knock it off, and tell me what's going on. After everything I've gone through, your big-bad-vampire routine isn't frightening." *Much.*

Killian made an amused noise at the back of his throat. "Fine, then maybe you'll understand this: you are no longer worth the investment."

*That* caught my attention.

Killian, with his manipulations and conniving plots, was a lot more likely to pull back if he judged that the bottom line wasn't worth it. "What do you mean?" I cautiously asked. "I've fought my way to your top five vampires."

Killian leaned against his desk, his dark eyes glittering. "You have plenty of fighting power, but I don't need more of that. What I wanted was a way in with the wizards. Celestina told me of your conversation with Mason, which means I know you are no longer Adept of House Medeis."

I curled my hands into fists as I tried to sort through his words. Was this some kind of joke? Or was he serious?

"I considered keeping you on regardless," he continued. "But the Elite's reaction made me realize just how useless an endeavor that would be. No one would trust you because of your association with the Drake Family."

A bitter taste filled my mouth. "I don't believe you—or any of this. I don't get what you're trying to accomplish right now, Killian, so just tell me what's *really* going on."

I thought a muscle jumped around Killian's left eye, but it was so fast I couldn't be certain. He stared at me for several long moments, his expression unreadable, then turned his back to me. He sauntered back to his desk chair and plopped down, arranging himself in a lounging position that showed off his vampire grace, then stared at me with cold, hard eyes.

"You certainly show off the wizard trait of stupidity to its fullest potential. Dissatisfied with the explanation? Fine. Not only are you no good to me since your chances of regaining your House have fallen, you are no longer trusted among your own. Therefore, you are useless to me. Admittedly, it was my mistake in backing you so strongly, but what's done is done. I have no mercy for those I can't use, so I am removing my offer of protection and ending our contract."

That felt too possible to write off. I bit my tongue as I tried to hold in the hot burst of emotion that threatened to tear me in half. Rage and hurt seesawed back and forth, each stabbing Killian's words a little deeper into my heart.

"If this was your big plan, why are you telling me?" I fought to keep my voice strong and calm rather than let my anger or the throb of pain give me away.

Killian stared at me, his face expressionless. "Because I know there's no possible way you can take back House Medeis by yourself. And once it's known I no longer back you, your fellow wizards will lose all interest in you. You are without friends and family, now. There is no place for you to go, so it doesn't matter *what* I tell you."

Oh, now *that* was a lie. I swung around, opening my mouth to tell Celestina to back me up.

That was when I realized a backpack hung from her grip. The red of her eyes was the same cold red of glittering rubies—beautiful, but distant. She wasn't smiling, wasn't frowning, instead she stared at me as if I were a task she had to complete.

I turned to Josh, but he was just as expressionless and just as cold.

The silence of the office was so suffocating I could hear myself breathe as I slowly turned back to face Killian.

"Celestina has gathered your belongings. Take them and leave, now," he said.

I stared at him, studying the set of his eyebrows, trying to gauge the blackness of his eyes.

I still didn't believe it.

Not because I was stupidly optimistic, but because I was a trained *wizard*. No matter what original purpose Killian had for me, at worst I could still work for him sensing fae magic—something no one except a wizard could do, and something that would be extremely helpful given his ongoing feud with Queen Nyte.

But something had happened. Killian was turning on me out of a lack of trust. He obviously wasn't willing to tell me everything or ask for help. I didn't know *why* he wanted to run me out of Drake Hall, but what hurt me most—what caused the bitter taste in my mouth and the squeezing of my chest—was that after everything I'd done with him, and with the Drake Family, he still didn't trust me. *They* didn't trust me.

It felt stupid that their trust was so important, but it was.

I glanced at Celestina and Josh again—who were still expressionless.

Obviously, I had overestimated our closeness. I'd forgotten that as Killian's underlings, we couldn't ever *really* be friends. Not the way it was with Momoko and Felix. They would serve Killian until every bit of blood ran from their body, and they didn't care if they had to sacrifice me to do what he wanted.

*I'm such an idiot.*

"Fine," I said. I took the backpack from Celestina and started to turn to the door.

Killian scoffed. "Congratulations on finally accepting the obvious."

"No." I swung back around and pointed a finger at him. "It's too late. You can't hide it from me when you are masking yourself and your actions. I *know* you. You're up to something, and you don't want me around anymore, fine. Whatever. This is a clear wakeup call of exactly how much you trust and value me, and I'm not going to beg to stay where I'm not wanted."

Killian blinked. It wasn't a crack in his mask, but I was pretty sure it meant I'd caught him off-guard.

I waved my hand. "Good luck with whatever this *thing* is. I'm sure you'll be very happy with the result." I made for the door—intending to get out of the room before Killian could see me crack.

"I hope I never see you again," he said.

I paused in the doorway, and turned just enough so Killian could see my smile. "Then I'm afraid you're going to be disappointed. Well wishes with your ruling the Midwest vampires. It's obviously what you care about most."

I wanted to slam the door, but Celestina was right behind me, so that was a big nope.

I clutched my backpack. I didn't know what it was filled with —I didn't even have *shoes* when I arrived at Drake Hall—but it very obviously didn't have the one thing I wanted most: my katana. The fact they hadn't given it to me just showed how shallow our supposed friendship really was.

I couldn't believe I'd been so *stupid* to think *I* mattered to them the way a close friend would.

I was so angry, so *hurt* I could barely see straight as I stormed through Drake Hall. I only vaguely noticed that the few vampires I saw were jogging up and down the hallway.

When I shoved open the front doors, there was a huge motorcade outside—bigger than any of the processions I'd seen accompany Killian even when going to Regional Committee of Magic meetings.

Oh yeah, Killian was up to something all right.

"So where are you taking me?" I asked Celestina with clinical interest.

"Off Drake property." Celestina gestured for me to walk past all the cars.

I stepped off the sidewalk and onto the driveway, but paused. "Wait, are you literally just dumping me outside the gate?"

That awful, expressionless mask Celestina wore didn't even crack. "His Eminence is done with you," she said. "He has no responsibility to find you the means to reach wherever it is you wish to go."

I followed Celestina, but more out of shock than compliance. They weren't even going to give me a ride back into town? They lived in the country! Magiford was miles away! I studied Celestina's back, bitterness seeping into the raw mix of emotions that churned in my chest.

Not only was I not as close to her—or any of the others—as I thought. I was so very unimportant they wouldn't even bend Killian's orders to help me survive.

I followed Celestina down the snaking driveway, my emotions

building to the point where I was shivering by the time she opened the great dragon gate of Drake Hall.

I hitched my backpack farther up my shoulder and glanced at my guide. "Take care, Celestina. Thanks for the fun."

Her mask wasn't quite as perfect as Killian's, so I saw it drop for a second when her eyes widened before she slapped it back in place and was once again a perfect vampire with an expression that could have been chiseled out of marble.

I think she expected me to yell at her, and I wanted to.

But her rejection of me now wouldn't take back the laughter we shared, the times she had protected me, or—more importantly —the hours of training she had invested in me.

When I stepped onto the road, she shut the gate behind me with a rattle. No goodbye, nothing.

That hurt.

I took in a shaky breath, and was surprised when I heard a cheerful voice.

"Yoo-hoo! First Knight! Here you are!" Julianne trotted down the driveway, a bright smile on her face as she gazed adoringly at Celestina. "We're almost ready to leave! There's just one more inspection—would you come look at the back few cars?"

Celestina listened intently to Julianne and nodded as she let the cheerful vampire lead her away.

Julianne didn't even glance at me—she was wholly absorbed in Celestina...which was what made me realize Manjeet stood on the other side of the fence, a finger pressed to his lips in the universal sign of silence.

He glanced back at Julianne, then threw something over the wrought-iron fence at me.

I caught it just in time, the lacquered scabbard slapping my hands. I stared down at my chisa katana, then looked at Manjeet, surprised.

He winked, then slunk into the shadows of the trees, popping out by Celestina and Julianne and joining their conversation.

Through the spokes of the fence, I saw Julianne turn around to face the road.

I shuffled so I could cradle my sword in one arm and wave with the other.

She smiled at me—not her usual bright grin but something that was tinged with sadness—and then hurried after Celestina.

I was touched.

Julianne idolized Celestina. For her and Manjeet to team up and get my sword—which Celestina very obviously hadn't deemed one of my "belongings"...

I was still in my workout clothes and wearing my sword belt, so I secured my katana to my hip, then crossed the street.

What was I going to do? Did I really have no choice but to walk back to Magiford? But where would I even go once I got there?

"Did Celestina pack my cellphone? Probably not if she didn't include my katana..." I slipped my backpack off my shoulder and unzipped the pocket. It had the fancy clothes Killian had ordered for me—the ones that were stretchy yet padded so I wasn't forever getting bruises and scrapes in practice. And that was about it. No phone—so I guess calling an Uber was out—not that I had any money to *pay* for the ride.

Unfortunately it also meant I had no way to contact Momoko or Felix.

Cars revved behind me.

I jumped as the huge motorcade that had been lined up outside Drake Hall rumbled down the driveway.

The dragon gates swung open, letting the cars through. They turned onto the road—the majority of them being SUVs, Killian's favorite—and turned left, starting the route to the city. I stopped counting at the twelfth car, but I watched them disappear down the road.

Once the last car passed, the dragon gates swung shut, and—to really underline how much Killian wanted me gone—two vampires I didn't recognize took up guard posts just inside the gate.

"What a jerk," I muttered, clenching my teeth. My eyes stung as I stared into the backpack. A few tears escaped, leaving scalding trails down my cheeks before dripping into my backpack.

One of the vampire guards turned to stare at me, his eyes narrowed in suspicion.

I shouldered my backpack again and started the long walk to the city, walking on the shoulder of the paved road. I'd only been walking for a few minutes when I heard the distant purr of an engine: it was another car.

This one wasn't from the Drake estate, but farther down the road—a bright blue pickup truck.

I stepped farther into the ditch and wiped my eyes off on my sleeve, but kept walking.

The truck passed me, then slowed to a stop. The front door opened, and a pretty human hopped out. She was about my age with raven black hair and eyes so blue they almost bordered on violet. Her skin was a warm golden color—I couldn't tell if she was just tan from the summer or if it was her usual skin tone.

She had to have some fae blood in her—that eye color wasn't natural, and she had the willowy build and beautiful face structure for it, too. But she seemed overwhelmingly human when she squinted at me, scrunching her nose a little. "Are you okay?"

I couldn't feel any kind of magic coming from her, and her wardrobe—jeans and a plain t-shirt—was something a fae wouldn't be caught dead in. She probably was mostly human with a faint trace of fae in her family.

My suspicion faded, and I forced a smile. "I'm fine, thanks."

Doubt clouded her face as she looked from me to the fence surrounding the Drake estate—which was still visible. "You need a ride?"

I started to reject the offer, but almost crumpled.

I had no one. And if I wasn't careful I'd still be walking to the city after dark. Besides, the kindness of her soul practically radiated off her.

"A ride would be really great," I admitted in a small voice.

She flashed me a mischievous grin and slapped her hand against her truck door. "Then hop in!"

She climbed in easily, but I was quite a bit shorter than her and hindered by my sword and backpack, so I had to do more of an ungainly scramble. "Thank you." I tucked my backpack and sword into the area for my feet and wiggled to adjust in the huge seat. The truck had the faintest whiff of hay and dust.

"Of course! Are you headed for Magiford?" she asked.

"Yeah. You can drop me off once we hit city limits."

"I can take you farther in than that." She waited until I was buckled in before she started driving down the road. "I have to get to a farm supply store on the other side of the city, so I'll cut right through it."

Where could I have her drop me off? The Curia Cloisters, maybe? Despite what Killian had said, the Elite might be willing to help me. Or should I go to the library and hope the Paragon was holed up there again and hiding from the local courts?

"You own a farm?" I politely asked.

"Sort of," she said. "My parents have a hobby farm—my mom has chickens for the fun of it and has a garden so massive I swear one day it's going to be ground zero for a plant apocalypse, and my step-dad has a few horses." She glanced at me and grinned again. "I'm Leila, by the way."

"Hazel."

She gave me the side eye. "And you're a...wizard?"

Legitimately surprised, I gaped at her. "How did you know?"

She shrugged. "Us humans don't usually walk this close to the Drake estate, and you didn't seem like a fae or werewolf, and you're far too alive to pass for a vampire."

I had been wondering what kind of a person would offer a ride to a strange wizard with a sword. This explained a bit of it. "You live around here, then?"

"Yep—I'm neighbors with the Drakes," she said. "I'd never suggest trying to slip through their fence, but we don't have any problems with foxes, coyotes, or uncultured werewolves going after my mom's chickens. Predators don't like getting too close. And the Drakes keep some really nice dogs."

Dimly, I remembered Josh mentioning a neighbor, and a loud piercing bray that had scared the tar out of me months ago. "Wait —are you the neighbor who owns the donkey?"

Leila laughed. "Yep! He lives with the horses. He was supposed to be a guard donkey, but it's not really needed, so instead he lives a life of luxury and is doted on by my mom. He thinks he's the best even though he's about half the size of the horses and sounds like a drunk goat."

I laughed, but when the moment of humor passed I let my head sag back on my neck, pushing into the headrest as the truck bounced along.

"Are you sure you're okay?" Leila asked. "You look...lost."

It was hard to swallow, but I forced myself to, and then pushed a smile into my cheeks. "Yep!" My voice cracked, so I hastily cleared my throat.

Leila glanced at me, then turned on the truck's flashers and pulled over on the side of the road.

I wondered why, until she leaned across the bench seat and put her hand on mine. "It's going to be okay."

"What?" I blinked, and it was then that I noticed a few more scalding tears had escaped my eyes and dripped down my cheeks. I scrubbed at my face with my free hand, totally embarrassed.

Leila squeezed my hand. "Whatever it is that you're facing, you will get through it."

There was something uncanny about her—I couldn't quite put my finger on why or how, but I could have sworn there was magic in her words.

That was why I asked, "How do you know?"

Leila tilted her head. "Because you're strong—here." She tapped the spot over her heart and smiled. "You can see it in animals when they have the will to live—they fight for it. And you, Hazel the Wizard, have a lot of fight."

She fished a napkin from a fast food restaurant out of the truck's glove compartment and started driving again while I blew my nose.

We spent the rest of the drive in relative silence. Leila turned on the radio and hummed a few songs—her voice was weirdly soothing to listen to.

I spent the ride staring at my sword, trying to sort through my very limited possibilities.

The safest and best idea was to seek out the Elite and hope he pitied me, even though Killian had proved him right (or somewhat right).

However, based on my past decisions, I didn't always do the safest/smartest things. Which left a few interesting options.

Something Killian said had crawled into my brain and was echoing around in there.

"*...There's no possible way you can take back House Medeis by yourself.*"

Was. That. So?

I wasn't stupid. I knew someone as powerful as Killian—or even Celestina—could swat at me and kill me like a fly. But here's the thing.

Mason was an ant of a threat compared to the violent grace of Killian Drake. And I'd been studying an ancient book —*another* item Celestina hadn't packed up for me, thanks for that —and using magic techniques my parents hadn't even used.

I could take Mason. The bigger problem was all of his allies. House Tellier, House Rothchild—they could overwhelm me by numbers. And, of course, it was pretty likely Mason would try and use family members against me.

The memory of Felix's tired gaze the night of the Summer's End Ball, and Momoko's fragile smile the day I saw her outside of Tutu's, swirled through my mind.

It was unlikely I'd win.

But I could no longer hide. And my family—my friends I had grown up with—were obviously in a world of pain.

I had to try. And if I got to bash some heads and deal out a bit of retribution, that would be all the better with the kind of foul mood I was in.

"Do you mind dropping me off in a residential area?" I asked.

"Not at all!" Leila clicked the radio off. "Did you have a place in mind?"

I smiled. "Oh yeah."

# CHAPTER NINETEEN

*Hazel*

Later that afternoon, bordering on the early evening hours, I walked down the street carrying my chisa katana.

Leila had done even better than she had first offered, and took me to a cafe so I could get changed into my tougher, more durable fighting clothes while she got herself a latte that was the size of a wine bottle. She'd then dropped me off two blocks up from House Medeis.

I spent about ten minutes casing the area—something that wouldn't have occurred to me before living in Drake Hall.

Based on the cars in the driveway and those parked out on the street, it seemed there was at least one car of House Rothchild wizards and three carloads of House Tellier wizards hanging around House Medeis. The Telliers were easy to pick out—they had *bumper stickers*. Rothchild was a little more difficult to pinpoint, but the driver had left his wizard suitcoat on his seat. It was possible there was another car of Rothchilds, but I didn't think it was too likely. The Rothchilds were usually more productive members of society than the Telliers, and they usually worked in the agriculture industry, so it was a little early for them to be getting home.

I ran up and down the list of cars owned by House Medeis members, but given that they were all parked on the driveway, it seemed like everyone was probably home. (Usually everyone got off work and was home before 5:00, so I was probably right.)

Despite receiving the title, Mason hadn't had his Ascension yet—the House hadn't changed at all since the day my parents died. (I hadn't thought he'd have had the ceremony yet—you need the signet ring to bind you to the House, and *that* obviously wasn't possible.) Still, it was a little encouraging to see nothing had changed.

If I was doing this with the vampires, they'd insist we slip over the short fence—preferably waiting until night—and then probably kill Mason in his sleep.

But they'd kicked me out. And while I had gotten over my 'no killing' thing, taking Mason out when he didn't have a chance to defend himself didn't sit right with me, even if it was another example of being a 'virtuous idiot'. But I didn't have anything else besides my honor at this point, and I *wasn't* going to lose that.

I was going to do things my way.

I still hopped the fence—there was no way I was going to ring the doorbell like an outsider at what was rightfully *my* House.

I felt House Medeis stir as I crossed the lawn. It didn't do anything to help me, but when I climbed the porch steps it didn't make a hole and swallow me alive either.

I tried the doorknob and almost laughed when it swung open.

A Rothchild wizard came trotting down the hallway, eating a sandwich. When she saw me her eyes widened, and she tried to shout, but she choked on bread crumbs.

I raised an eyebrow as I lazily observed her, and leaned against the doorframe. "Adept Mason," I shouted. "You traitorous, spineless, sea slug of a wizard. I'm back, and I'm here to challenge you for your falsely claimed position!"

The House exploded with activity.

I heard the muffled thumps of running upstairs, shouts of anger, and the buzzy feeling of wizard magic permeate the air.

I trotted back down the stairs and backed up until I stood in the middle of the front lawn. The afternoon sun heated my back through my clothes, and I adjusted my hold on the hilt of my chisa katana as I waited.

Wizards poured out of the front door.

A quick count, and it added up to nine House Tellier wizards and two House Rothchild wizards. They were the first out, standing between me and my family who strained and pushed their way through.

"Hazel!" Ivy—Felix's toddler niece—made a run for me, her macaroni necklace bouncing. Her father scooped her up, ignoring her cries as she reached for me with her chubby little hands.

"Hazel, what are you doing here?" Felix shouted. "Run!"

I locked my knees and watched Mason casually stroll onto the front porch, an arm settled on Great Aunt Marraine's shoulders. It might have looked caring to an outsider—handsome Mason caring for an elderly member of the House.

But I saw the way his hand dug into her shoulder and magic spiked around his fingers as his wizard's mark surfaced. Great Aunt Marraine's face was pinched with pain, and her gray hair had turned more of a snowy white in the few short months I'd been gone.

"Hazel? Welcome home." He smiled charmingly. "It's so good you've finally returned to the fold." He nudged Great Aunt Marraine. "Isn't it, Marraine?"

Great Aunt Marraine snorted. "I hope you bite your own tongue and choke on it, you—"

"Enough!" Fire engulfed Mason's hand, and he held it so close to Great Aunt Marraine's face I worried her hair might catch on fire. "I am your Adept—you will *not* disrespect me."

Great Aunt Marraine fell silent, and Mason's smile returned to his charming variety as he shifted his gaze to me.

This is what I was afraid of—Mason could still hold my family against me.

But maybe I could use a shield? If I pushed it between them, he wouldn't be able to reach her...

"I don't see any of your *vampire* friends." Mason's tone was pleasant, but rotted through—like cake left out in the summer sun. "Unless you come bearing a message from your new *master*."

I unsheathed my katana. "I have a message, all right."

"Careful," Mason warned me. "We wouldn't want any *misunderstandings*, would we?"

A House Tellier wizard pushed through between two House Rothchild wizards, dragging Momoko with him. A globe of water balanced in his hand, then slowly floated up to settle over Momoko's mouth as she thrashed in his grasp.

This wasn't good. All House Medeis wizards were wearing the magic-blocking bracelets. And even though they outnumbered Mason's minions, wizards weren't trained for physical fighting. They couldn't fight back.

I could unleash an area lightning attack, but a few of my family members would get caught in it. Could someone like Great Aunt Marraine take a lightning bolt and survive?

"Drop the sword, Hazel," Mason ordered, his eyes crinkling with his smile.

I licked my lips and clenched my sword's hilt, pressing the wrappings into my palm. I took a breath and intended to lower my inner gates, opening me to magic, when I heard the rumblings of a car.

It backfired three times in a row, making a few of the House Tellier wizards jump, as it puttered along the road.

I risked a glance over my shoulder and watched in confusion as a battered, banana yellow Volkswagen bug screeched to a stop, parking on the curb.

The front door swung open, and the Paragon popped out, carrying a picnic basket and wearing one of those cloth baby slings. Only instead of a baby, a hairless cat with judgmental blue eyes peered out at the world with an expression that communicated her general distaste for the place.

"Hazel—hi-hi!" The Paragon set his basket down so he could wave to me. "I'm *so* glad I made it in time!" He bustled to the sidewalk gate, then *kicked* it open.

I thought the House might react, but the gate didn't even creak as it swung open.

A quick peek at Mason showed he was just as shocked and confused as I was. "Paragon?"

The Paragon set his basket down again and pointed at his bald cat. "And Aphrodite, too!"

The cat yawned, showing off her needle-like teeth, then meowed.

"She *insisted* on coming with to see you—she has become rather fond of you, I dare say!" The Paragon flipped the basket lid open and pulled out a full sized kitchen stool (how?), and a folded-up easel that he began wrestling with.

Once it was assembled to his liking, he set it up in front of him and plopped down on the stool, camping out on the patch of sidewalk just outside of his non-gate-hindered view of House Medeis.

Mason relaxed his hold on Great Aunt Marraine. He even went so far as to pat her benevolently on the shoulder. "Paragon," Mason began in his most charismatic voice. "Please allow me to extend an invitation, and explain what—"

The Paragon shoved his hand out in front of him and waved it, cutting Mason off. "Ah-ah-ah—that is not necessary."

Mason glanced at the House Tellier wizard, who had discreetly peeled the water off Momoko's face and was trying not to grimace as she ground her heel into his foot.

"You see, I am not here as the Paragon—the spokesman for

every fae Court in the United States of America, the ambassador for every fae creature, and the highest ranking fae in our country. No, not at all." Though the Paragon kept his voice sunny and bright, Mason and the House Tellier wizards turned progressively paler as he rattled through his list.

"I am here as an *observer*." The Paragon dug into his picnic basket again. This time he pulled out a sketchpad and a fistful of pencils. "Hazel Medeis has received unconventional training which has made her use of magic something of a throwback to our more ancient of days. I'm curious to see how she faces off against her own kind, so I am here to record it for educational purposes."

He smiled, showing surprisingly white and perfect teeth, and no one present believed a word of what he said.

The Paragon was throwing his political weight around, without strictly doing anything per se. I didn't think he'd step in and help me fight, but his sheer presence would keep Mason from threatening one of my family members as a way to subdue me.

Mason seemed to realize the same thing, because some of his charm faded away as his eyes flicked to me, and I saw anger in the lines around his mouth.

"You *are* going to fight, are you not?" the Paragon asked.

Mason's smile returned. "I believe you have misunderstood what's going on, honored Paragon. This is a simple dispute between Hazel and me, there is no need for a—"

"Because if you're not going to start right now that will give me a chance to phone up the Elite. I imagine he'd be interested in observing Hazel's unconventional use of magic as well!" The Paragon smiled so brightly I could see his fae nature.

It wasn't that he sprouted wings or shed pixie dust, it was in the way his words seemed so *harmless* and *sincere*.

Fae were masters of deception.

Granted, the Paragon wasn't doing much to screen his threats, but he appeared so *genuine* his words almost seemed logical.

Of course he would want to watch me use my magic. Of course the Elite would want to see, too. It took me a few moments to realize there was nothing logical about this, and how had he even *known* what was going on? Our only connection was Killian—who obviously hadn't called him after he wouldn't even let his people drive me back to the city.

Name-dropping the Elite's title wasn't because he really wanted to chat with the wizard, but because he was again indirectly blocking and herding Mason into a fair fight—or as fair as I would get without my own backers.

I eyed the Paragon with new respect, but he was more proof how out-of-my-league I'd been with Killian and the Drake Family. I had allowed his odd cat, his complaining, and his cheery facade to sway me, covering up his fae nature and his own maneuverings.

At least he was helping me. No one could accuse him of favoring me given that all he intended to do was sit there, but it was more than any of the other wizarding Houses had done for me—more than the wizard subcommittee had done.

Mason slightly tilted his head. "Perhaps we could put on a play fight for your sake—"

"Winner takes House Medeis," I said, blasting through the pretty veneer of his words.

"Until first bloodshed," Great Aunt Marraine said in a quavering voice that made my heart twist.

"No." I narrowed my eyes. "Until the other is incapacitated. We're settling this *today*, Mason."

"It seems rude to settle such personal matters in front of our guest." Mason's gaze strayed to the Paragon, who was arranging his sketchpad on his easel.

"Adept Mason," the Paragon said. "If you think the community as a whole is unaware of your feud with Hazel, and believe you can hide this, you are as stupid as you look." The Paragon's eyes glowed, and for a second he looked a century younger.

"*Fight*," he ordered in a terrible voice that reverberated in my bones.

Aphrodite meowed, and in the blink of an eye the Paragon was once again a harmless old fae as he fussed over his pet. "Oh my, Aphrodite—are you cold? Do you need a sweater?"

It took Mason several tries before he was able to swallow. "Well, then," he smiled. "It seems we will fight. But since you are the challenger, Hazel, I believe my allies should be allowed to help me."

"That's not fair!" Felix shouted.

"Naturally, those belonging to House Medeis will remain neutral parties," Mason continued in his charming voice. "We couldn't expect them to choose between the two of us, after all."

Mr. Baree growled like a bear. "Coward!"

Mason narrowed his eyes at him, and I made a quick inspection of Mason's allies.

Nine from Tellier and two from Rothchild—and Gideon the Idiot, AKA the Heir of House Tellier—was one of the nine. On top of Mason...could I handle them all at once? He clearly didn't think I could.

I opened my inner gates, letting magic swim through my bloodstream and burn my skin as my wizard's mark surfaced. "It sounds like you're not going to give me a choice."

Mason morosely shook his head. "We don't have to do this, Hazel. The House's prestige has risen. Isn't that more important than a few petty squabbles or disagreements? The House comes first, after all."

I looked past Mason, at the tired and hopeless expressions of my family, and something in me broke.

All my life I'd heard that horrible phrase. I hadn't ever liked it, but it seemed logical—the House was necessary for our survival.

But did we really *want* to survive if our existence was going to be miserable—like this?

"No," I said. "The House *doesn't* come before everything, at least not for me."

A gasp whirled through everyone gathered as House Tellier, Rothchild, and Medeis wizards gaped at me.

Gideon—who had been ambling across the lawn, abruptly retreated, and almost everyone turned to look back to House Medeis to see how it would punish me.

The House was still.

I smiled as I straightened my wrist, bringing my katana into a guard position. "Right now, I don't care about the *House*. I'm here because you're terrorizing my *family*. To me, they are my top priority. You can have the House if you want it that badly—but you won't take it. Because what good is a House without any wizards? So let's finish this *disagreement*."

Gideon looked to Mason. The Medeis traitor nodded, and Gideon ambled across the lawn again. "House Tellier, let's go!"

Mason swiveled to look expectantly at the two House Rothchild wizards—two women.

The women nervously looked from Mason to me. "It seems to me, that although we are allies, one House shouldn't interfere with the inheritance of another House," one of them nervously said.

Mason narrowed his eyes. "Are you afraid of her? Why? There are no vampires at her back."

The second House Rothchild wizard rocked back on her heels. "It doesn't matter if she's supported or not. We stayed out of it when you made your move. We'll continue to stay out of it now."

Lightning zipped up and down the blade of my katana. "Stop worrying, Mason, and get down here."

Mason smiled brightly and shook his head. "I think House Tellier can handle you."

I stared incredulously at him. "You're seriously not going to fight? What kind of a—" I cut myself off when Gideon summoned his favorite attack—a fireball—to his fingertips.

This changed things. I couldn't take them all out with one massive attack like I'd hoped. If I did that Mason might try to run or delay the fight, and I couldn't afford that since I had the element of surprise *and* the Paragon's presence to keep things at least halfway fair.

Gideon flung the fireball at me, starting the fight.

I ducked it and swung my sword through the air, making the lightning on it crackle and leap to the nearest wizard.

He yipped and backed up a step, but the eight other Tellier wizards closed ranks on me.

I forged a shield of pure magic and slid it around to cover my back, my thoughts tripping over themselves as I tried to both defend and come up with a strategy.

Gideon threw another fireball at me. I had just enough time to shoot off a stream of water, which hissed and evaporated when the attacks collided, filling the air with hazy steam.

I couldn't see them, but more importantly they couldn't see me *or* each other.

I held my breath as I listened.

Grass crunched under boots to my left, and I swung my hand through the air, shooting off a thin line of blue flames.

A woman yelped in pain, and I flung baseball sized chunks of ice now that I'd narrowed the area down.

She shrieked, and Gideon cursed.

"Someone clear this steam," he shouted.

A massive wind curled around me, almost knocking me off my feet until I stabbed my katana into the lawn and held on to its hilt.

The steam cleared out, letting me see my victim, who was clutching her bleeding head.

My hours of practice with my shield paid off. One of the wizards flung what sounded like a massive rock at it—which ricocheted off it and hit the attacking wizard with a painful thud. Eliciting an airless wheeze.

I glanced at Mason. He had his arms folded across his chest and was leaning against the porch railing with a look of expectation.

I'd have to lure him out—let him think House Tellier had me almost beat so he could make the finishing blow himself, and then I'd get him and all the Tellier wizards with the lightning attack that affected a large area—the same kind I had used on Rupert.

The trickiest part of that would be letting the Tellier wizards beat on me without getting badly injured so, when Mason finally stepped in, I'd still have the strength to defeat him.

The woman with the bloodied head was slowly crawling away —bringing it down to an eight on one fight, though a quick glance behind me confirmed the wizard who had tried to go through my shield was still plastered on the ground, struggling to breathe.

Four wizards rushed me at once, coming at me from the sides.

I ducked the fire attack and sliced through a dagger-sharp icicle one of them had thrown at my chest, my katana cleaving it like butter. The third wizard created something that looked like a prickly vine—even though it was Tellier orange—and flung it at me. I rotated my katana and cut through it, but instead of dissipating the attack, it separated, one vine wrapping around each arm. The thorny bits dug convulsively into my skin, creating rows of deep scratches and making it hard to hold on to my katana.

I clenched my teeth as I made blue fire dance up and down my arms, burning the vines to ash, but pain still rippled through my muscles. While I tried to adjust my hold on my katana's hilt, the fourth wizard tried to knock me to the ground by raising the turf beneath my feet.

I threw myself into a sideways roll, my shoulder taking the brunt of the force before I popped back to my feet, coming up just behind one of the wizards.

Scratch that—it was going to be equally hard to hold back

from using an area attack. *Eight* wizards was a lot of targets when I could only hit one at a time.

The closest wizard turned around, but he was so *slow* compared to the quicksilver vampires.

I rotated my wrist, swinging my katana so the hilt faced out, then popped him on the side of the head.

He went down like a sack of potatoes, which was pretty gratifying because for once I actually felt physically strong. (Let me tell you, it required a heck of a lot harder of a hit to take a vampire down!)

I was still stupidly celebrating this feat when one of the female wizards created a dozen dagger-sharp icicles and flung them at me in such quick succession I couldn't possibly block or duck them all.

I avoided the worst of them, but one skimmed across the top of my shoulder, slicing straight through my protective shirt and through muscle. It wasn't deep, but every arm movement made pain rip through that shoulder. Even worse, another skimmed the top of my hand.

*Memo to self—buy protective gloves, too.*

I didn't want to get a worse injury, so I swung my magic shield around so it was in front of me.

The wizard who had almost knocked himself out on my shield was standing on shaky legs—and we couldn't have that.

A chunk of ice to the knee dropped him again—this time with a painful crunch.

The wound on my hand trickled blood across my fingers, which made it harder to keep the correct hand positions on my sword.

I swiveled my shield to my back as I turned, taking quick inventory of the wizards.

"Now!" Gideon shot off his stupidly-beloved fireball at me, along with five of his wizards.

I jumped to the side, but they kept firing, and I *knew* I didn't have the footing for another dodge, so I threw my shield in front of me as I tried to recover my form.

It blocked the fire attacks, which bounced off its blue surface—raising shouts of surprise from the wizards.

Unfortunately, those shouts covered up the movement directly behind me.

The buzz of magic came too late.

The fire had been a trap—distracting me while another wizard threw a rock boulder the size of a watermelon at my head.

I dropped to my knees, but the thing smacked into the top of my head, scraping across it.

Pain radiated from my skull to my toes, and my stomach quivered as I dropped, my muscles giving out.

I could barely even think as the pain swam through my system. If that rock had hit me dead on, it probably would have killed me.

"Hazel!" That was Felix calling for me. I could barely hear him over the ringing in my skull.

Wishing I had been a bit faster and managed to dodge more of that attack, I shook my head as I tried to clear my vision of stars. Thankfully, the buzzing hum of my shield hung over my prone body, so the rest of the wizards couldn't pile on me, but my skull was seriously rattled.

I was now a fairly easy target for Mason. Hopefully he would take the bait—or I was going to have to gamble and get the Tellier wizards as a group and then chase Mason. There was no way I could take another hit like that and not drop.

I made a show of trying to regain my footing, and instead fell flat on my face. But my ploy worked.

Mason was slowly crossing the lawn, his charming smile growing with every step he took.

*That's right, come closer...*

# CHAPTER TWENTY

*Hazel*

Blood dripped down my temple as I watched Mason. When I looked past him, a part of me couldn't help but be irritated.

My family—who outnumbered Mason and his minions—all stood and watched me with pale faces.

Momoko was crying, her face pressed into Felix's chest, but none of them tried to help me.

I mean, they didn't have magic, and this fight was between me and Mason...and yeah, none of them had the physical strength or training I'd received at Drake Hall. But were they seriously just content to stand there without a fight and watch as I got the life beaten out of me?

There was something broken about that. I knew they loved me, but Medeis was a peaceful House. A *pacifist* House.

And we wouldn't survive if that didn't change.

Mason stopped just a few feet short of me. His wizard's mark burned across his skin as blue magic encased his fists.

"Unfortunately it seems you still aren't strong enough to run House Medeis," he said.

"Because you hide behind the troops of another House!" Mr. Clark shouted.

Mason swung around to scowl back at the House.

I gripped a fistful of grass and pushed myself onto my knees. My stomach was still quivering, and I had the faint desire to throw up. But I couldn't stop now—I could win if I just *kept going*.

A rancid taste filled my mouth. I tried to swallow it as I managed to stand. The ground seemed to swivel under my feet, but I mentally marked the House Tellier wizards.

It looked like I had subdued three of them. Gideon and the rest stood around me in a circle. *Hopefully* I'd be able to make an attack wide enough for all of them.

Mason gave me his attention again as I picked up my katana—my blood had turned tacky and sticky on the hilt. Cleaning it was going to be disgusting.

"You've learned your place now," Mason said. "You were never fit to run House Medeis. Neither were your parents."

"You say that as if you aren't the worst thing that ever happened to our House." I laughed, wincing when it hurt. I started to discreetly pile magic around my feet, building my power for my next—and final—attack.

Mason shrugged. "The wizarding community doesn't agree with you. The respectability and general rank of House Medeis has increased."

"Ahh, Mason." I pushed my katana into the ground again and held on. "Didn't I already tell you? I'm not fighting you for the House, but my family." I smiled. "Checkmate."

Mason frowned. "What—"

I unleashed my magic, causing massive lightning strikes that struck the area in a twenty-foot diameter around me.

The first struck Mason, instantly flattening him and making his clothes smolder.

The next hit Gideon—making the Heir yell in pain and

flinging him a few feet as the ground beneath my feet glowed blue with my magic.

Bolt after bolt struck, splitting the air, burning the ground, and the attacking wizards.

A few House Tellier wizards dragged themselves out of my circle. I got Gideon twice, but Mason I struck again and again as blue sparks danced around me and the area was such a violently bright blue it was nearly impossible to see.

The ground rocked, and the air trembled with electrical currents.

I yanked my sword from the ground, and the lightning bolts stopped striking and instead arced around me in a beautiful show of crackling lines and hissing sparks.

I wiped more blood off my face as I knelt down at Gideon's side.

He made a mewling sound, but he couldn't get his limbs under control to move away from me.

I dispassionately rested the edge of my katana on his uncovered neck, making his face turn red with fright and the veins in his neck pop. "This is your only warning, Tellier," I said in a cold, dispassionate voice. "Come after me or my family—or even *think* of helping Mason again—and I'll find you. And if that happens, it will only take *one* lightning strike to fix it. Do you understand?"

Gideon nodded.

I stood, pausing when my vision briefly turned blurry and my stomach again voiced its doubts.

For a moment I wanted to kick Gideon hard in the ribs for *all* those times he'd tortured me, picked on me, and made my childhood miserable.

But even though so much of what I had thought to be truths were lies, I knew if I did something like that, I'd be no better than Gideon.

I made my way to Mason.

He was in the worst shape. His limbs were still twitching, his clothes were smoking, and the lightning had actually torn one of his shoes off. He couldn't *stop* moving.

I didn't kneel by him, but I did rest the edge of my sword against his neck as I had with Gideon.

"Mason, do you agree it is your loss?" I asked with ice in my voice.

It took a few moments before he stuttered out, "A-agreed."

I slowly blocked off my magic pathways, and my wizard's mark flickered out.

"Hazel!" Momoko flew toward me, Felix right behind her.

"You did it—you crazy girl!" Felix messed up my hair, but guardedly watched the House Tellier wizards scrape themselves off the ground and edge toward the sidewalk.

The House Rothchild wizards stood awkwardly at the edge of the porch and were almost run over by the outpouring of House Medeis family members.

"Adept!"

"Hazel—you're home!"

"Welcome home, Adept!"

I laughed as my family crowded around me.

Franco—Felix's older brother—dabbed at the smeared blood on my hand with a washcloth. "We'll have to get you to the doctor."

"Surely we could afford a fae healing potion?" Great Aunt Marraine asked.

"Hazel, Hazel!" Ivy stretched her arms out to me, holding the macaroni necklace she tried to give me at my parents' funeral.

Behind me, Mason groaned.

I reached out a hand to brush Ivy's head, but grimaced at the dried blood on my hands. "Just a minute, Ivy."

I stepped back from my family and returned to Mason, watching him.

He was still in pretty bad shape. He'd need a doctor, but I was pretty sure he could speak without stuttering now, given that he was sitting upright.

"Mason." I did my best to imitate the icy, uncaring tone Killian used when he was at his worst.

It must have worked to some degree. Mason's skin turned ashen as he looked up at me.

I stabbed my sword forward—stopping just short of piercing his throat.

(This brought gasps from my House Medeis family.)

"You admitted your loss. House Medeis is mine—*as it always was*," I snarled.

Mason's throat bulged as he swallowed, and his hands started to shake again.

"Because I'm not like you, I'm willing to offer you mercy. You will leave House Medeis today, and by tomorrow I want you out of the Midwest Region."

Mason audibly ground his teeth, but I didn't care if he was angry.

"Your false paperwork that declared you Adept is no longer valid. From this moment forth you are considered an exile of House Medeis."

"Be reasonable—"

"You tore House Medeis apart with your selfish ambition, and terrorized the family we have grown up with." My voice was so frosty the air felt colder. "It's called *mercy* because I'm granting you something you are unworthy of, Mason. You deserve pain and suffering, but in the spirit of the Medeis I grant you this chance."

I leaned in so my face was so close to Mason's he could feel my hot breath. "*However.* If you attack me or any member of House Medeis again, I will kill you."

That raised another round of gasps and concerned murmurs—of course, fighting, much less killing, was *not* the Medeis way.

It didn't matter, though. Despite the pain he was obviously in, Mason's eyes still glowed with hatred.

Given that he hadn't killed anyone, and that House Tellier was just as guilty as he was, I wasn't expecting much of a punishment from the Curia Cloisters—though I would hound them endlessly until they booted him from our region, and I was going to embark on a rampage to figure out how the Wizard Council had approved Mason as Adept without officially meeting. But I'd be true to my word—*all* of it.

The Paragon clapped loudly. "Hazel Medeis is rightful Adept of House Medeis." He was still sitting out on the sidewalk, his quill pen clenched between his teeth. "And might I say, that was positively a *wicked* attack! I don't think I'd ever seen wizards use an attack that affected an entire area around them. Well done! Even Aphrodite was impressed!"

Aphrodite, still secured against the Paragon's chest in her baby sling, flicked one of her giant, hairless ears. "*Mmert.*"

I laughed and waved to the fae and his cat. "Please, Paragon and Aphrodite. I invite you both into House Medeis."

"Fantastic!" The Paragon got to work disassembling his easel. "I have some questions to ask you now that Drake isn't hiding you away in his Hall. Do you—"

"ADEPT!"

Some of the members of House Medeis screamed, but I'd already heard the scuff of grass behind me.

Days of drilling prompted me. Without looking back, I whipped my sword behind me, unflinching when it pierced flesh.

*Mason.*

I turned around, but his fate had already been sealed.

Mason had attempted to jump me from behind. Instead, I had stabbed him through the chest. He wasn't going to make it, because he had chosen cowardice and greed over my mercy.

A dagger slipped from his limp fingers—probably what he meant to kill me with—before he collapsed to his knees.

I stepped closer to him. The difference in our height meant I didn't even have to crouch when I pulled my sword clean. "Just because I offer mercy, doesn't mean I'm stupid."

Mason's eyes were still wide with shock as he died.

I wasn't happy with his death, but I wasn't going to regret it.

Mason had made a lifetime of poor choices. Ending it because he couldn't let go was *his* decision.

Judging by the shocked expressions of everyone from House Medeis, I wasn't sure they saw it quite the same way.

Great Aunt Marraine was shaking so hard I thought she might collapse, and Mr. Baree was watching me the way one watched a rabid wolf.

Momoko, however, had a hardened smile and a gleam in her eye that told me *she* understood, and Felix had a thoughtful expression settle on his face as he rubbed at the magic-reducing bracelet.

"What a mess." The Paragon peered over my shoulder. "Make no mistake—you acted in self-defense. I would be happy to testify such a thing, as I'm sure *any* of the fine wizards from House... what House are you again?" He turned to Gideon.

"H-House Tellier, Paragon." His legs shook as he bowed to the Paragon.

"That's right, the House of ugly color combinations. For real —your ancestors should have looked at a color wheel." The Paragon wrinkled his nose at Gideon, then pulled a cellphone with a neon green cactus cover from Aphrodite's sling. "I'll ring up the Elite and tell him some wizard reinforcements are needed to come down and handle everything."

I looked around for my sword scabbard, then realized it was useless—there was no way I was putting my katana away when it was spattered with blood. "Thank you, Paragon."

"Adept..." Great Aunt Marraine said in her quavering voice. "How could you...?"

"Things are going to change for House Medeis," I said simply.

"I'm sure. But you are injured, Adept." Mrs. Clark's face was white when she glanced past me at Mason, but the smile she gave me was still motherly. "We really should see to your injuries first."

The pounding ache that rippled out from the top of my head *was* starting to get distracting. "Okay," I agreed. "But we also need to find the keys to get those bracelets off you all."

"I know where they are!" Franco grinned at me. "Felix, come help!"

Felix glanced at Momoko, who curled an arm around my mid back, tugging me so I leaned into her. "I've got her," she said. "She'll be okay until we get these stupid bracelets off."

"I am not a child the two of you need to watch," I grumbled.

"I disagree, Adept." Mrs. Clark's face was sorrowful as she and Momoko guided me across the lawn. "You are still a child, who has been forced to deal with horrors no human should."

I didn't answer—I was busy holding my breath as we crossed the threshold of the House, wondering if it was going to smite me for openly saying I valued my family first.

Mercifully, it was silent, and I relaxed just a little.

"I happen to have a few fae healing potions on me," the Paragon declared as he shamelessly followed us inside and looked around. "Why don't you set Adept Medeis on a chair, and we can get one in her, yes?"

They settled me in the closest spot—a rickety wooden chair settled in the hallway.

The Paragon pushed a golden potion encased in a glass vial into my hands. It had that faint floral taste that always accompanied fae magic, but it also tasted warm and musical—like piano music.

And as I took a swig of my potion I peered up at the Paragon, and wondered how, exactly, he had heard that I was going to attack Mason, and that I was no longer in Drake Hall...

# CHAPTER TWENTY-ONE

*Hazel*

In the end, there wasn't any fallout from Mason's death.

As the Paragon had offered, he'd phoned the Elite, who sent out guards from the Cloisters to collect Mason's body.

The Elite had dropped the rank of all the Houses that had helped Mason and was lodging paperwork that barred them from serving on the Wizard Council for the next decade. I had formally broken off all alliances with the traitorous—but *for the moment*, I was most concerned with the mental/emotional wellbeing of my family, and House Medeis itself.

It seemed that even though Mason had the paperwork proclaiming him Adept, he hadn't been able to do anything to House Medeis.

Since I had the key to both the lockbox at Tutu's and the House vault that contained things like the family's social security cards, birth certificates, etc, he hadn't been able to force the family to officially ratify his position. And without the ring, he couldn't Ascend.

Which meant as a whole very little had changed for our House. Structurally, anyway.

My family was a lot quieter, and I noticed wrinkles and silver hair that hadn't been there before my parents died, as well as the occasional haunted expression.

House Medeis itself was silent. I felt its magic stir, but it didn't even cut me off from hot water.

No one seemed worried about this except me. I was pretty concerned this didn't mean the House was satisfied, but incredibly weak.

The House had essentially been without an Adept for *months*. Adepts were necessary to keep a House functioning because of the flow of magic, and House Medeis had been cut off since my parents had died.

Which was why, four days after I had won my House back, I was trying to draw all the necessary paperwork together to file for my Ascension.

I didn't have the ring, so it wouldn't be a real Ascension, but it would hopefully open the flow at least a little between the House and me so I could stir up some of its magic.

I chewed on my lip as I turned the two keys required to open the House safe, grinning when it swung open. "Here we go—the necessary forms of ID and registration." I triumphantly swiped a stack of papers from the small safe and brandished my prize in the air. "And you can *bet* I'm going to take at least five years before I 'remember' to go re-register and get my magic tested," I grumbled. "Or at the very least I should wait one year for every month the Wizard Council sat on their dusseldorfs and refused to help me."

I carried the papers back to my dad's desk—now my desk—and started sifting through them.

My parents had organized them so each household in the family had their own folder—the Clarks had one, the Barees another, and so on.

The Medeis folder was the thickest—which was kind of funny because we were the smallest household in the family since it had just been me and my parents.

But when I flipped our manila folder open, I discovered it was all because of a thick envelope pressed just in the cover.

Curious, I flipped it over, my heart stopping.

*Hazel*

I recognized the writing as Mom's. But what did they have in here that hadn't been left with the lawyers, or the lockbox in Tutu's?

Was it paperwork for when they had me sealed? But I'd gone through the safe with my parents just last year and never saw this stuffed envelope.

I paused, then grabbed my dad's old-fashioned letter opener, savagely ripping it open.

Inside were a couple sheets of white printer paper. I plucked them out and unfolded them to read, and they almost immediately fell from my numb fingers.

*Dear Hazel,*

*If you're reading this it means the worst has happened, and both of us are dead.*

It was my dad's handwriting this time—another slug to the gut.

I really didn't want to read it. I didn't even know what to think of my parents anymore after everything I'd been through. I couldn't tell where the lies ended and the truth began.

I wracked my brain, trying to recall if the lawyers had ever shown me a letter like this—I didn't *think* so. Everything had been squared away with the will.

A good five minutes passed before I gave in to my twisted sense of hope and dread, and started reading again.

*Which means we have so much to tell you—things that will hurt you, and things that might make you hate us.*

*To begin, your magic abilities were partially sealed by the fae Paragon as a baby.*

*While we have raised you and registered you as having very little magic talent, in reality you are a rarity in your generation, for you have about as much magic power as I do.*

*But you were sealed for several reasons. First, we wanted to shield you. Given that magic has lessened with each generation, it's shocking you were born with as much talent as you have.*

*Secondly...your mother and I wanted you to experience life with little to no magic, so you would know and understand how others have suffered.*

*We didn't do this out of a misguided effort to have you experience suffering at a young age, but rather because in the last decade, there's been a distinct shift to wizard politics.*

I had to read the line twice—I almost couldn't believe my eyes.

Being sealed...it wasn't about me personally?

*Since the 1900s, wizard Houses have banded together—first to stay strong against the other supernatural races, and then to stay strong when our presence was revealed to humans.*

*In general, Houses have been friendly. Records of fighting between Houses have been extremely rare—only a few cases in the century.*

*However, as magic has continued to die, desperation has begun pressing in on us.*

*Before you were born your mother and I could see it. The stronger Houses began banding together to vote on what would suit their Houses best, instead of what was best for the wizard community as a whole. And it's only gotten worse.*

I snorted. "That's for sure."

The incident with Mason proved it.

The other Houses had allowed Mason to go as far as he did because they didn't want me as Adept when they thought I was weak. By the time I had unlocked my powers it was too late. And even though Killian had been cruel in his delivery, he was right. The wizarding community would be eternally wary of me due to my connection with the Drakes if they were even half as concerned about preserving wizards as Dad thought they were.

*If this continues, the strong Houses will begin to prey upon the weak.*

*That cannot happen. It's not right, and I believe if it* does *get to be that bad, magic may collapse entirely.*

Why would he think that? I read on, but he skipped answering it, unfortunately.

*Which is why we sealed you. With so little magic you will understand what the less powerful Houses have experienced, and you will fight for them.*

Fight for them? That was another line I had to re-read twice.

*Fighting is not a part of House Medeis. It is so counter to what we have taught—even your mother and I have had it engrained in our hearts since we first learned magic.*

*You, however, have not.*

I blinked in surprise.

He was right, in a way.

My parents hadn't done a lot to help me when I got picked on, but even though we were a House full of pacifists, they never lectured me for the fights I got in. Not even the time I broke Gideon's nose and chipped one of his teeth.

*Having so little magic backed you into a corner. You had no other option except to fight. And that is why you can change House Medeis—it's why you are the* only *one who can change it. We have tried, but it seems like we can only prepare the way for you.*

*I won't lie, sweetheart, it's going to be difficult.*

*The other Houses won't want you to protect the others, and they won't like the change to Medeis. Some might try to harm you.*

*A few other Adepts in Magiford may suspect what we mean for you to do. We haven't been outright threatened yet, but I think it's coming. But it doesn't matter. As Adepts of House Medeis, it is our duty to protect our* family, and to achieve that means we must also do what we can for the wizarding community.

You, Hazel, are the greatest gift we can give, because you can change things for the better.

We're so sorry for the pain you've gone through because of us, for the fights you got into, and for the merciless teasing of others. But you are strong and powerful, and you are what we need more than anything right now.

As your parents, we know this is an unfair burden. Hopefully this letter will be unnecessary, and when you turn twenty-five we'll tell you about your seal and pass the House off to you—though if things continue as they have, we will try to tell you sooner.

The key to undoing your seal is to have the willpower to end another's life to protect someone.

It may appear to be an ugly, brutal key, particularly given our House's historical stance on violence. But I hope after reading this far you'll recognize the wisdom to it.

Hazel, there is no greater strength than defending another, but the cost for such strength is great. You must be prepared to fight—and indeed kill —for others. You will shed blood, receive injuries, and possibly be criticized for protecting those in need. But magic is no good to us if we do not use it to do what is right and to protect others.

That is the real purpose of House Medeis—of all wizard Houses—to protect. It's something we have forgotten in our fight for survival, but I hope it is a stance you will take, and teach to all of House Medeis.

Your mother and I love you so much, my darling daughter. You have made us so proud, and we believe that you are the only one who could shake off centuries of tradition. And after seeing what you have endured, I don't think anyone of House Medeis will reject the idea of protection.

With all our love,

Mom & Dad

I sat at the desk with tears dribbling from my eyes.

This was why...

It hadn't been out of malice, or for any real political motives. I really wished they had re-thought their plan—or *told* me about it. But all of this meant my parents were the good people I had believed them to be.

Perhaps even better.

Relief flooded me like my magic. It was all I could do to sit in my chair and let the tears come.

*Finally.* I was finally free of all those nagging fears and doubts. And it only bolstered my resolve to change things within House Medeis.

We couldn't continue on as we had. Things had to change, big time.

I cleared my throat and re-read the letter, pausing when I came to a particular line that had bothered me the first time through. *We will try to tell you sooner...*

Had that been why Mom called me the day they died?

Mom said they wanted to talk...and asked me to meet them at the Curia Cloisters. Did they plan to explain everything to me then?

I scrunched my eyes shut and rubbed my forehead. There was a fresh pain in my heart—going through this had again ripped open the wound of my parents' death, but there was some happiness as well. I finally had the answers I had wanted, and it was better than what I had feared.

I smoothed the multi-page letter out on my desk, pausing when I noticed an extra note on the final page—a tiny message scrawled at the bottom in the boxy letters of Mom's handwriting.

*PS: We gave the signet ring to someone for safekeeping.*

"Huh?" I frowned at that one.

The signet ring was in Tutu's—until I destroyed it. But the vault was hardly a "someone".

They must have changed their minds and not bothered to update the letter.

Someone knocked at the door.

"Come in," I called.

Felix opened the door and poked his head in, his niece, Ivy, hanging from his neck. "Do you have a minute?" he asked.

"Of course." I smiled, then glanced at Ivy, who grinned bashfully at me. "What's up?"

Felix held Ivy on his hip with one hand, and ran his other through his silky beautiful blond hair. "There appear to be some vampires watching the House."

I kept my expression bland. "Where?"

"We've caught sight of them lingering at the street corners—always on the opposite side of the street from House Medeis."

"How long?"

"Since the night you beat Mason." He grimaced. "Sorry. None of us thought anything of it until we started mentioning seeing vampires to each other at breakfast this morning. We didn't mean to withhold information."

I smiled. "I know." This was also a bigger reflection on how passive House Medeis had become. That they hadn't even thought vampires strolling around a confirmed wizard neighborhood was unusual was a pretty good indicator of how clueless my House was.

*You might be a sourpuss, but thanks for all the training, Killian! I will put it to good use.*

"Were they all wearing suits?" I asked.

"The three Momoko and I saw were, but I didn't think to ask the others. Do you want me to check?"

"Nah, I can ask at dinner. But I'm pretty certain it's vampires from the Drake Family. Although I don't know what they want."

Felix frowned a little—making him look dazzlingly concerned. "Are you sure it's not out of concern for you? I know you said things ended badly, but—"

"They're not watching out of personal concern for me," I said. "If anything, Killian is probably just shocked I successfully beat Mason, and is wondering if I'm on the verge of kicking the bucket. The Paragon probably blabbed about the whole thing the night I arrived—he'd *love* knowing something Killian doesn't."

I busied myself with gathering up my letter.

"If you say so," Felix said doubtfully.

There were several really awkward moments of silence.

"Can I talk now?" Ivy asked in a whisper that was about as loud as a normal speaking voice.

"Go ahead, Ivy." Felix—the ever-doting uncle—set Ivy down.

She skipped over to my side of the desk, brandishing her macaroni necklace. "I made this for you a long time ago."

It was hard not to rub her head like she was a puppy—her enunciation of words had gotten so much better in the few short months I was gone! "All for me? Thank you!"

Ivy passed it over, and I recognized it as the macaroni necklace she'd worn to my parents' funeral—the one with the metal loop that hung from the bottom to keep it weighted down.

I made a few humming noises of appreciation. "It's so beautiful! I will treasure it."

"The Adepts said I *had* to give it to you," Ivy said.

Felix and I froze. "What did you say, Ivy?" Felix asked.

"The Adepts," she repeated in her tiny voice. "They said I *had* to give it to you. You need it."

*No. It couldn't be.*

I took a closer look at the metal loop, my heart thundering in my chest.

The loop was actually a plain, unadorned silver ring...much like the one Mom wore.

But she had the consort ring, not the signet ring. This wasn't... it *couldn't*—

My chest squeezed as I untied the yarn and removed the ring. My mouth was dry, and I slipped the plain ring on.

Awareness bloomed at the back of my skull. I could *feel* every room in the House. Momoko's footsteps as she marched across the front lawn tickled my fingers, and a warm tingly feeling on my palm was someone running hot water.

What was most shocking, though, was that I could finally feel the magic of House Medeis itself. I could feel the dormant magic that lined its timbers and bricks, and I tasted the wild magic that condensed from the air around the property.

The House itself stirred. Floorboards creaked, a few light fixtures shook.

"I'm sorry," I whispered.

The House purred in my mind.

"Hazel?" Felix broke through the haze of my shock. "Is that...?"

"Yes."

"Then the one Mason destroyed?"

I stared down the silver ring. "It must have been the consort ring?"

"The consort ring is purely symbolic, isn't it?" Felix asked.

"Yeah. It has some magic to give the consort a connection to the House, but it's a more modern thing that uses a spell to piggy-back off the signet ring's power." I confirmed.

"And this has the power of a signet ring?"

"It *definitely* does."

Felix stared down at Ivy, his eyes almost popping out of his skull. "She's worn that thing almost every day, flouncing around in front of Mason. If he had any idea..."

"The Adepts made me promise!" Ivy brightly said. "Shhh, secret!" She shushed us and then giggled.

I let air leak out of me as I stared at my finger. "We should go tell the others."

Felix made a funny noise.

I finally raised my eyes so I could meet my friend's gaze. "Because now, I can move up the Ascension date."

"To when?"

"I'm thinking...tomorrow."

# CHAPTER TWENTY-TWO

*Hazel*

D espite every objection and complaint, I got my way, and we moved up my Ascension date to the following day.

No one from House Medeis objected, of course. But the witnesses that were needed to be present from the Curia Cloisters whined pretty much constantly from the time they arrived.

A bunch of wizards from other Houses showed up for the occasion. None that had helped Mason, of course. But there were representatives from a few Houses that lived a few hours away, and a couple of more local Houses that hadn't been involved with House Medeis before.

I made certain to send invitation emails to everyone on the Wizard Council. The Adept of House Luna made it, and so did the three Houses that had voted with her, but none of the others showed.

A few werewolves skulked around, as well as some wizards who weren't sworn to a House.

Ascensions were pretty public, firstly because attendees technically weren't allowed on property during it.

No one was except for the Adept. Everyone—including members of the House—had to camp outside on the sidewalks.

This is because Houses will change with each new Adept. Sometimes it might be something as unimportant as changing up the landscaping a bit, other times it might be as drastic as adding or removing a floor.

Regardless, it's pretty dangerous to stand on the House's lawn when it's going through the change, which is why anyone who wanted to watch could. The street got blocked off anyway, so there was plenty of room.

I narrowed my eyes and carefully searched the crowd.

There—at the very edge of the gawkers I spotted a black suit and bright red hair...

"Are you ready, Adept?" Great Aunt Marraine asked.

She and the other House Medeis wizards were lined up on the sidewalk—as it was their House they were given the best view.

I smiled at her. "Yes."

"You know the ceremony—you speak to the crowd for a moment before climbing the Beacon and presenting the House with the signet ring?" she asked.

"We went over this at least a dozen times last night, Great Aunt Marraine."

The older woman flinched. "I know—and I know you know. But...I'll feel better when you've Ascended and the House has officially bonded with you." Her lower lip trembled before she gave me a brave smile.

I hugged her, and it only took a moment before the doughy woman hugged me back, giving me an extra ounce of encouragement.

She wiped away a tear or two from her eye. "You look very impressive today!"

I grinned—I was wearing white pants with a blue dress shirt, white heels, a white suitcoat with the House Medeis coat of arms, and a white sword belt for my katana. (And yes, I carried my sword despite all the squawks from the Curia Cloisters representatives.)

"Everyone is out of the House, Adept." Momoko gave me a slight bow, all signs of humor gone. "You may begin the ceremony whenever you like."

"Thanks, Momoko."

"Of course. Come on, Great Aunt Marraine—we should join the others." Momoko guided Great Aunt Marraine to the sidewalk where the rest of House Medeis stood, watching me with a mixture of hope and worry.

I was pretty sure at least a few Medeis wizards were convinced the House was going to punish me for declaring that they were more important than the House. I couldn't blame them—the thought had occurred to me as well, given that House Medeis was touchy at the best of times.

I stood on the walkway that led from the street sidewalk up to the front porch and cleared my throat. "Thank you to everyone who has come here today to celebrate my Ascension, and this new chapter in House Medeis's history." My voice was loud, and I kept my expression fixed and stoic.

"I am so happy that, after the many trials and tribulations that have fallen on House Medeis since my parents' death, the time has finally come for me to claim my birthright and bond with House Medeis in this Ascension ceremony."

There were a few guilty looks in the crowd after that—particularly from the Curia Cloisters reps—good. They deserved to feel guilty.

"I'd like to take this opportunity to announce a change I intend to implement to House Medeis."

That got everyone's attention. I hadn't told anyone besides Felix and Momoko what I had planned.

Both of them innocently watched me while the other House Medeis wizards stirred, exchanging lowered whispers and furrowed brows of confusion.

"For years House Medeis has had a culture of peace...and passivity. We generally do not train with our magic outside of school, and we do not train to fight at all." I paused, meeting the gaze of my senior wizards. "That is a policy we will no longer follow."

The lowered murmurs became explosive exclamations—mostly among the audience. (The House Medeis wizards seemed preoccupied with gaping at me in shock.)

"Instead, we will train our magic *and* our bodies. We will become proficient at fighting—not so we can conquer or act as tyrants, but so we can defend, and so we can protect." I felt some magic slip past my control and make my wizard mark flare. "What has happened to us this year will *never* happen again. And as long as I breathe, I will see to it that it happens to no other wizard House."

The silence was deafening.

I could almost taste their rejection, and they didn't even bother to hide the scowls, shared looks, and elbow nudges.

The House Medeis wizards looked like miserable sheep clustered together, frightened and alone.

*This was the right decision.* Watching them only reinforced that.

The extreme to which House Medeis had taken our desire for peace made us rot from the inside out. We would still be peace-loving and kind—but rather than passive, our kindness would be *ruthless.*

I smiled.

It didn't matter who doubted us, or even if House Medeis ended up hating me as the Adept.

I cared about my family, and I'd do whatever I needed to, to make sure that next time we'd be strong enough to hold on to what was important.

"Thank you for listening," I finished. "I will begin the ceremony."

Alone, I walked into the House and climbed the staircase up to the third floor.

The House was silent, and even though I wore the signet ring, it didn't react to me.

I made my way to a small closet stuck between two doors in the top hallway, revealing a ladder nailed to the wall.

I climbed it and pushed against the wooden trapdoor at the very top, which opened up into the tallest turret in House Medeis.

The turret was open air, circular, and small enough that a really tall human could almost stretch their arms from one side to the other. The only thing in the tower was a stone stand, and a globe of blue magic laced with veins of gold—the House Beacon.

The globe was the center of House Medeis, and the source of all its power.

To complete my Ascension, I had to push the ring into the globe and place my hands on it, solidifying my connection to the House.

I set the trapdoor back in place and edged around the Beacon so I faced the street—and all of House Medeis.

I saw a few people point, then wave to me.

I smiled, even though they couldn't see it, then took a deep breath and removed the signet ring.

"Okay, House," I murmured. "It's your turn. You heard what I said, and I'm pretty sure you can judge my heart. Are we in this together?"

It didn't respond—but I figured its reply would be in however it morphed the House, so that wasn't unexpected.

My fingers shook as I dropped the signet ring. It passed through the Beacon's exterior with only the smallest of ripples, and a tiny chiming sound.

Now it was my turn.

I took a deep breath, and before I could over-think it, I slapped my hands on the globe.

Magic flared around me, lighting the area with a brightness that was so invasive I had to shut my eyes. It exploded outward, making the turret into a torch of blue and gold magic.

*This is it.*

The ring had connected me to the House, but now I could feel its foreign, magic intelligence. It brushed against me like a pet would...producing a purring vibration I felt in my bones.

It felt *pleased*. I could feel it in the way the light emitting from the Beacon curled around me. But was it just happy to finally have an official Adept?

As if it could tell my thoughts, the wooden flooring beneath my feet began to rumble. My heart sped up as I heard the sound of bricks and mortar crumbling, and wood groaned.

Was it *destroying* a part of itself? Was the House that mad with me?

Abruptly, the ground opened up, and another wing—wholly finished from the roof timbers to the ornamental stone edging—shot out of the ground. The tower I stood in grew taller, stretching high above House Medeis, before the two other turrets shot up in a similar fashion. Weirdly, I could feel the House at work in the taller turrets, installing what I thought was a telescope and wiring a security system.

I held on to the Beacon for dear life as the entire House *grew* another floor, and in my new connection with the House I realized...it had just built a gym in the basement.

The buzz of magic informed me the new gym was stocked with weightlifting equipment, treadmills, and more.

In the backyard, the decorative fountain with the diapered baby angels stretched out and deepened, turning into a lap pool.

The iron fencing that surrounded the House Medeis plot grew by about five feet, and the ends turned sharp and pointed.

A flower garden fell away and was briefly buried under dirt and soil, before the House spat up four targets, and two racks of swords, shields, bows, and different kinds of weapons I hadn't seen even in Drake Hall.

Where had the House even *found* those weapons?!

I watched in shock as a mini training ground was created on the front lawn while the House industriously settled its inner architecture. It had added dozens of guest rooms—did it expect that our number of members would be rapidly expanding?!—and had scrounged up a second fridge in the slightly expanded kitchen.

A few of the flower beds were sucked under to make room for the additions, and both the gate that opened up to the sidewalk and the gate in front of the driveway thickened.

For the most part the outside of the House was finished—it was still making some minor adjustments to the landscaping, and I was pretty sure it had just added a bunch of mats to the basement gym—but from the increased wing and story to the taller towers to the new shooting range on our front lawn, the House's response was pretty clear.

I finally pulled my hands free—my palms itched from the extra burst of magic.

The ring bobbed on the globe's surface. I scooped it up and slipped it on, blinking as the pet-like feeling of House Medeis stayed with me with our new connection.

"Thank you." I rested my hand on top of the Beacon. "I'll do my best to make use of what you've given me."

I tugged on the trapdoor, intending to shimmy back down the ladder, but House Medeis peeled back the railing of the Beacon and built what appeared to be a temporary staircase for me. I hesitated before I started down it, trying not to think too much as the House assembled the staircase about three steps ahead of me, and tore every step down as soon as I had passed it.

A few members of House Medeis were laughing. Some were hugging, and the youngest were bouncing up and down—but almost everyone my parents' age were smiling through tears as they watched me step off the temporary staircase and onto the springy grass.

I held my arms up. "What do you guys think? Do you think the House likes me?"

Medeis wizards surged onto the new lawn, coming to hug me and examine the changes to their home.

"Oh, Hazel. I knew it all along!" Great Aunt Marraine dabbed at her eyes with her tissue.

"You're going to be a great Adept, you brat," Franco said with a grin.

"I think this is the biggest the House has been in generations," Momoko said.

Felix smirked. "How badly do you think you freaked the other Houses out?"

I laughed and hugged every House Medeis wizard. With each person I saw my happiness grew, and I *knew* I was doing the right thing.

My family might not be so merry when I woke them up at six in the morning and got them started running laps before everyone left for work, but that was okay.

We would learn to fight, and the House would help us.

Once I hugged the last House Medeis wizard, I turned to everyone lining the streets. As I marched down the front walkway, the sidewalk gate swung open as the House anticipated my decision.

"Welcome to House Medeis," I said with a smile that was more teeth than glee. "Come in, so you can tell everyone *all* about it."

A few of the onlookers floated away—probably the ones going to report to my scoffers. The Curia Cloisters reps had to come in, and my more distant allies chose to as well. A few of the gawkers slipped through, but I didn't worry.

If they tried anything, House Medeis would lock them in a closet.

I stayed at the gate, greeting everyone who passed through to go gawk at the House, until there was only one other person standing on the far side of the street, a pale, red-haired man wearing a black designer suit.

I slipped my chisa katana from its scabbard and sent a crackle of lightning shimmering up and down the blade. My wizard's mark burned my cheek as I crossed the street.

"Get lost, Rupert. And tell the others I will no longer put up with them skulking around."

Rupert scowled at me. "You can't be everywhere at once."

I smiled widely. "I don't have to be. The House can take care of it."

At that moment the Beacon shot off a crackling starburst of light—a warning shot that passed high over the houses and buildings surrounding us.

"The Drake Family made their choice very clear to me," I said once the light had faded. "I have no desire to see *any* of you again. Stay away."

I rotated my wrist, twirling my sword—which almost sounded like a lightsaber with its crackling lightning—then turned around.

"Did you ever stop to ask yourself how the Paragon knew what was going down here, or why he decided to come?" Rupert's voice was as irritating as a fly in my face.

"What?"

"The Paragon happened to show up *just* as you approached the House, did he not?" Rupert asked. "And you *knew* Mason was gathering allies. And yet only two Houses were around when you made your attack."

I scowled. "What's your point?"

"That you're blind."

"*Excuse me?*"

"Particularly because you haven't even asked the most important question of all." Rupert tilted his head back, looking imperiously down at me. "Where was the Night Court—Mason's newly minted allies—when you were confronting him?"

I slowly turned so I wasn't frowning at him over my shoulder, but instead facing him head on. "I dropped in out of the blue. I don't expect the Night Court would have anticipated that."

"And you don't think Mason called them the moment he realized you were here?" Rupert tucked his hands in the pockets of his slacks.

I was silent for a moment as I turned the matter over in my mind. "A huge motorcade left when Killian kicked me out."

"Yes," Rupert nodded. "That was the attack party. His Eminence had us launch an ambush attack on the Night Court that afternoon. They didn't come because they were busy, fighting *us*."

"If you're implying he did that for me, you're an idiot."

"Why? He didn't chase you out because he tired of you. He was trying to spur you into fighting Mason."

"That's not a whole truth," I said. "Or he would have just *told* me to make my move against Mason."

"You're right," Rupert scoffed. "But you're forgetting about the attack."

I blinked rapidly. "Attack?"

"At the mall? Where you were almost hit with a paint ball?"

"Oh. That. Yeah, talk about deadly."

"It was the Night Court."

"I do recall that detail, yes."

"You don't get it—they did it as a warning. They were sending a message—they could have just as easily shot you with a bullet as a paint ball, and you didn't pick up on them because they didn't use magic. Celestina and Josh would have reacted in time, but you wouldn't have. There's a war brewing between the Drake Family and the Night Court, and Queen Nyte as good as told His Eminence she'd go for you first."

I figured there was at least a somewhat understandable reason behind Killian's behavior. I hadn't really expected it to center around me, but it didn't change anything. Killian could have told me all of this, but he didn't trust me, and chose not to.

And I wasn't going to waste my time hanging out with someone who didn't trust me, and friends who would drop me with a *word* from their boss.

I flicked my katana, ridding it of electricity, then slid it into its scabbard. "Why are you even telling me all of this?" I asked. "You *hate* me!"

"Because my loyalty is to His Eminence." Rupert narrowed his eyes at me. "And as distasteful and irritating as I find you, His Eminence holds you in some kind of regard—enough to make him act outside of his usual actions."

I raised an eyebrow. "You think I'll just go waltzing back to him if I know that?"

"Isn't that generally how females act?"

*I can't kill him. It would be so, so, so annoying to deal with. I. Cannot. Hurt. Him.*

I forced a pleasant smile to my lips, but I was irritated enough I think it came off more as demented. "I'd already figured out Killian had a reason for his actions, but it doesn't matter. I don't like dealing with crap. And trying to manipulate without telling me anything is exactly that, crap. Tell Killian whatever you want. But unless he apologizes personally, I don't want anything to do with any of you."

Rupert sputtered. "His Eminence *apologize*? To *you*? You must be out of your mind!"

"I probably am. Now, go on—bye, bye."

Rupert shook his head. "I don't know what he sees in you that is even remotely redeemable."

I snorted. "That's pretty rich coming from a vampire."

Rupert shook his head and skulked off, probably in search of his hidden, Drake issue black car.

"Hey, Rupert."

The vampire scowled back at me. "*What*, Rat-blood?"

"Thank you for telling me."

Rupert struggled for a moment, seemingly trying to decide if his facial expression should settle on disgust or indifference. He nodded, and the line of his shoulders was a little more relaxed as he strode off.

I meant what I had said.

Even if the Drake vampires were convinced Killian liked me, I didn't care. I required a fully functioning relationship with my friends and comrades.

I didn't expect him to spill his darkest secrets or anything, but mutual trust and respect would have had him *telling* me these things instead of trying to manipulate and then sending his minions to do his dirty work.

I knew it was a good boundary to have, and I knew I'd be happier in the long run for it. Even so, there was a small part of my heart that still ached.

If only...

I forcibly turned to face House Medeis, my soul a little soothed by its transformed appearance.

"It's okay," I said. "I'm back home with my family, and we're about to make some major changes. Everything is going to be okay."

I crossed the street, and if the skip in my step was forced, that was okay.

All of us had gone through a rough few months. It would take time to heal. It would take time for me to stop waking up in the middle of the night, thinking I was late for a training session.

# CHAPTER TWENTY-THREE

*Killian*

"She's continued getting her people up for early morning practice," Julianne reported. "And I've tracked a rumor that she has hired a werewolf as a mixed martial arts teacher, and a vampire slayer for weapons training, but based on outdoor demonstrations she seems to be the one drilling her people in magic."

I tapped the clean surface of my desk and tossed a used blood pouch in the trash.

I was almost certain the Paragon had given her the magic book. Celestina reported that it had gone missing from her room two days after Hazel's Ascension ceremony. If she studied the book closely enough, it was possibly the best teacher her House could have, given that it was from the Paragon's private collection.

"Any sign of trouble from the other Houses?" I asked.

Julianne shook her head. "It seems they are intimidated by the big changes in House Medeis. It is now the second biggest in the city and has made the rank and reputation of House Medeis rapidly climb."

I leaned back in my chair. "Well done. Continue with the observation."

Julianne bowed. "Yes, Your Eminence." She backed out of my office and closed the door behind her.

I scooped up the fresh blood pouch she'd brought. I poked the straw in and stood with a groan, turning to look out the windows.

As much as I regretted it, chasing Hazel out of Drake Hall had been necessary.

After the mall attack, Queen Nyte had sent a letter confirming that the paint ball had been her doing, and she didn't fail to underline how easy it would have been to swap the colorful ammunition for bullets.

In a war with the Night Court, Hazel would be the first target.

I knew Hazel would refuse to be safely hidden away in Drake Hall, but the mall had proved that perhaps I wouldn't be able to keep her safe.

Hazel wasn't a vampire. She likely wouldn't survive a bullet wound. She couldn't be involved in the war—somehow she had become too precious to risk in a war.

The night of the Summer's End Ball...I didn't know when I last *laughed* like that. Kissing her had been the natural thing to do. It was like finding a piece of me that had been missing for centuries that I had forgotten about—although, *no*, she was not *the one*. I wasn't stupid enough to believe I'd ever have that. But she was important to me.

And that was why I had to drive her out.

I had to make Queen Nyte think I had lost all interest in her. The easiest way to accomplish this was to make *Hazel* think I'd lost all interest in her.

It had been difficult, and holding back the Night Court so she could take back House Medeis without their interference *and* while still making that idiot fae queen believe I didn't care for Hazel had taken more plotting than I had used in politics since snagging the position of Eminence.

But I had accomplished it.

Hazel was now safe at her House—which, if my underlings' reports were to be trusted, had basically become a bastille with the personality of a starved shark—and Queen Nyte appeared to have lost interest in her.

I had achieved my plans.

And if I missed the rich, warm scent that was Hazel and sometimes found myself drifting in the direction of the training hall at the hours she used to train, that was an acceptable price.

I still wasn't sure I *liked* how important she had become. She was a potential weakness—something I didn't like.

*Once the war with the Night Court is over, I can seek her out again. Until then, this will be good for me.*

*Everything is temporary, and with all of my years I've learned everything—and everyone—can be lived without.*

*This will be a good reminder.*

Even so, as I glanced back at the reports that detailed Hazel's new life at House Medeis, I found myself wondering if I could move up my timeline and end the feud with the Night Court sooner than I originally planned.

*To be continued in Magic Unleashed: Hall of Blood and Mercy Book 3*

---

# A JADED VAMPIRE

---

## A Hall of Blood and Mercy Short Story

R upert hated humans.
They were obnoxious, reproduced like rabbits, and were *fragile*.

He put humans far behind himself as a vampire when they started dying off, forever leaving him alone.

He had a number of human friends—every one of them had left him feeling holes in his heart from their lost friendship. But the deciding factor that made Rupert vow to ignore humans forever was a young lady—beautiful, kind, and with the laugh of a fresh spring breeze.

She listened to him with a startling intensity and offered her clever thoughts and intelligent observations, smiled at him with warmth burned by love, and even though she knew what he was... had reached for him without hesitation.

With her, the world seemed a brighter place brimming with possibilities and joy. She was everything to Rupert. He knew it with his entire being that she was his *one*!

Then she died.

And she died *young*.

She passed away in a freak horse-riding accident just a few

scant years after Rupert first met her. Although she was his sun in the sky and laughter in his heart, he'd had been helpless to save her.

He would have sacrificed anything to protect her, but in the end her human fragility was too great to overcome, because they died too easily. He lost her—and her laughter, and her voice, and her smiles, and her sweetness, and everything that made him think life was wonderous.

And Rupert realized his cold, vampire heart would never recover.

He'd been lost and broken when the Elder of the Cotelleon Family, tracked him down.

Rupert had previously resisted joining the Cotelleon Family, even though he'd been turned by the Cotelleon Elder himself. But after losing *her*...their insufferable superiority and constant mind games were a welcome change to the ache in his heart.

Their derision towards humans meant they only kept them as servants—and for their blood, of course.

Rupert didn't mind—it meant he didn't see daily reminders of what he'd lost forever.

But the wound of losing his *one* never really healed...it festered in his heart. And so as he lived with his Family and the years turned into decades and the decades became centuries, Rupert came to despise humans for what he decided was their weakness.

Then the Cotelleon Family Elder made the biggest mistake of his immortal life, and began plans to overturn the Regional Committee of Magic.

Rupert heard whispers of it and knew it was a gloriously stupid plan.

Sometime over the last century, the age of the vampires had passed. Vampires had to join forces with the werewolves, shifters, and fae just to *survive*. The idea that they could plot against the Regional Committee, when the upper echelon of the Cotelleon

Family rarely left the inner sanctuary of their manor, was laughable.

Even so, he'd never betray his Family. So, he took care to travel away from France—his home country. He lingered in Britain and visited parts of Asia and Russia. He was just considering looping back to Scotland when Rupert was summoned before his home Regional Committee of Magic for the trial and execution of the *entire* Cotelleon Family.

Rupert was told that he'd be spared, but he'd have to be adopted. As the sole survivor of a Family that had turned on supernaturals, he was too dangerous to leave Unclaimed. But now he was also a pariah. Who would *want* him?

It was then that Rupert met Killian Drake, Elder of the revered Drake Family that had once torn Britain asunder, and was now the terror of America.

Killian wasn't yet the Eminence of the Midwest, but it was fairly obvious the charismatic vampire had plans. By taking in Rupert, Killian received a fairly large chunk of land in France, as well as all remaining Cotelleon resources. Rupert assumed that was the purpose of his adoption—to obtain these things.

And it was. Except Killian surprised him.

"Celestina will draw up a training schedule for you. Sword fighting, martial arts...you'll probably need a beginner's class in gun safety and handling. Unless...?" Killian's unsettlingly black eyes rested on Rupert, who willed himself not to shiver.

"I have never handled a gun, Sir."

"Of course. What Family would bother to learn the weapons of modern society?" Killian Drake eyed Rupert's clothes—reminiscent from the early 1800s. "Josh will need to take you to the tailor for appropriate clothes."

Rupert tensed under the gaze of his new leader. "What is wrong with these, Sir?"

Killian sighed and looked very put out. "I'd worry that you are an idiot, but the rest of our kind are just as blind and ignorant as you. What's wrong is that you look like a carnival renaissance actor, that's what. No member of *my* Family is going to wander around with a wardrobe that will embarrass me. Now leave."

Killian was beyond brisk or blunt—he was beyond *rude*.

But when a very shocked Rupert was shot during his third gun safety session because he wasn't paying attention, he realized Killian Drake didn't mean to adopt him in name only. He was going to be enfolded into the Drake Family whether he wanted it or not.

The Drakes did things differently. They trained.

In fact, they trained *all the time*.

Rupert used to live a life of leisure—mens' clubs, billiard games, glittering socials in the darkness of night with the other noble vampires. After his adoption into the Drake Family, he didn't have a moment to ponder more than the night's training schedule.

This, more than Killian Drake's vast power, inspired Rupert's loyalty.

Killian wasn't content to let the vampires fade into obscurity. He was going to forcibly take back power, and crush those who opposed him.

He was the kind of vampire the Cotelleon Family had dreamed of. Killian was hard, deadly, and cunning. He became the Midwest Eminence in record time, expanded the vampire base of power in the region, and was well on his way to becoming legendary.

And then Hazel Medeis waltzed in.

She stank of magic, was far too brave considering she was just a breakable, useless wizard, but the worst part about her was that she was *personable*.

She cracked jokes and ran around like a yipping dog while taking every bit of training the Drakes threw at her.

It was awful.

Didn't anyone realize how easy it was for her to die? Didn't they realize the hours of training they were sinking into her were going to be useless? Hadn't it occurred to them that in a few short decades she'd be gone? There was no point in training her, no point to investing anything in her at all!

Worse yet, Killian seemed weirdly *fond* of her. More so than any of the Drakes had realized, because when Rupert crossed a line and inflicted more damage on Hazel than was deemed necessary, Killian half killed him.

He probably would have just offed him, if it wasn't for that wretched puppy squeaking around Killian's ankles and asking for mercy on behalf of Rupert. (When he had just knocked her unconscious! Surely only humans—wizards included—could be that stupid.)

That occasion only gave Rupert more fodder for his comfortable hatred of the Wizard. It also meant the Drake Family stopped trying to push Rupert into training the smelly human— another blessing.

Rupert resolved to hunker down and ignore her whenever possible. It wouldn't be long until she'd leave. Or die.

But the yappy puppy's seemingly useless sniffing helped her bag Solene—the Unclaimed vampire that had been killing vampires and humans alike. And instead of telling a vampire about it and then scurrying to safety like a good human, she flung herself face first into a fight with Solene, even though she barely had the battle instincts of a rabbit.

Rupert would have felt vindicated in his assertion that she wouldn't be alive long, except not only did she sacrifice herself for the Drake Family's sake, she *won*! And she unsealed her magic! And it turned out, with magic backing her up, the puppy had some serious bite to her.

Rather, she could be downright *deadly*.

Rupert blankly watched Hazel Medeis electrocute a Drake vampire half to death with a sizzling bolt of lightning.

*She's a menace, and we're teaching her how to effectively fight against and kill us. This can only end poorly.*

And then the Wizard went and sacrificed her House signet ring, for Killian...and for Rupert.

She'd fought to claim it, and she *needed* it to free her family and get her House back. And she threw it away, destroying it to save Killian and Rupert from powerful and deadly magic that certainly would have killed Rupert.

He saw her later that night, red faced and puffy eyed, but she smiled when she saw him, and she never showed any signs of regretting her actions.

Rupert didn't know what to think after that.

And he didn't know how to react when Killian—acting by instinct—had her thrown from House Drake in an effort to cut her out of the impending fight between the Night Court and the Drake Family.

Obviously, the Eminence still cared for her—a veritable parade of vampires was sent to watch House Medeis and its scrappy Adept to guard it and report any signs of the Night Court.

One afternoon not too long after the Wizard's exile, Rupert was sent in Julianne's place when the beautiful vampire was forced to stay home to deal with some unexpected paperwork.

It happened to be the day of the Wizard's Ascension ceremony, which officially bonded her to her House.

As Rupert watched, the magical House changed from a quaint mixture of a French Chateau and a Victorian home, to a hulking behemoth of a building that had the same architecture, but somehow gave off the feeling of a fortress.

*Figures.*

When Hazel approached him with the obvious intent to shoo him off, to Rupert's surprise he disobeyed a direct order from the vampire he most respected—and feared—in the world, and *told* her why Killian had kicked her out, and how the Drake Family had raided the Night Court to keep the fae distracted while she settled things with Mason.

Even as he told her, he wondered if he had lost his mind and what possessed him to—in a way—betray his leader. For a *human*!

He didn't even like her!

(He didn't.)

It had to be because of Killian. The Eminence appeared to be...*fine* since Hazel's departure, but no one in Drake Hall sincerely believed this was the truth.

Yes, he told her for the sake of the Eminence. That had to be it.

But a small, tiny part of Rupert whispered that perhaps it was because although Hazel smiled and laughed, when she met his eyes he could see the pain and hurt in her eyes.

Rupert immediately snuffed the thought out.

Humans were beneath him. There was no point in fraternizing with them, no use in becoming fond of them. They only died on you in the end.

————

WEEKS LATER, Rupert stared gloomily at the monstrosity that was House Medeis.

No one had found out he'd disobeyed Killian and told the smelly Wizard that the Eminence had sent her off for her own safety.

...but no one had found out because nothing had changed!

The Wizard, apparently, had a head of rock! She hadn't made any attempt to approach the Drake Family, or even message Killian Drake.

*Perhaps a good smack would cure her bout of stupidity?*

But Rupert had seen her drill her people on more than one occasion, and he wasn't actually sure he could even beat her anymore. (It hadn't been a fluke when she beat him back at Drake

Hall, but Rupert had been confident he could still best her at least half the time. Now? Not so much.)

Rupert stuffed his hands in the pockets of his tailored slacks and wanted to whine.

He was a high-ranking member of the esteemed Drake Family. What was he doing, kicking up his heels on a street corner, peeking at noxious-smelling wizards?

Besides, when one of those wizards finally got around to telling Hazel that he was here, she was going to shoot lightning at him again.

Rupert sulked and wondered if he needed to be more obvious.

Killian was still solid, and his manner hadn't changed...except that he had gone back to rarely laughing.

Although Drake Hall smelled markedly better, apparently one yappy wizard produced a lot of noise—and opportunities to be laughed at.

Across the street, a wizard of House Medeis—the female black-haired one that was friends with Hazel—peered curiously at him from the sidewalk.

When Rupert boldly met her gaze, daring her to go tattle to Hazel, the young woman gave him a sunny smile and waved to him.

"The Adept is doing fine!" the woman shouted to him. "She might be overworking herself a bit, but she's having fun razzing the Wizard Council!"

Rupert was mildly insulted on behalf of all vampires and their aura of mystery that a *wizard* had figured out why he was there.

The feeling faded away as impatience jockeyed for the front— if the dark-haired wizard *knew* why he was here, why wasn't she harping at Hazel?!

The wizard had the audacity to *wink* at him before she swung the sidewalk gate open and hopped onto House Medeis land.

Rupert scowled at her back.

Yes, Rupert hated humans.

No other supernatural could match them in terms of obnoxiousness, fragility...and, perhaps, heart.

But, seemingly unlike his revered leader, there was no way he was reckless enough to let them back into his life. There was no way he'd ever allow himself to become friends with them again.

Another House Medeis wizard waddled down the sidewalk—this one an ancient woman with silvery hair blazed with a colored stripe. When she saw him she smiled and waved. "Hello, dear! Hazel is in fine health these days!"

Yes.

Not. A. Chance.

THE END

## HAZEL'S ADVENTURE CONTINUES IN...

Magic Unleashed- Available on Amazon!

It's funny how people—or vampires—you thought were your friends can value you so little that they are able to abandon you with no regret.

But I'm stronger than that!

After Killian Drake showed his true colors and kicked me out of his mansion, I was able to get my house back and finally free my family.

Now, my magical House has expanded, my family is thriving, and things are finally starting to look up!

...Until the fae attack Killian and his vampires in a political meeting that *I* happen to be attending.

I might still be furious with Killian, but no vampires are dying on my watch.

Unfortunately, I never stopped to wonder what the consequences would be for saving the most feared and deadly vampire in the Midwest. And it never occurred to me the lengths Killian might go through to win me back.

# OTHER SERIES BY K. M. SHEA

# ABOUT THE AUTHOR

K. M. Shea is a fantasy-romance author who never quite grew out of adventure books or fairy tales, and still searches closets in hopes of stumbling into Narnia. She is addicted to sweet romances, witty characters, and happy endings. She also writes LitRPG and GameLit under the pen name, A. M. Sohma.

*Hang out with the K. M. Shea Community at...*
kmshea.com

Printed in Great Britain
by Amazon

41106305R00165